This book is dedicated to Winifred Powell
(23.01.1914 – 09.03.2012)
a woman who was loved by all, who loved her family dearly,
and loved to read, too.

Maybe she can get this book from 'www.kindle.god', where,
of course, all books will be free.

The Falconer Files
by
Andrea Frazer

The Falconer Files

Falconer Files – Brief Cases

DRAMATIS PERSONAE

Of the Shepford Stacey Church of England Primary School:

Headmistress: Audrey Finch-Matthews
Teacher: Harriet Findlater
Classroom Assistant: Charlotte Chadwick
Dinnerlady: Stephanie 'Stevie' Baldwin
Patron: Rev. Septimus Lockwood
Caretaker: Saul Catchpole
Cleaner: Florence Atkins
Sundry pupils

Residents of Shepford Stacey

Allington, Meredith – married to Derwent, children Mercedes and Austin
Borrowdale, Martha – married to Seth, children Isaac, Jacob, and Maria
Bywaters-Flemyng, India – married to Hartley, son Sholto
Baldwin, Stephanie 'Stevie' – dinner lady, barmaid, and mother of Spike
Baldwin, Patsy and Frank – Stevie's parents
Baldwin, Elsie – Stevie's grandmother
Course, Caroline – staying in one of the holiday cottages
Darling, Ernest – married to Margaret and owns the Ring o' Bells pub. Son David
Gorman, Vera and Letty – sisters. Both run the village post office
Greenslade, Robbie – landlord of the Temporary Sign pub
Hammond, Chris – married to Ann. Daughter Isobelle. Runs the village shop
Leclerc, Gabriella – married to Morgan, son Lorcan
Macpherson, Maura – married to Cameron, son Angus
Smithers, George and Kathy – elderly couple staying in one of the holiday cottages
Snoddy, Adrian – married to Pippa, son Milo

The Officials

Detective Inspector Harry Falconer
Detective Sergeant 'Davey' Carmichael
Sergeant Bob Bryant
PC Merv Green
PC Linda 'Twinkle' Starr
PC John Proudfoot
Superintendent Derek 'Jelly' Chivers
Dr Philip Christmas
Dr Hortense 'Honey' Dubois

Introduction

Shepford Stacey is a relatively nondescript village. One can drive through it and not even notice it, for there is simply nothing to make it stand out from the other more picturesque villages of this area, and it is usually ignored by the tourist trade.

It had originally grown up just south of a monastery, but that was before Henry VIII had his huge snit and instituted the Dissolution. He believed that if you didn't like the rules of the club you were in, then you ought to start a new one and write the rules to suit your own tastes, which is exactly what he did: an example followed by a certain Mr Cromwell, who also destroyed rather a lot of history and architecture, to the great loss of the public at large.

The sacking and burning of the monastery, however, did not mean the end of the settlement, as much agriculture had developed around the village to serve the monastery, and although the usual lines of commerce were disrupted by the destruction of the main customer's headquarters, there were other markets in larger surrounding communities, to take their spare produce and turn it into hard cash. Thus the village survived.

If we fast-forward to the present, the old monastery ruins and the site of its gardens are still there, protected by National Heritage, but it is one of those sites that has little to recommend itself, except as a perfect place to let young children run and climb (suitably supervised) to their hearts' content, and burn off as much energy before tea-time or bedtime as possible. For anyone who is not a child wishing to run around until he or she drops, it has little to offer. There is, therefore, no little booth selling tickets; there are no kind elderly folk offering to walk around the site with you, explaining how life used to be lived there. There is no twee shop lurking, selling postcards and tacky souvenirs, guidebooks and leather bookmarks (*suitably illustrated with the name of the place visited, and a crummy illustration done in gold, black, and white, to remind you of what it might have looked like if you had taken your glasses off and squinted horribly while you were there*). Admission is free and unsupervised.

Although it is fenced off, the site is accessible through a pair of wide gates that, at the moment, have allowed ingress to a caravan with three occupants. Whether or not the caravan has been granted permission to park on such a site is a matter of much gossip in the village (for there is not much happening at this time of year, and any distraction is appreciated). Only the three occupants – or at least the two grown-ups – comprehend the viability of their presence there, and no one has had the radical idea of just *asking* them. The English ideal of never offending by prying holds dear in this little outpost of English life, thus prolonging the life of gossip, and giving it more 'legs' than it would have had if someone had just posed a simple question in the first place.

The village itself is built around a crossroads, with St Anselm's Church at one corner (a ghastly Victorian Gothic revival), and the village shop diagonally opposite. The other two corners are occupied by the village's two public houses. The one between the church and the shop on the south-east side is called The Ring o' Bells, and it is not difficult to understand how it got its name. The pub on the corner on the north-west side is called, rather more puzzlingly, the Temporary Sign.

It had been known for many years as the Coach and Horses, and very happy everyone was with this – until the new landlord arrived, and decided that the sign was getting very tatty and needed repainting. Having hired a firm to carry out this procedure, he was instantly fascinated by the temporary sign they hung in its place to indicate that it was still a viable public house, and not closed down, as are so many country pubs these

2

days (*due to the fact that if one imbibes little more than a thimbleful of any alcoholic beverage, he drives at peril of losing his licence forever, suffering a hefty fine, and being imprisoned for about a decade. Murder often carries a lesser penalty, it would seem!*)

The landlord, infatuated with the rather unexpected renaming of his establishment (which he considered 'trendy'), cancelled the repainting and paid to keep what was to have been a – well, a temporary sign. The company he dealt with were perfectly happy with the arrangement, because they got paid without having to produce a masterpiece, and the landlord was happy because he had had his little joke, and hoped that it would bring customers in just to enquire about it.

There was a small post office, but this was scheduled to close at the end of the year, unless a suitable location could be found to rehouse it, as the postmistress was due to retire, and the present post office was situated in what would become, and had been before, the main reception room of her house. To this end, it still retained its attractive bow window, for when it reverted back to its original usage.

The only other village amenities were a riding school, just south of the main village, and Blacksmith's Terrace; five tiny dwellings that had been cleverly converted into holiday cottages by the couple that ran the riding school. Thus, could they provide not only the mounts for a horsey holiday, but the accommodation also, and collect on both fronts.

With these two sides to their business, they managed to make an all-year-round living. There were always people who liked to get away in the winter, even if only for Christmas and the New Year. There were also those who liked to hack around the countryside in the winter crispness. If one combined these with the local children who clamoured for lessons to such a degree that there was a waiting list, and the many gymkhanas that took place in the county to be practised for, and you have a healthy business, most of the income coming in the summer, but sufficient from winter lets, lessons, and hacks, to keep a family going all year round.

3

The only building likely to catch a casual passer-by's eye was the terrace of alms-houses in The Main (literally the main street). Named boringly and predictably the Victoria and Albert Alms Houses, the architect had been a fan of Elizabethan architecture and, given a free hand by the village's benefactor, had included mullioned windows and beautiful barley-twist chimneys in his plans. (*The result was nearly as eye-catching as that close of houses near Wells Cathedral that has had so much cinematic attention, and never fails to project one into a past century from a mere glance down it.*)

As was stressed at the beginning of this introduction, there was little to attract a passing traveller and cause him to break his journey for a stay here. It was just a little village – not a hamlet, for it boasted a church, no matter how ugly – that got on with its existence without a huge influx of tourists in the summer months, and it was glad of that. Life was tranquil and peaceful.

(Author's Note: author's comments are in italics & bracketed)

4

Chapter One

Thursday 31st March

'Good morning, Imogen. You know where the cake tin goes, don't you, Charlotte?'

'Good morning, Spike. Yes, I can see that Mummy's been busy in the kitchen. Isn't that lovely?'

'Use your handkerchief, Milo dear, not your sleeve. Not a problem, Mr Snoddy. I can understand how difficult it is for you, living in a caravan like that. Why not hang on at the end of school and buy something delicious as a treat?'

'Yes, Mummy will be cross if you scuff your lovely new shoes, Mercedes. Pick your feet up, dear, and walk properly. What a grown-up boy you are, Austin, carrying that big plastic box. In the foyer, Mrs Allington. The table's just on the right.'

'Angus MacPherson, don't you let me hear you use that word again, or you'll be staying in at playtime for the third time this week.'

'Isaac Borrowdale, I want that chewing gum *straight* in the bin when you get inside. Do you understand? Straight away! I will not have a repeat of what happened on Monday.'

'Don't worry, Lorcan. I expect it's the chilly wind. Thank you so much, Mrs LeClerc.'

She called into the school foyer, 'Mrs Chadwick, do you think you could let Imogen see herself into the classroom? Lorcan here has had a little accident. Spare pants in the usual place. Thank you.'

As the children were delivered to the school door, many of the parents shot through the doors with tins or plastic containers, for there was to be a bake sale that day, as the school was breaking up for the Easter Holidays – and breaking up very late, for today was Maundy Thursday, the double Bank Holiday weekend almost upon them.

Thus did Audrey Finch-Matthews, long-since widowed headteacher of Shepford Stacey Church of England Primary School, welcome her charges, and call her thanks to the contributing mothers, on the last day of the spring term. As she cajoled and upbraided the youngest of the pupils, she patted her dark brown (dyed) curls into place and allowed herself a moment of smugness. Hers was a popular school and, although numbers were low at the moment, she had not an ounce of worry that it would close. The vicar had recently opened a waiting list, allowing children from other villages to apply to attend the school, and they should be packed to the rafters in September.

On the other side of the entrance, Harriet Findlater, fifty-seven-year-old spinster of this parish and teacher of the upper school class (seven- to eleven-year-olds), held court with the mothers delivering their offspring to school on this bright spring morning. Her mind was also on the school and its future, for Audrey Finch-Matthews would reach her sixtieth birthday this year and Harriet hoped, with a burning fervour, that she would retire and give her a chance to run the school, before she had to retire herself.

'Come along, Sholto, and stop pulling on Mummy's arm so. If you don't get a move on you'll be late, and then where would we be, eh?' Audrey asked, seeing India Bywaters-Flemyng struggling to insert her son through the school gates.

Picking up his pace, the five-year-old stopped in front of Mrs Finch-Matthews and asked, 'Where would we be, Miss? I expect you know, 'cos you're a teacher,' his face a mask of innocence.

'Sholto! Mind your manners! I'm sorry, Mrs Finch-Matthews, but we do encourage him to be inquisitive and ask questions,' Mrs Bywaters-Flemyng explained, a sly smile twitching at the corners of her mouth.

'Hm! Well, perhaps you ought to teach him the difference

between a genuine enquiry and an enormous piece of cheek. Young as he is, I'm convinced he's bright enough to tell the difference, even if Mummy isn't,' the head teacher answered, being completely un-enamoured of India's superior ways and attitude to others. She wasn't the only one around here with a double-barrelled name, and she was just going to have to live with the idea.

Really, the cheek of the little imp, and his mother hadn't upbraided him with even a look of disapproval. Whatever was the world coming to? When she was Sholto's age she would have been awarded a clip round the ear for such facetiousness, followed by another one, when her mother heard about what had happened. How times had changed since she herself had started school.

There was not usually impertinence of this kind from the pupils: it was something that had arrived with Sholto Bywaters-Flemyng and, if she had anything to do with it, it would end with him too. She had always been very strict about respect for adults, and that pint-sized chancer and his arrogant mother were not going to change anything.

'What extraordinary names the children have these days, don't you agree, Harriet?' she asked, as they entered the school after the last of their pupils, and closed the doors on the outside world for the last time this term.

'Oh, I do agree, Audrey. It was all Susans, Lindas, and Jennifers in our day: and good old Steven, John, and Peter for the boys. Life was so much simpler then, like the names.'

'I couldn't agree more, Harriet. Just look at the Allingtons. Their six-year-old (bless her cotton socks) is called Mercedes, and their two-year-old is called Austin. Have they got some sort of subconscious car fetish, or is it just me, unable to keep up with the times?'

Treating this as a rhetorical question on her own part, she continued, 'Do you remember those pretentious parents who sent their *ghastly* precocious twins here a couple of years ago? And we had to take the extraordinary step of permanently excluding them, the little devils?'

7

'Castor and Pollux,' confirmed Miss Findlater.

'I always thought of them as Bastard and Bollocks, I must admit,' confessed Mrs Finch-Matthews in a stage whisper.

Blushing at this unusually strong language, Harriet contributed, 'I understand they go to that private school on the other side of Market Darley, now – as boarders, I believe.'

'I presume they have a psychiatric dorm, if they've taken those two,' opined the headteacher, lifting a wry eyebrow. 'Now, let's see if we can locate Charlotte Chadwick to get her to put these cakes into some sort of order, and get prices on them.

'Which reminds me: the decorators are arriving just before we close for the term, so we'd better get Charlotte to brew an urn of strong tea; they always seem to need so much of it. Well, they'll just have to pour their own, and be grateful that we even have such a thing as a tea urn. Hmph!' she concluded, with a rebellious expression on her face.

An aerial view of Shepford Stacey would have revealed a number of individuals moving away from the school premises and off and away to attend to their business for the day.

Maura MacPherson and Martha Borrowdale walked together, living next door to each other just across Back Lane from the school, in Creepers and The Vines respectively. Martha Borrowdale was thirty-six years old, determined to be happily married, and had three children. Isaac, her five-year-old, she had just dropped off at the school, along with Jacob, his ten-year-old brother who was in the upper class. Maria, her two-year-old, obediently held her mother's hand as they strolled slowly back home.

Martha was overtly respectable, and was viewed as a terrific snob, a wife who spent a lot of time ignoring the shortcomings of her husband, who was no stranger to the inside of a police cell, although all that had been a long time ago. She kept her nose in the air, and constantly kidded herself that people had either forgotten all that business, or had never even heard of it. If only she could keep him on the straight and narrow, she could live the life she pretended she was already living, but she was often in a state of low-grade fear, that something else would jump out of the woodwork at her, concerning either his past, or his far from crystal-clear present.

He was supposed to be working from home at the moment, but at what, she had no idea. She just knew he spent an inordinate amount of time on the computer, and had files on that Machiavellian machine that she had no access to, and this fact existed as a low-grade worry at the back of her mind. But she didn't want to be distracted by thoughts like that now, and brought her thoughts back to the present with considerable effort, tuning in again to what Maura was saying.

Maura and Cameron MacPherson had only the one child, Angus, who was also five, and their house was only half the size of the Borrowdales' residence – but one would never have guessed if one had listened to Maura MacPherson. Given her endless monologues on the trials she had bringing up her one 'wee chick', and the amount of labour she expended on her home, one would have thought that she had a brood as large as Victoria and Albert's, and a residence to rival the size of any of those inhabited by Victorian royalty.

Adrian Snoddy wandered slowly up Sheep Pen Lane to the caravan he shared with his wife, Pippa, and their five-year-old son, Milo. He was not in any hurry to get back to the doubtful comforts of the caravan that they had lodged on the site of the old monastery gardens, and rather doubted his sanity when they had decided to have a year-long adventure, living as travellers. Both had moneyed parents, and he was losing his conviction that one should try to live as others live for a while, to give one a balanced view of life.

He'd just decided that he would inform Pippa that they would see the school term out for Milo's sake, and then return to their familiar familial roots, when he heard his name called from across the road, turned, and saw Gabriella LeClerc waving at him. 'Do you fancy a coffee before you go home?' she called, holding her hands one either side of her mouth in the way of an improvised megaphone. 'The kettle's on, and I've got Jammie

Dodgers.' How could he resist?

Turning on his heel and heading across the road in the direction of Chimneys, he waved to indicate his consent, and a smile lit his previously gloomy countenance. He'd have coffee and Jammie Dodgers with Gabriella, then he'd go back to the caravan and inform Pippa of his decision about their living arrangements. If she didn't like it, she could stay in that clapped-out old biscuit tin on her own. He didn't see why he had to be part of realising her gypsy-life dream any longer.

In Forsythia Cottage Stevie (née Stephanie) Baldwin had just got back from dropping off her son Spike at the school. She would be returning there after the school day was over, to give it an extra-thorough clean as it was the end of term, but before that, she had her shift behind the bar of one of the two local pubs.

She was a single mother, only twenty-two, and she lived, still, with her parents and grandmother, who all lent a hand in Spike's upbringing, and were very generous with their time while Stevie went to work. Patsy and Frank Baldwin had not exactly been delighted when their only daughter had informed them, at the age of seventeen, that she was pregnant, and had no plans to marry the baby's father, but since Spike's birth, they had doted on him, as had Frank's mother Elsie, who was now eighty years old, and thoroughly enjoying the amount of waiting-on to which her age seemed to entitle her.

'Shall I get the cakes at the school sale?' Stevie called, hanging up her jacket and slipping off her shoes in preference for a slipper. She had need of only one, for comfort. 'I can get there a few minutes early and get the pick of the selection. I can give them to you to bring home, Mum, when you collect Spike, and we can all have a nice little treat before I go into work this evening, can't we?'

'Nice one, Stevie,' called her mother, re-boiling the kettle for tea, now that her daughter was back from the school run. 'Go and give your grandmother a shout, and tell her I've got the tea made, and she'd better get a move on getting down here or all the chocolate biscuits will be gone.'

In Paddock View on Four Stiles, Hartley and India Bywaters-Flemyng were taking an overview of the bookings for both the riding school and the holiday cottages; a terrace of refurbished properties called Blacksmith's Terrace and located on Forge Lane.

'We've got number one vacant until after Easter,' Hartley stated, he being the one who was responsible for the bookings and maintenance of the little cottages. 'The Cliftons in number two are taking advantage of the extra days free at Easter, so they won't be off until Tuesday, and then I can get that prepped for the next visitors. The Smithers and Mrs Course don't go until Tuesday either – that's three and four – and I've got a couple arriving anytime now for number five – staying for the long Easter weekend and through to the following Friday. What've you got?'

'No lessons after today till Tuesday, then I'm just about booked up,' replied his wife India. 'You know how the little ankle-biters love their ponies and horses, and I'm up to my eyes in extra lessons. There's also a booking for Wednesday for a group from Fallow Fold to go hacking for the day. That's a nice little earner, and it'll help to make up for the four days without my regular customers.'

They were a tall handsome couple, she, twenty-nine years of age, he thirty-five, but they were not popular. They exuded an air of superiority and arrogance, and the little exchange India had had with Audrey at the school entrance was typical of their relations with the other residents of the village. They had no friends locally, and didn't socialise, deeming themselves of superior breeding to the local turnips who had lived there all or most of their lives, never having left to get a university degree, as they had done, and they did not differentiate for any newcomers either.

Their aloofness alienated them, but as their main aim was to make a success of their twin businesses, they neither noticed nor cared. That part of their aloofness stemmed from the fact that Hartley suffered from a serious stammer, they were reluctant to admit.

11

In The Rectory, now that their daughter Dove was safely in school, Rev. Septimus ('Child number seven – don't ask!' was his usual response to enquiries about his name) and Ruth Lockwood were having a full and frank – in fact, frankly, loud – discussion about the change in the rules for admissions to the school.

'I don't care how you try to justify it, it's going to ruin yet another one of the village schools with just a couple of classes – they're dying out and will soon become extinct. And you want to admit children from other parishes? You know what it's been like here, with all and sundry buying up the properties, and turning up at church for a couple of weeks, then expecting to get a place for their child in the school, as if it's their right.'

'Ruth, you have to understand that if it's not opened up in some way, the school will close, and that'll be even worse. We've got less than thirty pupils registered, and that's covering ages five to eleven. There's no way we can remain open if numbers don't improve. I've told you, it's been discussed with the school staff, the parent governors, and at Diocesan meetings and, if we want the school to survive at all, we have to be less narrow in the criteria of our admissions system.'

'It's awful enough as it is – all those pretentious women with their ghastly children's names, making register sound like it's for some mini-RADA. They only come here so that they can get the sort of education their children wouldn't be exposed to if they went to an ordinary state school. They're getting the good quality of a private education, without having to pay for a private school, and I think that's cheating. If you want your child to go to a Church of England school, then you should be a practising Christian.'

'Don't be ridiculous, Ruth. What has the Christian religion got to do with anything in this country any more? Tell me that! Our beliefs and traditions have slowly been whittled away, to the point that virtually no child starting at a local authority school has the faintest idea what a Christmas carol is – the nearest they can guess is 'Merry Xmas Everybody' by Slade.

'Do you know what one woman said to me the other day?

12

She said that the likes of us shouldn't go about trying to ruin the fun of Christmas with all that religious clap-trap, and what was the point of it all anyway? I tried to point out to her that without the 'Christ' there would be no '-mas', but she told me it quite upset her little grandchildren to have to be hauled off to the kiddies' nativity service, and miss all the cartoons on the telly about Santa Claus and Rudolf the Red-Nosed Reindeer. At her age, she should have been setting an example, and I can tell you, it's the closest I've ever come to giving an otherwise sweet, grey-haired old lady a 'fourpenny one' right on the nose.

'And as for the Easter message – I absolutely give up. For most families now, it's just about 'bunny-wunnies' – or that ghastly American Easter Bunny, I should say – cakes with little chicks on, and chocolate eggs.'

'So that's more reason than ever, then, to keep the intake just to those who live in the parish and attend church on a Sunday,' shouted Ruth, not caring who could hear her.

'Why can't you see that the solution's the complete opposite, woman? The more children we let in who haven't been exposed to a Christian upbringing, the more children we get a chance to influence, and educate in the ways of a Christian life.' Septimus' voice was raised too now, and they were both red in the face, glaring at each other across the desk in his study.

One corner of Ruth's mouth twitched just a millimetre as she struggled to maintain her expression, but her husband noticed it, crossed his eyes at her, and poked out his tongue. 'Race you upstairs!' she challenged, shooting out of the study door and stamping up the staircases with all the grace of a pantomime horse. Bringing up the rear of this animal, rarely spotted outside of December and January, bounded Septimus. They may have been married for eight years, but the passion of their union was undiminished, and this argument was going the way of most arguments in their household – towards a very sweet resolution.

Things were almost as sweet in the sitting room of number two Victoria and Albert Terrace, as Flo Atkins poured out tea from a bone china pot and offered chocolate biscuits to Saul

13

Catchpole from number three, whom she had invited round for a 'little visit' this morning. She had been the cleaner at the school and he the caretaker for a number of years, and she felt, on the eve of the holidays, that it would be nice if they planned a couple of little outings together; something for her to look forward to over the next couple of weeks except for her own company. Her daughter was going to Tenerife for a fortnight, and her son worked in Manchester and said he couldn't get away.

'Drink up, dearie,' she exhorted him, 'and I'll top the pot up with boiling water. And help yourself to another biscuit. Don't want them going off now do we, duckie?'

'Quack, quack!' Saul whispered under his breath, but he helped himself to two more biscuits, and drained his teacup while Flo was in the kitchen dealing with the teapot. He was seventy-two to her sixty-six, and although they lived next door to each other now, that had only been since she was widowed six months ago, and they were gradually feeling their way as neighbours. He didn't really know how he felt about her, but she'd certainly looked after herself, and it did banish the loneliness he had felt since his wife died five years ago. Any port in a storm, he reckoned, as long as there was safe harbour, and Flo didn't look as if she would bite.

In the old monastery gardens' site, in a rather tatty caravan, a tiny elf of a woman was pegging out clothes on a dryer suspended from the bottom of one of the caravan windows. Her wavy hair was long, but sadly neglected, and the dark brown cascade down her back was marred by split ends and rats' tails. Out of the corner of her eye, she spotted her husband, taking his time coming back from the school run, and hailed him as he approached the pedestrian entrance to the site.

'Where on earth have you been, Adrian? I need to get the bedding to the launderette in Market Darley, and you know I can't handle that big car. I can't drive anything without power steering, Milo's school breaks up today for over two weeks, and there you are, away with the fairies, dawdling along the road as if you had all the time in the world.'

14

'Well we do, don't we? Neither of us has a job, or a hobby, or any voluntary work, or neighbours, or a social life, or anything at all, really, do we?'

'What's eating you now?' asked Pippa, unable to ignore the signs that he was going to throw one of his moods, and her with so much to do.

'Oh, I've just about had enough of all this. It's not as if we need to live like a load of gypsies. We've both got perfectly respectable – no, well-off – families, who'd love us to give up this silly charade of yours and live a normal life with our son.'

'And what's wrong with this way of life, might I ask?'

'It's simply not us: we're fakes! At the end of the school year I'm leaving this sardine can, which nearly froze me to death this winter, and I'm taking Milo back to civilisation. He shouldn't have to grow up with his parents living hand-to-mouth like a couple of drop-outs, when there's plenty of money in the bank, and he doesn't have to. Say what you will, it's going to happen whether you like it or not!'

'Oh, good! I wondered how long it'd take to wear you down, and get you to act like a man instead of a quivering jelly.'

'What do you mean? *You* don't want to do this either?'

'Of course not! I just wanted to see how far I could push you, to do something that was basically against your wishes. I wanted to be married to a man, not a mouse. Thank God you've stood up to me at last. Now, carry on like that, and we'll be all right. But you're right about seeing the academic year out. It's better for Milo to complete his first year there, and it'll be a lesson to your parents, not to forbid you to do anything. Really! At your age!'

Adrian Snoddy was all of twenty-eight years old, his wife, two years his junior.

Life was emerging in the two village pubs, diagonally opposite each other at the crossroads that marked the centre of the village.

In the Temporary Sign, Robbie Greenslade was already on his computer, putting together what was to be the first pub quiz

15

under his management, and, if it increased sales sufficiently, he hoped to make it a monthly event. Robbie always had an idea or two on the go, and this was his latest one.

In the Ring o' Bells, Ernie Darling was collecting the last of the glasses from the previous night, his thoughts already on his next task; clearing the ashtrays from the smoking shelter in the car park. If he didn't know better, he'd swear that the car park was livelier than the pub some nights, and rued the day they had banned the habit on licensed premises. At least if his smoking patrons had still been allowed to indulge inside, it would have increased their drinking rate. As it was, they got chatting, and couldn't be bothered to go in for another round for an age.

His wife Margaret made her way unsteadily down the stairs, one hand on the bannister to keep her balance, the other covering the top of her head, as if she expected it to fall off. As indeed it felt it just might, after the amount of gins she'd downed the previous evening. This running a pub lark after taking early retirement might be all right at nine or ten in the evening, but at the same hours in the morning, it wasn't so hot. She'd have to alternate with soft drinks for a night or two, until she was feeling back on form. 'Ernie! Don't crash those glasses around so noisily. My poor head feels like it's going to burst,' she pleaded.

'Serves you right for filling your boots. You're always the same when that old Catchpole feller is in. It looks like I might be having to keep my eye on you, when he's about.'

'Don't be so silly, Ernie. More like me having to keep an eye on you when that Florence Atkins is around. I've seen you sniffing round her like a little dog. And you know damned well what's wrong with me.'

'Don't be so ridiculous, woman. Take some pain killers, get yourself a mug of strong black coffee, and then come back in here and help me to make this business a success. It's the only way we're going to make any real money for a properly-funded real retirement in a few years' time. You're going to have to pull yourself together and live with it.'

Back at the school, just a few minutes after the children had finished assembly and returned to their classrooms, a battered white van pulled up at the school gates, ladders secured to its roof, a scraped and battered sign painted on its side that read:

Colin GREENWOOD,
exterior and interior painter and decorator.

Three men jumped enthusiastically from its cab and made their way through the entrance, visibly eager to get on with a job with a set fee, and not one to be charged by the hour. The boss, Colin Greenwood had high hopes of this one, and hoped they could knock it off in good time to make a decent profit. It might even lead to further work in the same vein. You never knew.

Five minutes later, they exited the building again with instructions not to start work before four o'clock today. If they started opening paint and white spirit this early in the morning, there was no telling what the children would get up to during playtimes and lunchtime. Audrey Finch-Matthews had told the vicar to make it perfectly clear that work could not commence before that hour. She had worked in schools all her working life, and there weren't many tricks she wasn't *au fait* with. Paint during school hours was a 'no-no'.

The van backed out of the school premises, turned left on to Sheep Pen Lane, and straight into the car park of The Temporary Sign. Robbie Greenslade had taken advantage of the legislation that relaxed the hours of pub opening, and was ready and eager for their order.

As the smoke from the van's exhaust pipe dispersed, Anne Hammond from the village shop trotted energetically into the playground with a biscuit tin in her hands. Her daughter Isabelle was twelve now, and had left the village school last September, but, like others who no longer had a direct connection with it, Anne liked to contribute what she could, and a tin full of vanilla butterfly cakes was the least she could do. The place had given Isabelle a sound grounding for her senior years at school, and after all, a great deal of her custom came from the

17

schoolchildren and their parents.

A number of figures had approached and left the school at intervals during the morning, taking note of the sign in the foyer asking them to leave their offerings on the table provided, and they would be collected later in the day for pricing and display.

Charlotte Chadwick was one of the stragglers, and returned home to bake. She was a classroom assistant at the school and would have to be there just before lunchtime to help out voluntarily. Her official paid duties did not commence until after the lunch break, but she liked to give a little free time to such a good little school.

She had delivered her six-year-old daughter, Imogen, to the school, and strolled back to Laurel Lodge opposite Blacksmith's Terrace, to fill her kitchen with the smell of individual treacle tarts, and lots of them. These were now cooled and stacked in the tin that she carried carefully towards its destination.

Approaching the school gates for the second time that morning, she was surprised to see Lorcan LeClerc, one of the older infants from the lower class, out in the playground and walking towards her uncertainly, not a supervising adult in sight. Not quite sure what to do, she smiled at him as he approached, and asked, 'Is Mummy coming to collect you for something?'

'No,' he replied, in a tiny voice. 'I was on my way to get Mummy.'

'Why, whatever for, Lorcan?'

'It's Mrs Finch-Matthews. I ... we ... don't think she's very well.' The last five words came out in a rush, and his face had a strange sort of hurt look to it.

'And what makes you think that, Lorcan, dear?'

'Well, she's lying on the floor, instead of reading a story to us, like she always does at this time of day. And she's got something in ... in ... in ... her ... eye.' He gabbled the last word, as if there were something about his head-mistress' eye that he didn't want to think about. Ever again.

'And what is everybody else doing while they're not being

told a story?' Charlotte Chadwick asked, taking him by the hand and leading him gently back towards the school building. 'Angus MacPherson covered her eye with her scarf, Dove Lockwood said a little prayer for her to get better, and then we told everyone to do some silent reading until somebody came to help us, and tell us what to do. It was my idea to go and get Mummy.'

'Why didn't you just go and tell Miss Findlater, Lorcan?'

'Don't know,' he murmured, grimacing as he remembered. 'Didn't want to upset her,' he explained, and began to resist her urging towards the school library, where story-time always took place. 'I'm not going in there again!' he said, quite forcefully, and dug his heels into the tough corded carpet of the corridor. 'You can go in, but I'm not going to. I'm going to go and read silently at my desk,' he stated emphatically, unattached his hand from hers, and went back into his classroom, walking like an automaton, his face an unhealthy putty colour.

Placing her tin of cakes tidily on the table indicated by a cardboard sign, Charlotte walked tentatively into the school library.

Chapter Two

Thursday 31st March – later that morning

In what passed for Detective Inspector Harry Falconer's office in the Force's temporary accommodation, two things happened simultaneously. His telephone rang, and the door to the office slammed open, to admit a figure that made the inspector utter a little scream, as he reached for the telephone receiver.

It had been decided by 'the powers that be' (*or 'lack of will' on the author's part for a long-winded explanation of who was involved*) that Carsfold Police Station would become an 'office hours only' service, with the paper records still not digitised to be stored on the premises, and that there should be a transferral of staff to the Market Darley building, which needed extensive modifications to be suitable for a sizeable influx of staff.

All personnel, therefore, had been moved out while alterations took place, and were now housed in premises in the High Street that used to be the seat of business for 'Mr Bankrupt'. The 'mister' had been metaphorically removed from the name, as the business had gone under like so many others, and the floor space available had been deemed sufficient to house those officers currently without an official work station while the station was being altered and enlarged.

Two of these personnel happened to be the afore-mentioned Harry Falconer, DI, ex-army, forty years old, single, and surrogate father to three pampered pussycats. He was of average height, with a nice olive tone to his skin, dark-haired and dark-eyed, said eyes currently almost popping out of his head as he stared at what had just entered his office.

Detective Sergeant 'Davey' Carmichael was six-feet-five-

and-a-half inches in his enormous cotton socks, had recently married a young widow with two sons, and was the unquestionable master of the unexpected.

'Good morning. Detective Inspector Falconer speaking,' the older man intoned into the phone, while his eyes were still fixed hypnotically on his recently-arrived partner who revolved his lower jaw slowly as he hung up his coat. He had had a dental appointment first thing this morning, and was suffering from a new filling, or rather the effects of the pain-killer that had stopped him screaming his head off as the dentist had drilled merrily away at a lower left molar.

Five minutes later, as the phone connection was severed, it finally came. The explosion was loud, but mercifully short. 'Carmichael! What the bloody blue blazes are you doing coming in here with blond hair?' shouted the inspector, hardly able to believe his eyes, and wondering if he ought to pinch himself to see if he were dreaming.

'I fanthied a change, thir. For thpring, like. Tho Kerry got me some thtuff when sche went schopping. Sche done it for me last night. What do you think?' The anaesthetic had obviously not yet worn off, and his speech was somewhat slurpy, and damp for anyone standing too close to him.

'?!' Falconer found himself speechless, and not for the first time, in Carmichael's presence.

'What wath that, thir? I didn't quite catch it.'

'?!'

'I thought that'th what you didn't thay,' replied Carmichael, fully comprehending his inspector's unspoken sentiments.

On the way out of the building they had to endure the usual jeers of the un- or under-employed who hung around the town centre, smoking roll-ups and swilling cheap lager or cider, not quite daring to light up a spliff in such proximity to so many police officers.

'Didn't know yer could 'ave a pig farm in the middle of town, did you, Pinky?'

''As the Force gone financially as well as morally bankrupt, then?'

'Place used ter be run by scum. Now the filth's in charge. Not much change there then, is there? Except the tone's gone down a bit.'

'Taken any good bribes lately, Occifer?'

But such remarks had become commonplace in a very short space of time, and the two detectives just tuned the voices out, as they exited the building. They headed for Carmichael's car, as Falconer's gaze was so hypnotically drawn to his sergeant's new hair colour that he reckoned he would not notice the usually abhorrent state of the young man's Czechoslovakian dustbin on four wheels – and, in any case, his own car was in need of fuel.

'Why, Carmichael?' was all that he could muster, as they paced across to the vintage Skoda, which only seemed to be kept in one piece by rust, dollops of old chewing gum, and elastic bands.

'It'th nithe to have a change now and again, thir. Don't you think tho? You'd feel really different if you had thome low lighth in that dark hair of yourth.'

'Urrrrrr!'

'Not for you, then, thir! By the way, where are we headed, and why?'

'A place called Shepford Stacey – the school. Headmistress seems to have got something in her eye.'

'You're joking, thir.'

'No I'm not. It's a skewer. But at least she won't have to worry about a headache. She's dead.'

'It wathn't one of the kiddieth, schurely?'

'You never know, these days, but I sincerely hope not.' (*Pause.*) 'No. Don't be daft, Carmichael. I know society has broken down considerably since I was that age, but these kids are aged between five and seven. Most of them probably couldn't even reach that high. And don't distract me with ridiculous ideas. Low lights! The very idea! That's women's stuff!'

A few minutes later:

'Do you want to hear the current word on the beat, thir?'

23

'On the street, surely.'

'No, thir. On the beat. I got thith shtraight from PThee Green.'

'Go on.'

'Apparently Thuperintendent Chiverth hath been having a chinwag with the Chief Conthtable, and the Chief Conthtable thayth that your arrival here hath turned the area under hith jurithdiction into the murder capital of Europe, if not the world, and would you kindly schtop attracting all thethe murderth.'

'I don't believe you. You're making that up!'

'Am not, thir. I heard it thtraight from Merv Green'th mouth.'

'Then he was pulling your leg.'

'Actually, I think it wath more *your* leg he wath trying to pull, thir. And it worked, didn't it?'

'No comment, Sergeant, and wipe that smug grin off your face this instant. And if you speak to me again before that dratted anaesthetic wears off, I shall need the use of an umbrella. So shut up! Now!

'Yeth, thir.'

It was the last day of March, so they should be seeing the end of the March winds and the beginning of the April showers, by weather tradition. This year, though, the two months seemed to have made a pact to see the change of month pass with no change in the weather. During their drive over, the wind had risen and was now gusting strongly, driving a bank of battleship-grey clouds over from the south-west, and the first spots of rain began to fall as they pulled into the school car park.

By the time Carmichael had finished shunting his petrol-powered wheelie-bin back and forth to a position he approved of for parking, bright coins of rain were spinning off the tarmac as the last rays of sunlight were quenched by the clouds. They left the car with as much haste as they could muster, and headed for the school entrance doors at a run, pulling their collars over their heads to gain a little shelter from the sudden cataract of water.

It had been a good ten miles' drive along windy narrow roads past Upper Shepford and through Shepford St Bernard to reach their destination, and as they ran, rain now glittering soaking through their clothes, Falconer calculated that it would have been quicker for someone from the Carsfold station to have attended initially, Carsfold being only half that distance from the village – except that Carsfold station now only functioned during office hours, and with a skeleton staff who were only empowered to deal with minor matters and petty offences.

And that's exactly why the Force in Market Darley was now situated where it was, while builders altered and extended their previous building, so that it would accommodate the over-staffing left from the reorganisation at Carsfold, and a few other rural stations like it. The case would have landed in his lap eventually though; and he dived through the doors, standing open in readiness for their precipitous entrance, in search of shelter from the precipitation that necessitated it.

Charlotte Chadwick stood at the open doors to welcome them, her face grave and distressed. 'Thank God you've arrived!' she exclaimed, somewhat suitably for a Church school. I'm Charlotte Chadwick, by the way. My six-year-old Imogen's in the lower class. I called the vicar when I found out what had happened – after I'd done the 999 business and fetched Miss Findlater to gather all the children into the hall. He's here with his wife, and everybody's in there now, including Stevie, that's Miss Baldwin, the dinner lady, who arrived in a very timely manner, when I was trying to get Miss Findlater calmed down, and before the vicar arrived.'

'I think we'll just remove our wet things before we go ...' Falconer attempted to stem the flow, which was as merciless as the rain outside, but was unsuccessful, as Mrs Chadwick, once more, took up her tale with relentless determination.

'I found little Lorcan – that's Lorcan LeClerc, he's only five years old – all on his own in the playground, looking around for help, so I took him back inside; I was just delivering a tin of

25

cakes for the sale this afternoon.' She paused to draw breath, but as Falconer inhaled in readiness for speech, she held up her right hand, like a traffic policeman, to halt him, and continued,

'It was dead quiet in the school – oh, I'm so sorry, I should never have used that word! Anyway, all the 'uppers' – that's the eight- to eleven-year-olds, were in their classroom with Miss Findlater; she doesn't cope very well with very young children's behaviour. There wasn't a sound, and I asked Lorcan to take me to Mrs Finch-Matthews, asking him where the rest of the 'lowers' were – that's the five- to seven-year-olds, and he led me straight to the room outside Mrs Finch-Matthews' office where the little library is located.

'And what a sight met my eyes when I looked round the door. You simply wouldn't believe it!' Falconer would have welcomed the chance. Carmichael was in his element, however, his notebook in one hand, enthusiastically-licked pencil in his other, leaning against the wall, scribbling notes as if he would set the paper on fire.

'There she was, lying on the floor in front of her chair – it's story-time, you see, just before lunch. It gives the other staff a chance to set the hall out with the tables and chairs and other stuff for the school lunch, which must have just been delivered, because I noticed the metal containers stacked at the back of the hall when I took a little peek in there a while ago.'

She must have been breathing through her ears by now, for she hadn't made a noticeable pause for breath for quite some time, and Falconer was now building up a head of steam. 'Now, don't let me get distracted. Where was I? Oh, yes; Mrs Finch-Matthews lying on the ground. There was a silk scarf with scenes from Paris lying over her face, and the rest of the children from the class were all sitting cross-legged on the floor in front of her, with their 'silent reading' books, and when I asked why they were doing that, Lorcan told me that Angus MacPherson had told them to do it, while Dove Lockwood – the vicar's daughter, and a very sensible girl – had 'shushed' them all into silence.

'I'm sure they all just did as they were told because they

were so shocked and frightened, and if they were looking at the pages of their books, they weren't looking at that awful figure on the floor. They just waited for a grown-up to show up, I guess.'

At last the flow was stemmed, and Falconer was furious to discover that he had forgotten what he was going to ask her originally.

'Is the vicar around?' Carmichael asked, for him, having already decided from their loquacious lecture, that Miss Findlater would probably prove a bit of a washout. It appeared that he could now speak again without hindrance of dental injection, and this cheered him somewhat.

'That's exactly what I was going to ask,' cut in Falconer, not wishing to relinquish his seniority in front of a member of the public. And I shall need to know if there is somewhere suitable for setting up an incident room. We can't work out of Market Darley – it's far too time-consuming at this distance. It's all right, Mrs Chadwick, we can sort something out with the vicar when we know exactly what the situation is here,' this last to forestall his new playmate, who had drawn in a breath to interrupt.

'Now, quick as you can: where is everybody? I'm sure you've already told us, but it's slipped my mind.'

'In the hall, like I said, but they can't stay in there, because there's all the tables and chairs to set out, like I mentioned, and the food will be getting cold, and they'll all be very hungry by now ...'

'Enough! Now please get me this dinner lady person – Stevie, did you say her name was? – and start moving the children into an empty classroom; they must have come from somewhere, and they'll have to go back to it again for now. No! Not another word. Off with you!'

Charlotte Chadwick complied, with a little smile that seemed to indicate that she liked being taken charge of, and returned a couple of minutes later with Stevie Baldwin.

'Before you say a word,' Falconer said, holding up a hand in imitation of the gesture that Charlotte had used on him just a few minutes previously, 'I realise what the priority is here. Summon whoever you can, to assemble the dining room and get the meal served, then we'll decide how this is going to work. Shoo! Shoo! Off you go! You've got lots of empty tummies to fill, before we can even catch our breath and get started.' Falconer was surprised at how bossy he could be in self-defence, and realised that he had not issued so many orders in such a short space of time since he had left the army. It felt good!

Carmichael surveyed the inspector with respect. 'Tummies, sir?' he said. 'I never realised how child-friendly you were.'

'Am I?' he asked, puzzled; still lost in happy memories of shutting that woman up before he punched her in self-defence.

While the children ate, in uncharacteristic silence today, Stevie and Charlotte supervised while Rev. Septimus Lockwood and his wife Ruth contacted the parents of those in the upper class and arranged for them to be collected early.

Apart from the parents' obvious shock at what had happened, they were almost as concerned about what would happen to all the cakes that had been baked for the sale, due to take place that afternoon. In the circumstances, the vicar felt obliged to promise that he would lend one of the unused rooms in The Rectory tomorrow, so that the event could take place without any disappointment or wastage.

Ruth would have to run that particular bun-fight, as Good Friday is quite a busy day in the Anglican Church calendar, and he had a few worthy stalwarts who would expect him to supervise the Stations of the Cross – all of them elderly, and High Church to a man (or woman).

After the arrival of the parents of the children from the upper class, the parents of the lower class were summoned, as the children would have to be questioned in case they had seen anyone or anything, perhaps through a window, and their parents were required to be present for this. It was lucky for them that several of the pupils were missing at the moment, due to the annual visitation of the chickenpox virus, making their task quite a bit lighter than it otherwise could have been.

The final phone call of that session was to the parents of Miss Findlater, who had been almost hysterical since the body had been discovered. Not only was she not very good with the behaviour of young children, but it seemed that she hadn't attended even a short course at the School of Hard Knocks, and was still weeping into a handful of tissues in her, by now, empty classroom. They would have to speak to her later, when she had pulled herself together and recovered her dignity.

'Why on earth did she become a teacher?' Falconer hissed to Carmichael, as Stevie and Charlotte ushered the older children out of the door and into their parents' tender care, without being subjected to too much of a third degree. The parents knew that, if the bake sale was taking place the next day, and at The Vicarage, it would also be a free-for-all for gossip as well as cake purchases, and were content to wait until then, to allow more information to become assimilated and made ready to share.

'How on earth should I know, sir? I've never even met the woman before,' Carmichael hissed back, astonished, never having being taught the niceties of dealing with rhetorical questions.

Without another word, the two men entered the small room that served the school as a library, and contained, in the far right-hand corner, the glass panels that enclosed the office of the head teacher, such an arrangement not only ensuring silence while books were being chosen, but an extra buffer of space in the case of anything really private being discussed within said office.

Just outside the front glass-panelled wall of this structure stood a wooden chair and, a few feet in front of it, and prone on the floor where she had fallen, was the shell of Audrey Finch-Matthews, the Parisian-patterned scarf covering her head and face, just as described by Charlotte Chadwick.

Stepping forward, Falconer whisked away the scarf and revealed what it had hidden; what had been so appalling to a child that it had needed to be instantly extinguished visually.

29

The hair was slightly tousled from its impromptu covering, the make-up barely smudged by the indignity that had been suffered.

It was the skewer sticking out of the eye-socket that was so out of place and so disturbing. In fact, its presence was so incongruous as to appear obscene to anyone not expecting to see it there. 'I want this videoed and photographed to the nth degree when the SOCO team gets here. I want nothing missed. It's absolutely grotesque.'

Falconer's mobile phone rang, and he spoke briefly before returning it to his pocket and turning to Carmichael. 'The SOCO team is here already, and so are the uniforms, waiting outside in their vehicles, and Dr Christmas is on his way. You stay inside and I'll go out and organise them. I won't be more than a few minutes, then we can start to take statements.'

The SOCO team he directed straight in to the relevant room. In addition to these bodies, he had been sent PC Starr, and PCs Green and Proudfoot, the latter not having crossed his path since he had worked on a case in Castle Farthing last year [See: Death of an Old Git].

'Ah, PC Proudfoot, we meet again,' he greeted the constable, a dangerous twinkle in his eye, as his memory served him a little snack of 'previous circumstances'.

'Good morning, Inspector. Our paths have, indeed, crossed once more,' he replied, somewhat inadvisably, as it turned out. A salute would have been more diplomatic.

'And have we let any vicars through to the crime scene on this occasion, Constable Proudfoot? Are there any clerics in the vicinity heedlessly obliterating valuable forensic material? Any vicar-ing vandals marauding around the premises?'

'No, sir!'

'Any reverend gentlemen at all, to cavort around and destroy physical evidence of the crime?'

'Absolutely not, sir. You know how sorry I was about that, sir.'

'Not even a retired lay preacher? Or a loose canon?' Falconer was rather proud of this last one, but knew no one present would appreciate its subtlety but himself.

'No, sir,' Proudfoot replied again, his face a big red football that threatened to steam if it got any brighter in colour.

'Good man, Constable. Keep it up, and you and I shall get along fine.'

'Yes, sir. Thank you, sir.'

'Absolutely no bishops or arch-deacons! I'm trusting you on this one, Proudfoot.'

'No, sir. Absolutely none, sir,' replied PC Proudfoot, hoping that his ribbing for the day was over and done with now, and he would be left in peace to proceed, unmolested, with his guard duty.

Carmichael squirmed for the poor man on his behalf. He, of all people, knew what it was like to be on the wrong side of Falconer's tongue, and his look towards the uncomfortable constable was pregnant with fellow feeling.

Abandoning his sarcastic banter, Falconer got down to business, and ordered Proudfoot to remain on duty at the school gate, to make sure that the only people admitted were parents of the children still inside the building. A quick word with Green and Starr established that the interviews would take place, split between the two main classrooms, thus allowing the hall to be cleared up, and providing a waiting space for those waiting to be spoken to.

The lower class children would be interviewed in their own classroom – familiarity might help to unlock any reluctant jaws – with a parent present and PC Starr in attendance. The staff members and anyone else adult would be interviewed in the older children's classroom, and PC Green could sit in on that one while he, Falconer did the interviewing. Carmichael could speak to the children. Although probably seen as the BFG by the children, he was more at ease with small people than Falconer, and with PC Starr as a further softening presence, they should be able to extract any necessary information.

Leading his troops in behind him, he re-entered the building ready to solve a crime, went through the lower class door, and immediately shut it behind him, in an unplanned attempt to give

Linda Starr an unexpected rhinoplasty. He must be hallucinating, and if he was, he didn't want PC Starr *not* seeing what he was *not* seeing, because it wasn't *real*.

Before him, over by the window on the opposite side of the room was quite a large rocking horse, and it was occupied and darting backwards and forwards at an alarming rate. As the bang of the closing door echoed down the corridor outside, he assumed his previously-employed hissing tones, and whispered hoarsely (*!*), 'Carmichael! What the hell do you think you're doing? Get off that thing this minute, before anybody else sees you. And don't do it again! Ever! Even if I'm not looking!'

Carmichael complied reluctantly, looking momentarily crestfallen now that his mood had been broken, and barely glanced in PC Starr's direction when she entered the room. Falconer could tell that his colleague was disappointed, because when they had set up the little conversation space in which the interviews would take place, he did not remove his notebook until the first child was ushered into the room.

When Falconer left to start his own interviews in the adjacent classroom, he saw Carmichael take one last, wistful glance at the large wooden rocking horse over by the window. Judging from the look of glee on the younger man's face when Falconer had entered the room, he reckoned the sergeant was, in his head, about to win the Grand National – Lester Pillock approaching the finishing line, to the jeers of the crowd.

After what felt like a rather bizarre period dominated by the unusual presence of 'short stuff', Falconer had PC Green check that the school was clear of parents and pupils, and assembled the remaining adults in the dining room. Luckily for him, Stevie Baldwin had whipped her Spike and Charlotte Chadwick's Imogen off to her parents', returning as soon as she could so that they could have a quick pooling of knowledge, before the police contingent returned to Market Darley.

They made a formidable sight, seven adults crouched on tiny infants' chairs; six tigers crouched for the pounce, and one XXXL grasshopper, with its knees around its ears. If it decided to rub its legs together, they would all be deafened, and with this thought twitching at his lips, Falconer found he was glad that PC Proudfoot was still on the gate. The thought of having to heave that sphere of a man to his feet would, somewhere along the line, need the application of a block and tackle.

The only representatives of the school present were Charlotte Chadwick (classroom assistant) and Stevie Baldwin (lunchtime supervisor), and after making a time-line for the events of that morning, there was little else they could do. It was down to the SOCO team, the pathologist, and a fingertip search of the grounds, to see if there were any clues to the identity of the person who had pushed a barley sugar twist, 1950s skewer through the left eye socket of Audrey Finch-Matthews, sometime between half-past ten and a quarter to twelve that morning.

Little had been learnt from the interviews at the school, but Falconer was confident that they would learn more when they widened their net of interviewees, and spoke to people in their own homes, where not only would they feel more comfortable, but would have recovered somewhat from the shock.

Chapter Three

Good Friday, 1st April

The previous afternoon had been a period of writing up notes, hoping for developments to occur without benefit of catalyst, but this latter had been in vain, and although today was a Bank Holiday for most people, for Falconer's team, it was just another day at the factory, with a murder to solve.

With a rush of déjà vu, Harry Falconer looked up as the (temporary) office door opened to admit Carmichael, and elicit from the inspector, for the second day in a row, a high-pitched, almost girlish shriek.

'What have you done now, you idjit?' he boomed, eyes once again glued to Carmichael's scalp.

'I just thought I'd try it, as it's my birthday today. Happy birthday to me, happy birthday to me, happy birthday to me-ee – happy birthday to me!' he carolled, executing a little (*large!*) twirl on the spot, before taking a bow.

'Many happy returns of the day, Carmichael, but why the colourful forelock?' Falconer asked, once again raising his gaze to his sergeant's hairline. 'Why have you got a clump of bright blue hair, as if blonde were not enough?'

'Because, in my job, red would have looked too much like blood, sir.' A perfectly logical reason in Carmichael's opinion, but the inspector still had no idea what he was talking about.

'Explain it to me, Sergeant, as if I were a dimwit,' he asked, visions of role-reversal dancing in his head.

'Food dye, sir. Yellow wouldn't have showed: red, as I said: green would just have looked as if I'd got grass in my hair. So it had to be blue.'

'Why did it have to be anything, Carmichael?' asked a still puzzled Falconer.

'I told you, sir: because it's my birthday. Happy birth …'

'Don't start singing again! I'll just not bother to ask in the future,' he sighed, facing defeat in the face, and simply not caring any more. They must have broken the mould after they'd made Carmichael, not because he was so wonderfully unique, but because he was so terrifyingly so, and they didn't want to make another one by accident!

And how typical of his sergeant, to have his birthday on All Fools' Day. He couldn't make up his mind whether this was absolutely fitting, or wildly ironic. It simply didn't matter: the day was Carmichael's, by right and by birth, and he didn't really want to spoil it for him.

Ruth Lockwood had worked like a demon to make The Rectory fit for the school's postponed bake sale. It really could not be held at the school – not only because of the decorators, who had also been postponed, but because it was an official crime scene. So she had dutifully thrown open the double doors between the sitting room and the dusty dining room, run round with a can of polish, and collected as many chairs as she could find.

If she set an urn of tea and one of coffee on the kitchen table, and left an 'honesty' bowl in open view for the money, she had no doubt whatsoever that the ladies of Shepford Stacey would linger with a hot drink, sampling wares that they had not yet bought in bulk, but just might if they proved tasty enough morsels.

And with that ghastly murder the day before, there was plenty to gossip about. Every vicar's wife knows that gossip breeds money, if only you can find something to sell while it goes on – preferably something either edible or pot-able. The money from the cakes was to swell the school coffers, but the money from the teas and coffees could go into the parish fund, as a reward for her, for stepping into the breach in such a timely fashion. After all, this was supposed to be over and done with the day before, and nothing to do with her whatsoever.

Thus, she comforted herself as she dragged yet another heavy old wooden chair through from the downstairs lumber room, remnants of a previous incumbent that had received no place in their home. That it was all down to her, she had been aware the day before, when it had all been agreed, for Septimus would be trapped in the church all day – fourteen Stations of the Cross, and not a public convenience on any of them, for his bodily relief!

Her last preliminary duty was charging the urns and making them ready to dispense the beverages for which they were labelled. The rest of the surface of the kitchen was covered in cups and saucers, most of them utilitarian white, some of them slightly cracked or chipped, all mustered numerously to slake the thirst of the gossiping hordes.

She opened The Rectory's double front doors at ten o'clock sharp, her loins girded for two hours of being rushed off her feet selling cakes, tarts, and biscuits, and having her ear talked off by her customers.

Saul Catchpole, the elderly school caretaker who lived in Victoria and Albert Alms-houses, was first over the threshold, as he was at any sale that involved home-cooked food. Flo Atkins, his next-door neighbour and the school cleaner, was hard on his heels. They both lived alone, and neither could be bothered too much in the way of cooking; opening a tin or heating up something was more in their line, and they relished the thought of home-made sweetmeats for the next day or two, which would be a tasty addition to today's hot cross buns.

Being quick off the mark enabled them to occupy the comfiest chairs in the sitting room area, the cakes being ranged upon the dining table at the other end of the double room. From here they were lord and lady of all they surveyed, and could engage in their beloved pastime of people watching, while indulging in a little mild malice and sarcasm, while they sipped their tea and nibbled at the cakes they had chosen, to go with their hot drinks.

'There's that Harriet Findlater over there with her mother,' Flo pointed out to her companion. 'What's the use of a woman that still lives with her mum and dad, when she's old enough to have grandkids of her own?'

'Waste of a life, if you ask me,' Saul concurred. 'Here, did I tell you about the right ding-dong they had a couple of weeks ago?'

'What was that all about, then? And what were you doing, eavesdropping?'

'I was putting a new washer on one of the sinks in the boys' toilets, and you know her office is just the other side of the partition wall.'

'That sounds fair enough to me, Saul. Go on.'

'Well, that Findlater woman is a few years younger than the late lamented. She wanted to be recommended to take over as Head when Audrey Finch-Matthews retired.'

'Sounds reasonable enough, I suppose. She's spent just about all her working life at that school, from what I've heard.'

'It did sound reasonable, the way she put it. She would only be able to remain in the job for two years before she herself retired; she had always wanted to end her teaching career with a headship, and they could get someone younger and more up to date when she'd had her turn at the wheel, as it were.'

'And what did old Audrey say to that little request, Mr Eavesdropper?'

'Now, you won't believe this, but she just laughed. She sounded half-demented for a moment, and little Miss Findlater sort of spluttered and faltered, trying to say something she couldn't get out.'

'The old cow!' judged Flo, making a face that conveyed a suitable amount of disbelief.

'That's what I thought. In spades!'

'So what happened next? I'd never have known this had happened, from what I've seen of them recently.'

'Old Audrey starts going on about how weak Harriet's discipline is; how she can't face teaching the lower class because of the behaviour of the young children; how she bursts into tears if there is any unpleasantness, finally running off to Mummy if things get really unpleasant.'

38

'Still, she could've let her have her turn, couldn't she?'

'She said she wasn't fit to be a teacher any more; that she'd got worse with age, and that when she, Audrey, retired, she was going to recommend that Harriet be offered early retirement on mental health grounds!'

'Oh, my Gawd! And how did she take that?'

'Burst into tears, called old Audrey an 'unspeakable lady-dog' – her very words – then rushed off home, presumably to Mummy and Daddy, to have her tears dried and her hand held.'

'So why weren't they at each other's throats?'

'For one, Harriet's that timid, she wouldn't say boo to a goose, and for another, I was just going into the Ring o' Bells the next lunchtime for my daily half, when I saw a van draw up, and a big bouquet of flowers being delivered at High Gates – no doubt from 'er Ladyship to old Droopy Drawers, by way of apology, or for being so honest, if you ask me.'

'She's that soft, that would probably have shut her up. I'd 'ave thought that the last thing she wanted was that poor wet hen snivelling and weeping all over her for goodness knows how long.'

'Well, we'll never find out, will we, now that 'er Ladyship's been murdered?'

The words were hardly out of his mouth, before they both inhaled sharply and turned to stare at each other, faces horrified.

'She never!' hissed Flo.

'She wouldn't! Would she?' hissed back Saul.

Sitting at the kitchen table, now almost stripped of all its cups and saucers, sat little Maura MacPherson, her Celtic-red, curly hair pulled back in a fluffy bun at the nape of her rather sturdy neck, and Stevie Baldwin, taking time-out from the crowd in the other rooms.

Maura opened the conversation. 'These cakes will stop their mouths, when they've eaten all the hot cross buns at home, won't they?'

Stevie smiled as she agreed. 'I don't think any amount of cakes would be enough for my gran, so I'll need to take plenty home with me.'

Niceties dealt with, Maura got straight to the point. 'Ghastly business, that, yesterday!' she declared sparingly.

'Unbelievable,' answered Stevie, leaning down slightly to scratch just below her right knee.

'Who on earth do you think could have done such a thing?' Maura asked, making it clear that this was a blatant opening gambit for a good old gossip.

'Off hand, I really couldn't say. Whoever it was must have hated her very much,' returned Stevie, in acceptance of the invitation. 'Have you got any idea who might have had it in for her; who might have had a motive for wanting her out of the way?'

'It's funny you should ask that,' Maura said innocently, knowing full well that that was just the question she had wanted to be asked, for she was bursting with a theory, and wanted urgently to test it on someone other than her husband. 'My Angus told me a very strange little tale only last week, but I think I can see the sense of it now.'

'What was that?' Stevie asked, rubbing at her leg again.

'Is that thing giving you trouble?' Maura asked, having noticing her scratching a couple of minutes ago.

'Oh, you know how it is. These National Health prostheses aren't very comfortable, but I'm saving up for a state-of-the-art one that not only looks better, so I can wear a skirt again, but is much more comfortable to wear.' Stevie made very light of the loss of her lower right leg. 'Anyway, go on.'

'Well, wee Angus said that Isaac Borrowdale was being silly, and Mrs Finch-Matthews saw him, and told him not to be a little scamp. Angus said that Isaac seemed to clamp on to the word 'scamp', and proceeded to tell the headteacher that he wasn't a scamp because he didn't have to send money to his daddy.'

'What on earth does that mean, Maura? It's just a load of gobbledygook.'

'Hang on a wee minute and I'll unravel it for you. It seems that Daddy works from home, for which I myself can vouch.

Well, lately, when the mail comes, there seems to be a lot for him, and he overheard his mother say what he thought was, 'More money from your scamps'. Well, It made no sense whatsoever, until I heard the local news last night, and there was a piece where they were asking people to be extra vigilant about computer 'scammers'. What do you reckon, Stevie?'

'I reckon you could be right, Maura, for I'll add my twopenn'orth now, but it's come in a rather roundabout way. Let me explain. My grandmother is a friend of Miss Findlater's parents; they're of an age, and have known each other for a long time. Harriet confides her little snippets from Audrey to her mother, who usually passes them on to my grandmother, who usually passes them on to my mother, and finally to me at the end of the line.

'It would seem that Seth Borrowdale acquired a criminal record as a juvenile, and wasn't really dragged onto the straight and narrow until Martha got her claws into him. She's a strong-willed woman with a lot of pride, and she'd be mortified if he was caught for anything else illegal after all this time: in fact I think she'd swing for him if he tarnished her holier-than-thou reputation. But can a leopard ever change its library books, let alone its spots?'

'Don't be so silly, Stevie! It wouldn't be able to hand over its card with paws like that!' Maura had unintentionally joined the game.

'Just as I said,' smiled her companion, pleased at the witty reply to her rather silly comment. Anyway, it would seem that when Seth was at school, and it was this very village school that he attended, he was one of Mrs Finch-Matthews' first pupils when she began teaching. And it would appear that he was a 'scammer' even then. She caught him buying Dinky cars from the new in-take of five-year-olds, with bubble gum for payment, then he went on to sell them to his friends in the upper class for their pocket money.

'Apparently he was strangely possessive about his own toys, and actually kept two sets of cars and trucks and things. This, I think, came from Seth's own mother to either Harriet or her mother. It would seem that when other children came round to play, he would get a collection of battered old toys out to share with them.

'When he was on his own, however, it was a different matter. He had a pristine set of playthings, kept immaculate, and in their boxes. These were for when he was playing on his own. He didn't like to share the good things with other people, in case they damaged them. Now that's damned odd in a child so young, don't you think?'

'Not only is that weird,' Maura agreed, 'but I think the business about using bubble gum as currency, to get his hands on hard cash, at that age, is positively criminal. I bet the mothers of the little boys who swapped their cars were livid.'

'No doubt, but what could they do about it? Their little darlings had, as it were, chewed the gum and found it good. That particular kind of currency had been confined to the waste bin or swallowed out of devilment, long before they found out what had been going on.'

'But that just backs up what I said, and confirms that he's been a bit of a wide boy since he started school. I wonder he doesn't have a criminal record.'

'Maybe he has, and we just don't know about it. You know that stuck-up bitch of a wife would cover for him, just so she could retain her air of superiority and respectability.'

'Come to think of it,' Maura commented, a look of deep thought on her face, 'there have been a couple of times when he's been away on business, or so she said, for a few months at a time. I wonder if he could actually have been "doing time"?'

'Wouldn't that be great?' Stevie asked, with a laugh. 'That'd knock Little Miss Snooty off her pedestal, and no mistake.'

'Aye!' said Maura, with a wicked little twinkle, as she rose to go back into the dining area to buy a few more cupcakes to replace the ones she'd unconsciously eaten while chatting to Stevie.

Meredith Allington, from Cobwebs, and India Bywaters-Flemyng of Paddock View entered the fray, one just a few seconds after the other. Thus they arrived simultaneously at the display of cakes, which was already showing signs of being depleted. They were each one half of two local couples, and had known each other since starting school.

Meredith Allington, an avid gossip-hound, the end of her nose twitching as it did when she scented prey, opened the conversation. 'Well, what do you think of yesterday? Just desserts or what?'

'I say! That's a bit harsh, isn't it? She was just a harmless old biddy not long off retirement.'

'Harmless old biddy – my arse! That's not what you've been saying all these years, and I still can't understand why you let your Sholto go to that school after what happened.'

'That was a lifetime ago. I haven't thought about it in years.'

'No, of course you haven't.' Meredith's voice was dripping with sarcasm. 'I remember the things you used to say about her: the way she treated your other half, and half scared him to death, until he developed that stutter. And he's not that much better now. You told me that he said he used to wet his pants every Monday morning, just at the thought of going back to school after the weekend.'

'Let's get these cakes sorted out and bought, and we can have a chat in a minute,' countered India in self-defence, pretending an unnatural interest in a blood-red strawberry tart.

'Tinned fruit!' was her friend's reaction. 'Let's away to the kitchen for a coffee when we've made our purchases, and we can have a good old chew of the fat.'

Knowing Meredith's unerring instinct for rumour and her love of dissecting any gossip in the offing, India agreed, and chose a Victoria sandwich and three sticky lardy cakes for their tea that afternoon. Sunday would bring endless chocolate, and this should satisfy the sweet teeth of both her son and her husband until then.

Meredith pounced on the strawberry tart from which she had just distracted her friend, and even had the grace to look a little guilty. 'Sorry! I just love tinned strawberries. I can't seem to help myself.'

Once settled in the kitchen with mugs of coffee – the cups and saucers had run out, and were piled in the sink and on the draining board in an ever increasing mountain – Meredith was off again, like a terrier with a scent. 'Look what she did to him. He had no speech problems before he started at that school. And you only stayed in the village because you could run the businesses as you do.'

'Well, it helped that Hartley's aunt died and left us that pile of a property of hers. That's what got us started; nothing to do with his 'communication problems'.'

'And it's jolly lucky you did inherit from her. What else could he have done?'

'He doesn't have a stutter when he's at home.' India was feeling decidedly defensive of her beloved spouse now.

'No, but you know you have to handle all the customers for the riding school and trekking, and do the welcoming and the hand-backs of the cottages, because he can't get a word out.'

'Oh, look! There's a couple from one of my holiday homes, just gone through the hall,' said India, pointing in a way her mother had always told her was bad manners. 'I think I'll go and have a word, see how they're settling in.' Where Meredith Allington was concerned, she had to take her opportunities to escape where she could, and with a quick wave, she disappeared back into the other room in search of sanctuary.

Her quarry was surveying the goodies on display while her husband was leaning against the wall pretending indifference, although he kept a close eye on what his wife was selecting.

'Hello there!' India cooed in her quarry's ear, making her jump slightly. 'It's Virginia Grainger, isn't it, from number five? And this is your husband Richard,' she added, as he moved away from the wall to join them. 'India Bywaters-Flemyng – I handed over the keys to your cottage when you arrived.'

'Of course. How nice to see you again,' smiled Virginia, indicating that she would take four scones and four jam tarts. 'There seems to be a lot of chat going on here. Is there something on in the village for Easter?' she asked, innocently.

44

'Nothing so inviting, I'm afraid,' India replied, n/
being the bearer of news, having a friend like Meredith. ᴵ ᴵⁿ
afraid the headmistress of the local primary school was
murdered yesterday, and we're not used to such sensations in
such a quiet backwater as this.'

At the word 'murder', Virginia's face had drained of colour,
and her husband's had assumed a strange blank expression.

'You've had a murder here?' Virginia asked, in a tiny voice.

'Yes. Yesterday. At the school. Down the road and across
the crossroads from where you are.'

The holidaying couple exchanged a horrified look, and
Richard took his wife's arm. 'I think we'll be returning the keys
to the cottage to you later today.'

'But why?' India was mystified by their reaction. She hadn't
even had a chance to go into the gory details yet.

'We came here for a break because, if you must know, we
recently became entangled in a double murder, and now we've
barely settled in here only to find there's been another one just
down the road from us. I don't know about you, Virginia, but I
don't think I could bear to be in close proximity to another one,
could you?'

'Absolutely not, Richard. Let's go and pack. Oh, we don't
expect a refund or anything like that,' Virginia added, looking
in India's direction and, hanging on to her husband's arm, they
made their exit, almost forgetting, in their haste to grab their
bag of sweet goodies, but pausing, of necessity, on their way
out, to return their cups and saucers to the kitchen.

'Extraordinary!' exclaimed India, immediately disengaging
her mind from this meeting and leaning forward to ask Ruth if
they had any hot cross buns.

'Certainly not,' was the reply. 'If we sold those, Anne and
Chris Hammond would be after us for trying to put the village
shop out of business.'

India gave her a comprehending look, for it didn't do to
tread on the commercial toes of another business in the village;
if, that is, one wanted to stay in business oneself. With a wary
glance towards the kitchen, she managed to slip through the

door and out of the house without being caught by Meredith again, to her obvious relief.

Miss Harriet Findlater had more or less recovered from her conniption of the day before, and turned up about an hour into the bake sale to choose something for a treat for herself and her parents. She had thought it better to get out and about as quickly as possible after the awful shock she had suffered, and she never failed to support anything the school had organised.

After selecting three blueberry and three chocolate muffins, she carried her purchases to the kitchen, where she found Stevie Baldwin at the sink washing and drying cups and saucers, and stopping momentarily to lift her right leg from the floor to ease the pain where her prosthesis rubbed.

'Hello, Miss Findlater,' she called. Don't have one of those clunky mugs. Here – I've got a nice clean cup and saucer for you – much more refined, if rather utilitarian. Help yourself from the urns. They're labelled. I'm just getting this done before I refill them.'

'Where's Ruth?' asked Harriet, glad to be in familiar company.

'Having a cuppa herself. She deserves it: it took ages to get all this set out, and with it being Good Friday, Septimus couldn't be here to give her a hand. I say, what do you make of that awful business yesterday?'

Harriet Findlater groaned, and sank into a chair at the kitchen table with her recently filled cup. 'I don't know what to make of it. In fact, I don't want to think of it at all: it was just so awful,' and with this declaration, she ran her right hand over her face as if to brush away an irritant.

'I know how you feel, but *someone* did that to her, and I'd rather we knew who it was, so they can be locked up before they do it again.'

At this, Harriet looked aghast, as if the thought had never crossed her mind, then asked, 'But who? It was so barbaric. I can't think of anyone who would do something so ... so ... savage. Can you?'

46

'No, but your memory of Mrs Finch-Matthews goes back much further than mine. Can you think of anyone who would bear her a grudge so strong that they would do something like that?'

'No, of course I can't.'

'I bet you could if you tried. You know you've got a marvellous memory, and you know more than anyone else about our little school now.'

Flattery always produced results, and Harriet Findlater propped an elbow on the table, her chin in her hand, and began to cast her mind back. 'Well …' she began, tentatively.

'Yes? Go on! What?' Stevie encouraged her, drying her hands and sitting opposite her at the table, where she placed a pile of saucers and a few cups.

'It's such a long time ago, my dear. I'm sure it can't have any relevance after so many years.'

'You let me be the judge of that. Now, don't tease. Tell me what you're thinking about before I burst.'

'It's the Darlings. The couple who run the Ring o' Bells.'

'She can't have taught them; they're much too old.'

'No, not them: their son. He would be about thirty now – David – and he went to the village school while both Audrey and I were teaching there …' She paused here, looking back through time to the little boy who was always in trouble.

'Come on! The suspense is killing me. What about him?' asked Stevie with growing impatience.

'He was always up to mischief: getting kept in at playtime, being made to clean the blackboard, and put up the chairs at the end of the day. It seemed he just couldn't behave himself. And he was really behind all the other children: didn't seem to get on with reading and writing at all, so he spent most of the day disrupting the other children from their learning and generally getting into trouble of one sort or another. A real nuisance he was.

'He had a vivid enough imagination, and he was articulate enough. You should have heard the names he used to call Audrey. I'd just started working there, and I found out he'd

47

been sneaking back into the school at playtime and stealing from the coats and blazers in the cloakroom: from satchels too, if there were any left unattended out there.

'He was always the one who would initiate a food fight at lunch time, or who would start an actual fight. He was argumentative and defiant, and yet I felt that he wasn't such a bad boy. I told Audrey that I thought there might be something wrong with him that might explain his behaviour, but she said he was just a wrong 'un who would end up a functionally illiterate adult, always in trouble for the rest of his life, and she washed her hands of him.'

'And did he?' Stevie interjected, trying to get to the point of the story.

'Halfway through his senior schooling he was diagnosed as severely dyslexic. But by that time it was too late for him to change. He'd been branded by too many people as an unruly tearaway. He started getting into trouble with the police shortly after he left our school, and just went further on down that road.

'Last month he was jailed for four years for his part in a string of burglaries, where he'd got off with a few months here and there before. I know it hit Margaret and Ernie hard, although they don't talk about him. They're contemporaries of mine, and I go in sometimes with Mummy and Daddy for a little drink, and I always have a little chat with her about when we were all young.

'I've noticed that since he was sentenced, she's rather been on the sauce, if you know what I mean.' Harriet Findlater blushed as she used this slangy expression, but it sounded better than just declaring that the woman had become a serious drunk.

'I don't really go in there,' Stevie replied, 'so I wouldn't know. If I go for a drink, which isn't often, as I'm saving for my new leg, I go to the Temporary Sign. As I'm a barmaid there, I tend to know all the customers, so I feel at home, and don't have to answer any questions about it.'

At this, Harriet gave a small titter of laughter. 'I'm sorry, my dear, but what would outsiders think of us if they could listen in. Here we are talking about cold-blooded murder in the old

News of the World style, then you say you're saving up for a new leg!'

Stevie's face crumpled in on itself, as she saw the ridiculousness of the situation, and they both laughed at the sheer absurdity of what life could throw at ordinary folk in the course of a casual conversation.

After a few seconds to regain their composure, Stevie had a question. 'You don't think she could have come over here in her cups and done for Audrey, do you? I mean, it's a pub, and they do food. There's bound to have been several skewers lying around in the kitchen.'

'If there are, and they're the same sort as was used,' here, Harriet shuddered. 'then I'm sure the police will find out. It's not for us to poke our noses in, now, is it?'

'Definitely not!'

As Harriet got to her feet, she glanced out of the door and did a double take. 'I'm sure I recognise that face through there, but not from recently,' she muttered, more to herself than to Stevie.

'What was that?' Stevie asked, also rising, to continue the washing-up.

'Oh, nothing. I just thought I recognised someone, that's all. I'm probably mistaken,' was the teacher's final comment as she went back into the other room to say her good-byes.

Ruth Lockwood had done another turn selling the baked produce, and was at this moment talking to another of the holiday cottage residents who had kindly brought a plate of freshly baked fairy cakes with her to the sale, to boost stock. 'That was a very kind thought of yours, Mrs Course,' Ruth cooed, doing her 'very bestest vicar's little wifey-poos' act.

'It was no trouble at all, Mrs Lockwood, and do call me Caroline, as we shall meet again at church this Eastertide,' the other woman suggested.

Ruth agreed – politely, of course – but made no such counter offer, merely handing her a bag containing her purchases and taking her money. 'I do hope you enjoy your stay in our little village.'

'No doubt I shall. I'm very interested in ecclesiastical architecture, and shall spend some time in your delightful little church admiring its internal adornments.'

As the woman walked off, Ruth gave a sigh of relief, followed, about ten seconds later, with a bellow of rage. 'Saul Catchpole, don't you dare pour the dregs of your tea into my cheese plant! You killed the last one I had stone dead after the cheese and wine party. Go and get a fresh cup if necessary, but no funny business with my green babies, or I'll … I'll … I'll throw hymn books at you after service on Sunday,' she concluded, laughing at her outrageous threat in defence of her houseplants.

Chapter Four

Good Friday, 1st April

The morning of Good Friday in the temporary police building in Market Darley was spent a little more seriously. Notes from the previous day were produced and collated, and there was the opportunity to check out the residents of the village that they had a note of, whether met in person the day before, or mentioned by one of those interviewed. The prime objective was, of course, to see if anyone in Shepford Stacey had a criminal record and, if so, for what.

'I've got something on David Darling,' Falconer announced, staring at his computer screen.

'I haven't found anything yet, sweetheart,' answered Carmichael, drawing himself a darted glare of disapproval. 'Sorry, sir, but it is April 1st.'

'And don't I know it, spending it with Blue-Bonce the pirate,' muttered Harry Falconer to himself.' Then, raising his voice to an audible level, he announced, 'he's inside at the moment on a four year stretch for a long list of burglaries, but he's got loads of previous form, from shoplifting when he was a kid to TWOC-ing, demanding money with menaces, and simple nicking – years and years of criminal behaviour. A real bad apple, by the looks of it.'

'But he can't have anything to do with it, sir; not if he's inside,' Carmichael countered.

'Agreed, Sergeant; but what about his parents? They run the Ring o' Bells pub at the crossroads. We'll have a word with them when we go back. Maybe it's a case of delayed revenge for something in his childhood. Run along and see if there's anything about to go live, or any other irons in the fire concerning this cove. But there's only so much we can learn from the past. Sometimes the present has a lot more bearing on things than we give it credit for, so we've got to give that a fair crack too.'

Carmichael left the office, happily humming 'Happy Birthday' and skipping like a child. Falconer admired his energy and enthusiasm, but feared for the ceiling of the floor below beneath his sergeant's thumping great feet. It was no way for a detective sergeant of nearly thirty to act, but at least no one but he could see it; with which thought he realised that he was beginning to feel protective of his partner, and was surprised by this discovery.

Carmichael himself would have suffered no embarrassment had his actions been witnessed by others, but Falconer realised that he would have, if it had been him. It must be that inner child that his sergeant mentioned sometimes, bringing out the protective side of his nature. If he wasn't careful he'd start viewing Carmichael like one of his cats, and then where would they be? In the asylum, that's where, with a wind-up mouse and a bowl of Kitty Crunch.

The DS returned fairly promptly with the information that there had been some contact with Trading Standards and from a couple of other forces about criminal misrepresentation and fraud on the internet, and the name that kept coming up for these scams, although not directly, but constantly, was Seth Borrowdale.

Falconer checked the computer where a file was kept, alphabetically, for names never nailed, but known, and there he was – Seth Borrowdale Esquire, of The Vines, Cat Hanger Lane, Shepford Stacey. He'd sailed pretty close to the wind on more than one occasion, and had been in trouble as a juvenile, only escaping arrest and conviction as an adult by the skin of his teeth and the fact that any evidence to his detriment was either hearsay or circumstantial, neither of which would get the go-ahead from the CPS. He'd do a PNC check and see if they had him on the DNA Database. It was an outside chance, but one never knew.

'I think we'll have a little word with him, too,' Falconer said decisively, which prompted Carmichael to enquire when they might be returning to said village.

'Not this afternoon, I don't think. It'll be bad enough going round bothering people tomorrow, tomorrow being the weekend, but to turn up on a Bank Holiday, when there doesn't seem any immediate risk of another killing – you understand that this is my gut feeling talking, Carmichael: I just don't get that hint of a psychotic serial killer here, more an old grudge being settled – where was I? ... turn up on a Bank – ah, yes. To turn up on a Bank Holiday would receive a grudging if not downright hostile reaction, which is something we could do without.

'We'll probably get a load of moans and complaints as it is, this being Easter weekend, but the sheer fact that there has been murder done should be a fairly strong mark in our favour.'

'In that case, and because it's my birthday, can I take you to see my Uncle Pete? It would be a sort of birthday treat for me – I haven't seen him in ages – and I'd love to show you his dogs.'

'What dogs?' asked Falconer, his eyeballs straying briefly to the window to identify weak sunshine outside, and not even a hint of the stiff breeze that had been blowing the day before.

'I mentioned him to you in that case we covered in the New Year. Do you remember? I told you he bred dogs; beautiful animals they are. He shows them sometimes.'[1]

'I do have a vague recollection, now that you come to mention it. It *is* a Bank Holiday after all; and your birthday. Come along Carmichael, I quite fancy looking at some well-bred dogs out in the fresh air.' Whatever was coming over him, to actually volunteer to venture into bandit country, where all sorts of dirty and muddy traps awaited his dapper appearance?

'Great, sir! I'll just get my ...'

'You won't need Mr Hat today, Sergeant. It's a lovely mild

---

[1] See *Inkier than the Sword*

53

day, unlike yesterday which was an absolute stinker. We can use my car, and I'll even let you drive it.'

'!' (*Carmichael was speechless.*)

So it was true! He was out of his mind, and he had to drag his thoughts away from things like, 'the lad deserves a treat', and others in a similar vein. He really was a sucker for sunshine.

Carmichael, after a fairly hair-raising drive which had had Falconer stamping on an imaginary brake on the passenger side and holding on to his seat, while trying to look relaxed, drew up in a lane beside a ramshackle thatched cottage, with a nameplate outside bearing the legend *Pups for sail – inquire within*.

'So this is your uncle Pete's place is it?' he asked, staring out of the car window at the overgrown garden, the mossy roof, and the clumps of grass growing out of the guttering.

'This is it,' Carmichael confirmed. 'The dogs and kennels are out the back. He spends more time out there than he does in the house.'

Falconer could believe it. 'It doesn't look like any other dog breeders' establishment that I've visited. I always used to go with Mama when we needed a new pup, and none of the places looked even remotely like this.'

'I 'spect they were all poncy places, sir, meaning no disrespect. Uncle Pete's is just a reg'lar country breeder's establishment, like you'd find in many a village. Let's get out of the car and go round the back. I know he's in 'cos I can see his car over yonder,' Carmichael suggested, pointing to a rusting heap in the shape of an old – a *very* old – Land Rover a little further down the lane, just inside a pair of drooping wooden gates. For a moment there, the sergeant had gone 'native' in his speech, and Falconer was a tad unsettled by this.

But he wasn't going to pass judgement. They had gone out for a nice afternoon, and a nice afternoon they were going to have, come hell or high water. Gritting his teeth, he locked the car and followed Carmichael's loping scarecrow figure to the rear of the property, still optimistic; trying to drown his doubts at birth.

He'd walked too far before he realised it. The weedy terrain stopped abruptly at the corner of the house, and the rear was a sea of mud and puddles from the autumn, winter, and spring rains, topped up nicely by yesterday's downpours.

Of course he had stopped too late, expecting to find a large concreted area surrounded by regimented rows of kennels. What faced him across the mud were the much-patched remnants of two truly venerable garden sheds, boasting a rainbow of coloured patches garnered over the years, and worn with pride.

Looking down as his feet, which had suddenly begun to feel cold, he found both of them planted in the middle of a puddle, deep enough to lap water over the laces of his hand-made Italian brogues. Carmichael, being a few seconds ahead of him, had found a pair of wellington boots (which by some miracle fitted him), probably from outside the back door, and was prancing around the sheds without a care in the world.

Trying to move his feet proved trickier than Falconer had thought, due to the sticky consistency of the earth at the bottom of the puddle, and as he lifted one foot, a spray of liquid mud which may or may not – but his nose told him the balance was towards may – have the benefit of added dog poo, sprayed up and made join-the-dots patterns on his linen trouser bottoms.

Hastily putting down his airborne foot for the sake of balance, he found he had put it in a small but seriously rural pile of something unidentifiable, and tried not to think what it might be. Unable to free his other foot from the cloying mud of the puddle, he lifted the foot from the pile of whatever, finding himself balancing on one foot again. And it wasn't long before he found out exactly what the 'whatever' was.

'Carmichael! Come here and give me a hand!' he yelled, standing on one leg like an unusually formally-attired flamingo in fancy dress, flapping its wings in distress.

From a little further away from Falconer, a little old man – Uncle Pete, presumably – yelled, 'Hey, what are you a-doin' wi' my chicken shit? That was for my compost 'eap. It was gonna be a treat for my garden later this year.'

So that's what it was!

Carmichael turned and moved towards Falconer, but not quickly enough. As the inspector put his free foot on what appeared to be solid ground, and pulled at his still imprisoned foot, the 'safe' foot – safely trapped in the mud, that is – began to slide away from him, threatening to turn him into a human wishbone. The stuck foot suddenly freed itself in a great spray of stinking water, thus adding momentum to the sliding foot while, at the same time joining it in its journey, but in the completely opposite direction.

Falconer's flamingo wings increased their flapping in a vain attempt to regain his balance, or even maybe to set off unreasonably early for his flight south for the winter, but nothing made any difference. As Carmichael arrived to make a grab for him, he was on his way down, his eyes popping out of his head as he surveyed what he was destined to land in.

Carmichael's brave attempt to grab him merely resulted in changing the direction in which he fell by a few inches, and he landed with a sickening thud in a slimy heap of black and white 'stuff', with his nose flattened on the muddy top of one of his sergeant's wellington boots.

''E's gorn and fallen right in my pile o' chicken shit,' complained the wizened old man, who had wandered over to see what was happening with this alien creature who had arrived with his great-nephew. 'Iss taken me ages to get tha' collected, an' pu' in a noice toidy 'eap, an' 'e's made a roight ole mess onnit. Where's tha wellies, Maister? Tha do need tha wellies cummin' in 'ere wi' all the rain we've 'ad,' asked Uncle Pete, chewing on an old straight pipe and rumpling his unruly hair with one grubby paw.

'My wellington boots are in the cupboard under my stairs,' explained Falconer through gritted, nay, *gritty* teeth as he lay beached, surveying the state of his jacket and shirt. His tie had disappeared, presumably burrowing into the chicken doo-dah in the hope of starting an independent colony.

'They be no good in there, Maister. You shoulden 'ave them on, cummin' 'ere in this weather,' Uncle Pete advised sagely, nodding his head at his own wisdom.

'I didn't know I was coming here!' he shouted in exasperation.

'Well, where d'you think youm was a-goin', then?' Uncle Pete was obviously rehearsing for a forthcoming crosstalk double act in the hope that variety shows would make a comeback, and had landed his stooge partner right in his own back yard. 'An' lookit you done to my chicken shit! My pile's all over the place now. There be a great gobbit on yon poncy jacket o' yourn. You can scrape that orf before you leaves.'

'Carmichael! Get me up, get me out of here, and get me home so that I can fumigate myself and change into some less excrementally blessed garments. Now! That's an order! Please?' What had started as a shout had deteriorated almost to a whine for mercy, and the sergeant grabbed him by the wrists and began to heave.

There was one ghastly moment when both of them nearly lost their balance at once, and surveyed the now flattened pile of chicken shit in trepidation, but with a monumental effort on the part of the younger man, they both arrived safely back on firm(ish) ground, Falconer with a remarkable resemblance to his cat Tar Baby's namesake.

'Do you want to see the puppies now, sir?' Carmichael asked, and had to cover his ears at the reply he received.

'Get that great lump off'n 'is trousers, Davey boy, and that clump off'n the bottom of 'is coat. Like liquid gold, that is, on the garden, an' I won't put up with 'oity-toity strangers in fancy Lunnon clo'es, cummin' on my land and tryin' to steal it from roight under my very nose.'

As they walked back to the car, round the house and across the weedy front garden, Carmichael was bombarded with questions, but not about his uncle's dogs, and not questions to which he knew the answers, offhand.

'Do you know how much this jacket cost?'

'No, sir.'

'Do you know how much it will cost to get it cleaned and properly pressed – *if* it can be rescued at all, which I highly doubt?

'No, sir.'

'Have you any idea of the price of hand-made Italian shoes, Sergeant?'

'No, sir.'

'Or of a Jermyn Street shirt?'

'No, sir.'

'Or a hand-woven silk tie?'

'No, sir.'

'Or Irish linen trousers?'

'No, sir.'

'Do you think you could get a blanket out of the boot, because I can't sit in the car seat like this?'

'Yes, sir!'

'Oh, and by the way, Carmichael,' he added, his shoulders beginning to shake (whether from the soaking he'd got, or from suppressed mirth, we shall never know.)

'Yes, sir?'

'Happy birthday!'

'Thank you, sir.'

'And please don't make me visit any more of your relatives. Your wedding nearly killed me, and today, I consider you to have made a second attempt on my life. If this doesn't stop, I may have to arrest you.'

'I won't, sir.'

'And your blue forelock's run where you got splashed!'

'Thank you, sir.'

Later that day, along with a great deal of steam, a steady stream of expletives wafted out of Falconer's shower cubicle, along with words like 'banjo,' 'dimwit', 'bumpkin', 'turnip,' and 'throttle'.

As Harry Falconer was scrubbing himself clean in the shower, fresh clothes laid out neatly on his bed for when he was dry, the

58

two pubs in Shepford Stacey were receiving the first of their evening regulars, both establishments hoping for a good evening as it had been a Bank Holiday and the next day was Saturday.

In the Temporary Sign, Stevie Baldwin was behind the bar, awaiting orders, as Robbie Greenslade, the publican, wandered around the one large bar replacing beer mats as needed, as he went. His was usually the bar of choice for those in the holiday cottages, because there was always an atmosphere in The Ring o' Bells that the locals had grown used to with time, but which made new customers feel uneasy, and happy to cross the road for somewhere with a more welcoming ambience.

Robbie was big on ambience. The lighting in his establishment was subtle, the colours rich, and a sexy saxophone album was usually on repeat play, but quietly, as background music should be. Its job was to soothe the ears, not drown the voice like a juke-box. He also put small bowls of peanuts and crisps on the bar at regular intervals, realising that this may affect his sales of such snacks marginally, but the salt in them would encourage folk to take in more liquid, and the only place they could obtain liquid refreshment in his establishment was from behind his bar. On balance, he won, hands down.

The food on offer was also a little less run-of-the-mill than most village pubs in the area, and his bar snacks included black pudding or gesiers salad, and poached eggs in Madeira sauce garnished with crispy lardons. All in all he gave value for money, but at slighter higher prices than the rival establishment.

His first customers of the evening drifted in, coagulating nicely around one big circular table. Stevie's parents were first in, greeting their daughter with waves and big smiles. Frank and Patsy Baldwin liked to get out a few evenings a week, to give them a bit of a break from Frank's mother, Elsie, who lived with them. If they went out on a Sunday lunchtime they always took her with them, but in the evening it got them away from her over-loud television and shouted commentary on what she was watching.

59

Next in was Anne Hammond, one half of the couple who ran the village shop. There was a 'gung-ho' film on the television that her husband Chris had particularly wanted to watch, so she had left him in charge of their twelve-year-old daughter, Isobelle, and grabbed the opportunity for a change of scene and livelier company, for she was a gregarious woman.

The final couple to complete the table entered just a minute or two after the others, and Vera and Letty Gorman from the post office joined the merry gang, out on parole from their various duties and obligations.

'When shall we five meet again? And you can't say it's bad luck, because I said 'five', so it wasn't quoting.' Anne Hammond opened the proceedings. 'What news, my dears? Oh, I'm feeling quite Dickensian, now. Anything from the school, Patsy? Has your Stevie heard anything?'

'I don't think so. Nothing she's mentioned, anyhow,' replied Patsy Baldwin, turning to glare at her husband, who was sitting beside her, muttering into his drink.

What he had actually uttered was, 'Why don't you ask her yourself, you nosy old biddy? She's only over there at the bar,' but his wife didn't want their evening out soured before it had even begun.

Vera Gorman, the younger sister by two years, and the one registered as postmistress for the community, also had a question for the table at large. 'Did anyone see the detectives? What are they like?'

'Stevie said they were very good with the children, especially the really tall one. She said his name was Car … Car … Car … Carmichael – that's what it was. She said he was quite young to be a detective sergeant in her opinion, and that he had bleached blonde hair. The other one was all right, she told me, but didn't really seem comfortable with children, and acted a bit grumpy with the other one – detective, that is. That's all I know. Now, who on earth do we think could have done it?'

'Tramp passing through, or a wandering psychopath,' was Letty Gorman's contribution. 'It so often is, in these detective stories. The detective spends two hundred pages suspecting everybody in sight, then it turns out to be somebody who hasn't been in the story at all, and I think that's cheating.'

'It might be cheating in books, Letty, but it would be so much better if such were the case, here in our own village. Who wants to think that someone they know, someone that maybe they see every day, is capable of such a wicked deed?'

'True, Anne; I hadn't thought of it that way. I just get so frustrated when I've taken the trouble to walk to the mobile library van when the books I get out don't play fair. A whodunit should be a whodunit, with no cheating.'

'Are you still on about your blasted library books, Letty? Well, you won't need to make a trip next time. You've got your very own whodunit, right here on your doorstep, and all the gossip goes through the post office, so you might have the opportunity to turn yourself into a real-life Miss Marple,' said Frank Baldwin, smiling a little cruelly into his beer.

'I should coco!' added Letty's sister, with a snort of laughter. 'Catch our Letitia here facing up to a desperate murderer. She'd pee her pants in fright!' and she laughed anew.

'I'd probably do a lot worse than that,' was Letty's opinion. She had decided to take the teasing in good part. 'I only want to read about murders: I don't want to be caught up in one.'

'Now, back to who might have done it.' This was Frank Baldwin, deciding to take the matter seriously. 'Do any of you remember that huge row between Audrey F-M and old Catchpole?'

Anne Hammond dredged her memory. 'About the milk money?'

'That's right. He was responsible for paying the milk bill for the kiddies' milk. If you remember, the school carried on ordering it for years after the state schools stopped. And he used to settle up with the dairy half-termly. Then it came to light that he had been fiddling the order somehow, and skimming a bit off here and there, so she gave him his marching orders.'

'I do remember, now you come to mention it, but I can't remember what the outcome was. He's working there again now.' Anne asked, still frowning in an attempt to recall.

'It was mended in the end, when the old vicar stepped in. No one else wanted to do the job, what with the hours spread all over the place, and the pay being so low, and Saul simply couldn't manage on his pension, and was glad of a second chance. She had to back down and offer him his job back, which she didn't like at all, but had no other choice.'

'I bet she didn't. And I'm willing to bet he didn't like having to go back there, after what had happened. There was always an atmosphere, Stevie said, if they happened to bump into each other; which, of course, didn't happen often, because he wasn't around too much in the parts of the school where she was.'

'And there were those awful twins with the funny name, that she expelled,' interjected Anne Hammond, recalling an unpleasant conversation with the twins' parents after a number of petty shop-lifting incidents, courtesy of their little darlings.

'Bastard and Bollocks,' added Frank Baldwin, grinning.

'Language, Frank!' exclaimed his wife in surprise.

'That's what Audrey F-M used to call them. It really amused Stevie. Their real names were … umm …that's it! Castor and Pollux! Pretentious load of old rubbish, if you ask me.'

After a short interval of polite laughter, Vera Gorman posed the inevitable question. 'But, surely their parents, or one of them, wouldn't come back here after all this time and stab her in the eye?'

'You never know what folk'll do, if driven to it.' And this was the final comment on the matter uttered by Letty Gorman, so steeped in detective fiction was she. But not so much that she didn't know which way was up. 'Your round, I do believe, Frank dear.'

'Did I hear a desire for more drinks, me dearies?' asked Robbie Greenslade, arriving at the table like a magically summoned genie. 'And which of you delightful customers is the murderer?'

'Robbie!' exclaimed five voices in unison.

'I only asked, didn't I? For all you know, it might have been me, with one of my own kitchen skewers, because she slated my giblets salad, and it infuriated me into a homicidal rage.'

'That was in very bad taste, Robbie,' Anne Hammond chastened him.

'Not at all, my dear lady. You haven't tasted my giblets when they're not fried to a crunch!' he quipped back, not in the least embarrassed. 'Same again all round? I'll bring it over to you, save all those wrinkly old legs under my table.'

'Robbie!'

'I know: shut up!' And he was gone in a whirl of incorrigible bonhomie.

In the Ring o' Bells, there were five people sharing two tables in one untidy group, and three others in the family room. At the two tables placed side-by-side were Saul Catchpole and Bill and Edith Findlater at one, and Flo Atkins and Margaret Darling at the other.

The Findlaters were a bit like the Baldwins across the road in the other pub, in that they occasionally sought refuge from a relative in a public house. In their case it was from their daughter, Harriet, who had been going on about what had happened yesterday, and then treating them to a blow-by-blow account of how she had been affected, and how she was feeling now, and how she would probably feel tomorrow.

It wasn't that they disliked their own daughter, really, but she *did* get on their nerves, and they had never quite forgiven her for not leaving home, like other peoples' offspring did. Why, Mrs Findlater had had a perfectly delightful afternoon with an unexpected visitor who had consented to share a pot of tea and a plate of chocolate biscuits, and she hadn't said a word to Harriet about it.

She couldn't get a word in edgeways, so she'd just leave her in the dark, and hope the incident was followed by a repeat performance, then she'd be able to show off a friend that her daughter knew nothing about, and she could say, 'well, I tried to tell you, but you were too wrapped up in your own feelings to listen'. That would teach her!

Switching off this satisfactory mental image, she tuned back into what was going on in the here and now. It would appear that everyone in the group had empty, or nearly empty, glasses in front of them, and surreptitious glances were flitting round the two tables, trying to sus out who would get stung for the next round.

'I'll get these – on the house,' announced the landlady, breaking the deadlock, as she had known she would have to. She knew the Findlaters would stand their round, but Saul and Flo would try to see the evening out without having to put their hands in their pockets at all. Not only a near necessity, it was a kind of game with them, to see who could spend the least in the course of an evening at the pub. 'I'll get doubles, shall I? Save time?'

Four nods of assent greeted this query, two with wickedly triumphant expressions. Margaret had also got the first round, was getting them doubles for the second, and, no doubt, Bill Findlater would feel obliged to get the next. That would be the point at which two members of the little quorum would move to the bar, to engage someone else in conversation, in the hopes of a last free drink or two before they tottered up the road to the Alms-houses.

'So,' said Flo, to get the conversational ball rolling again. 'Who's prime suspect for doing the old dear in, then? It wasn't you, Saul was it? I remember that barney you had with her over the milk.'

'It most certainly was not, and shut your mouth, you gabby old woman. There might be a bobby in here in plain clothes, just waiting to hear what we're talking about.'

'And the moon is made of green cheese, you stupid old fool! Look around you. We're so early, we're the only ones here, apart from Ernie behind the bar, and you're never going to convince me that he's a bobby in disguise.'

'I was only saying! And what about that couple of old biddies down at the post office? Do you remember all the uproar there was about banking the dinner money there? That silly old Letty Gorman couldn't add up for toffee. And then she lost one of the bags that the money was handed in in. Laugh? I nearly had kittens.'

'It was all sorted out, Saul, and you know it,' pointed out Edith Findlater. I know, because our Harriet told us all about it, although I'm not sure the atmosphere was ever right again between the school and the post office. Mrs Finch-Matthews opened a building society account shortly after that, and had to drive over to Carsfold on a Monday after school to hand the money in. I couldn't see the point myself, but apparently she did it on a point of principle, and damn the inconvenience.'

'Well, I can't see Letty Gorman as chief suspect, can you?' Bill Findlater asked of the table at large, just as Margaret returned with a tray laden with glasses.

'What are we talking about?' she asked, setting it down in the middle of the table as the others lifted their empty glasses to make room.

'Murder!' growled Bill, in a low sinister tone that made Margaret's face drain of colour.

'I say, are you all right, old girl?' he asked, wondering that his little joke comment could have had such startling results.

''M fine,' she mumbled, putting both hands out to steady herself on the table. Probably a bit too much of mother's ruin, but then if I can't indulge when it's my own pub, it's a rum do, isn't it? I said: it's a RUM do!' she repeated, and gave a queer strangled laugh. 'Joke! Drink up, me dearies, as the treat's on me.'

'We were just discussing who could have done that awful thing to Audrey up at the school,' explained Edith Findlater, offering an 'in' on the conversation.

'The Baldwins!' Margaret declared baldly, and took a swig of her very large neat gin – no pub measures for her, not even doubles, these days!

'The Baldwins? What, all of them, or just one?'

'Just one,' Margaret replied, her composure now completely recovered.

'Which one in particular? Stevie? Frank? Patsy? Old Elsie? Little Spike?' Saul Catchpole enquired, listing all the runners.

'Don't be ridiculous, Margaret.' Flo Atkins also rose to the family's defence. What happened to Stevie was a pure accident, and no one can say otherwise.'

'But if Madam had followed the lead of all the other schools in the area, instead of going her own way, saying there was no problem, then Stevie would still have two legs.' This was Flo Atkins, adding an opinion she had held since the incident first happened. 'You surely don't think one of them suddenly got a bee in their bonnet about something that happened years ago, and turned homicidal, do you?'

'I'm not sayin' as I do, and I'm not sayin' as I don't. I merely put it forward as a theory. Have any of you lot got a better idea?' Margaret's enunciation was beginning to deteriorate, as she tried, once again and unsuccessfully, to find the answer to whatever was bothering her in the bottom of a glass.

'What about you?' asked Saul, with a wicked little chuckle. You always said it was her that turned your darling David – geddit? darling David Darling – into the jailbird he is now.' This was dangerous territory, and Saul had, in fact, entered a minefield from which he was not to return unscathed.

'Get out of here, you filthy liar. Get out of here with your accusing mouth and your lies and implications. You're barred from this pub. You're barred for life. How dare you implicate ... How dare you insinuate ... Get out of here! Get out! Get out! Get out!'

'There, there, Margaret. Calm down and keep the noise down, will you? Do you want to drive all our other customers away?' Ernie Darling had appeared at their table from behind the bar. His hands on Margaret's shoulders, he crouched down and stared into her face, his countenance as expressionless as a stone mask, his eyes pleading for her to behave herself.

Saul Catchpole slunk away from the table, making beckoning motions with his head to Flo Atkins, but she pretended not to see them, and sat where she was. There was a chance of another free drink here, to calm down Margaret, and she for one was going nowhere until it had materialised.

All this was, of course, audible in the family room, where

Adrian and Pippa Snoddy sipped a half of bitter each, and their son Milo sat crunching the contents of a packet of crisps, his head cocked to one side, while his excellent five-year-old ears acknowledge the argument just through the doorway from them.

'I'm glad that nasty old lady is dead,' he said suddenly, making their heads whip round in his direction, and then added, with no discernible break in his thoughts, 'and I need another orange juice. Can I have one Mum, Dad, please? We only ever get one of anything, and I want everything to be the way it used to be when I was little.'

Both parents spoke at the same time. 'What's wrong with the way we live now?' his mother asked, sensitive to anything that criticised her decision to let them experience a bit of real life for a change, even if they were going back to reality in the not-too-distant future.

'Why didn't you like her, Milo? What did she do that you didn't like?' Adrian was more concerned with what had produced this unexpected animosity in his son. Although they had already decided that they were getting out of that ghastly caravan at the end of the academic year, they had failed to communicate this to their son with all the to-do about the murder.

It had been a joint decision not to sit around and see Milo or themselves subjected to deprivation and discomfort. He didn't like the way they lived, Pippa didn't either, it had transpired, and now they knew that Milo felt exactly the same. He didn't like being different either, being marked out from the other children as someone abnormal; someone who didn't live in a house.

'Sh-sh-she was always on at me, Daddy,' with a slight stutter that made them think of Hartley Bywaters-Flemyng down at Paddock View.

'He does that a lot now,' interjected Pippa, referring to the stammer.

'She always n-n-nags me the way you don't like it when M-m-mummy does it to you.' Out of the mouths of babes!

'What does she get on to you about?' asked Adrian, ignoring

67

his son's reference to Pippa's frequently restless tongue.

'She says I've got nits; that I need a haircut; that I need proper shoes; that my uniform is dirty, or too small or too big; that my fingernails are dirty; that I eat too fast at school dinners, but I'm really hungry, Daddy – really, really hungry, because Mummy doesn't really do breakfast, does she? Cornflakes are no good when I've got footie in games, are they?'

'Did you know anything about this?' asked Adrian, turning towards his wife, whose face was bright red.

'A bit,' she admitted, and then, when Adrian continued to stare at her, 'Well, yes, but there wasn't a lot I could do with our lifestyle. I just wished she'd give a little more thought to what we were trying to do, and cut me a bit of slack, the vindictive old bitch. I'm so glad she's gone. That Findlater woman is a lot more sympathetic and understanding.'

'Hang on a minute. Don't try to change the subject, Pippa,' Adrian commanded, raising his voice slightly, and realising that their quiet couple of hours out, was in danger of turning into a major row. 'You're responsible for our way of life at the moment. I told you some time ago that I'd had enough of it. That means that you're responsible for the cleanliness of our son and his clothes, his general appearance, and the way he's fed.'

'Does that mean he's not your son, too?'

'Of course it doesn't, but you've had me here, there, and everywhere, doing odd jobs so that we can make ends meet. On day-to-day care, it's your territory.'

'That's not fair!' Pippa fairly screamed at her husband.

'Nothing's ever fair in your eyes, is it? It wasn't fair that we had a very comfortable life before, so you had to make us go off and live like travellers. It's not fair that the caravan is so cold and small, so you nag at me day and night, and the innocent victim in all this – our child, our own flesh and blood – is the one suffering the most, and with no power whatsoever to change things. Well, we've all had enough now!

'And after what I've just heard, there's no way our son's going to see out the academic year at that school, and do another term in that clapped-out old caravan. We're leaving here next week, and if you've had a change of heart, and don't like it, or don't think it's fair, then I'll leave that filthy old mobile slum for you and you can stay there as long as you like, and rot, for all I care.

'We made a deal, and I expect you to stick to that, even if I have changed the timing a bit. We can stay with my parents until we get a house sorted out, if necessary,' Adrian declared in his most manly, head-of-the-family voice, but his wife was lost in another world.

'He was never hungry ... Well, never *that* hungry.' Pippa had been really stung by the revelations from her son, and was trying to imagine how it must have felt for him, trying to live her stupid dream, and never saying anything about how he was treated at school.

'And he never told me when he'd got mud or paint on his uniform until the next morning when it was too late. I hated that woman. She never gave Milo a chance, or cut him any slack. It was all so personal. I knew she disapproved of the way we lived, but it wasn't fair to get at me by criticising a little boy.'

'Well, it won't be happening again,' Adrian stated, 'because we're leaving Shepford Stacey and going back to a life we understand and enjoy.'

'It won't be happening again,' added Pippa, with a faint expression of triumph on her face, 'because the old hag is dead.'

'Pippa!' Adrian stared at her as if he didn't know her, as he heard a quiet voice tentatively ask,

'Can I have my orange juice now? And are we really leaving? Can we live in a house again like we used to? And can I go back to my old school? I miss my friends, Daddy.'

'Yes. Yes. Yes. Yes. And I know, son. I miss mine too!'

Harriet Findlater was glad to see the back of her parents. Over the years they'd become very hard, with barely any fellow feeling for what she had to go through, term after term, at that school. The children's behaviour was just getting worse and

69

worse as the years passed, and she was finding it more and more difficult to cope with a full-time classroom role.

She had spoken to Audrey, who was due to retire, about Audrey maybe recommending her for the soon-to-be-vacant position of head teacher, but she had, to her surprise, been rebuffed. She had thought that her many years at the school would count in her favour, and the change of position would give her a little more time out of the classroom and away from the children, doing the administrative work which she had grown to love.

But Audrey had quashed her request, stating that she thought maybe Harriet ought to take early retirement, so that they could go at the same time, and leave the school free for a completely new broom. She considered, correctly as it happened, that Harriet had lost her passion, and had little or no ability to discipline children of any age, and that, effectively, her career was over.

Audrey knew her colleague would get a good pension, even if retiring early, and it would free her and her parents to live wherever they wished, as it was only Harriet's job which had tied them to Shepford Stacey for so long, and had been surprised when Harriet had launched into a tirade about traitors and turncoats, and hidden enemies within the gates, which she was barely able to understand.,

By the time it had been explained to her, they had had a full-blown row about Harriet's teaching abilities – both perceived and actual – and Harriet had put a full-stop to the whole situation by bursting into tears and running out the school and home, leaving her colleague of many years angry, but more puzzled as to where she had gone so badly wrong with her suggestion. The woman was living on a knife-edge, in her opinion, and if she didn't retire soon, she'd have to go on health grounds, another basket case created by society's little darlings.

Had Miss Findlater but known it, her parents would have been absolutely horrified to find that Mrs Finch-Matthews saw the three of them walking off into the sunset together holding hands. Mr and Mrs Findlater had very different ideas on the subject, and were, right now, gathering information about apartments in the Algarve – *one-bedroomed* apartments – and were sneakily going about planning a retirement for two, far away from cosy English village life.

If Harriet didn't like it, she would have to lump it. And if she needed someone to live with, she could go to her Gran's. Her grandmother might be ninety-eight, but she still had all her marbles, and would probably welcome a bit more company than that provided by the district nurse and the home help. They'd done the crime and done the time, and now it was time for some parole for them. Harriet definitely needed a hard shove in the back to get her off the nest, or she would never fly, never give them any peace.

Oblivious of all this robust and abundant sub-text to her life, Harriet was sitting in the dining room at the rear of the house, working on next term's final version of the school timetable, which she assumed was now her sole responsibility, when she thought she heard a rustle of the just-budding shrub branches outside the window, and a tentative rattle at the back door handle.

Jumping to her feet, she looked towards the window, the curtains of which were not yet drawn, and thought she caught sight of a face, although it was in fact more an impression of a face: a blurred white oval which her brain interpreted as human.

Such was her mood that she forgot to be timid, and rushed out through the hall and into the kitchen to investigate, throwing the back door wide open, before her natural character took over and, not even closing the door behind her, she ran out of the back gate, down the pathway that edged the paddock and straight to the Ring o' Bells, towards the safety of her parents.

So precipitate and unexpected was her arrival on their 'night off' that Bill and Edith had insufficient time to fix on their usual smiles of welcome, and both greeted her with grimaces of dismay, hurriedly curving their mouths upwards and crinkling their eyes before she had a chance to say anything. Fortunately Harriet, in her panic, did not notice.

That, of course, was the end of the senior Findlaters' night of

71

freedom, but it didn't really matter too much tonight, after that nasty business with Saul and Margaret and, to be honest, they'd be glad to get out of the atmosphere that that had created, which was an uneasy one, to say the least.

Of course, there was no one in the garden at Forsythia Cottage, and no one in the house, although, as Mrs Findlater declared after they'd made a thorough search, that was all down to sheer luck, as Harriet had left the back door open wide, and anyone could have come in and helped themselves to just about anything they wanted.

'I'm sorry, Mummy, I was scared, so I just ran to get you two,' her daughter explained, tears forming at the inner corners of her eyes, a pathetic figure of a woman approaching retirement age and acting like a schoolchild.

'Well there's no one to be seen, you silly girl. You're going to have to be a darn sight braver for the next few days. Remember we're off to see Gran, and we're staying over the Bank Holiday weekend. You're going to have to fend for yourself then, whether you like it or not.'

'Couldn't I come with you?' Harriet asked, with a note of pleading in her voice.

'No, you certainly can *not*. This is our little trip, and we've been looking forward to it now for weeks.'

'But I'd like to see Granny, too. I might not get another chance, with her being so old.'

'Then you'll just have to go up sometime next week, if the good Lord spares her, while there's still no school. And look at it this way: instead of getting us all at once, your gran can look forward to another visitor when we've gone.'

'But I don't like long drives.'

'Then take the train.'

'But the train goes from Market Darley.'

'We'll give you a lift.'

'But I won't get back till late at night.'

'We'll pick you up as well. You're in your fifties, Harriet. For God's sake take charge of just a tiny bit of your life and stop relying on us for every little thing.' Harsh words, thought

Mrs Findlater, but necessary in this case.

Put like that, Harriet could hardly argue, and gave in with a bad grace, pouting like a five-year-old and stomping off to bed.

'No wonder she can't control the new intake at the school. She acts like one of them herself sometimes,' commented her mother, going into the kitchen to put the kettle on. 'When they said children were for life, I didn't think they really meant it!'

Chapter Five

Saturday 2nd April

In what passed for his office these days, Harry Falconer was scanning, with a wry smile, the report that informed him that there had been no fingerprints on the skewer (surprise, surprise!), and that it was the metric equivalent of six inches in length, and quite old; more than half a century old, in fact, and had a lazy barley sugar twist to the metal that was instant nostalgia for those of a certain age.

He knew the style well, because his mother had several such relics from her own mother's kitchen, which would be no good today to a modern housewife, who thought that skewers were for making kebabs, and had no idea whatsoever of the conductivity of metal, and its uses in the cooking of lumps of meat. In fact, not many modern housewives would know what to do with the lump of meat either.

No clues there, then, was his conclusion as the door opened to admit DS Carmichael, who had washed the rest of the blue food dye out of his forelock, but not with one hundred per cent success, leaving one clump a shade of pale green dangling down his forehead. This gave the impression of a sand dune with a small clump of grass growing out of it, but it wasn't that that grabbed the inspector's attention.

Carmichael removed a perfectly respectable mackintosh to blind Falconer with trousers that were a cross between luminous yellow and lime green. Above this, his shirt was in a pattern of broad vertical stripes of light blue, dark blue, red, and white. To add insult to visual injury, his tie was grey with an orange blobby pattern on it. *(Author's note: I have actually seen somebody in this garb, but unfortunately, I didn't manage to keep it to myself, and let slip to Carmichael about it, so it's all my fault!)*

'What in the name of God do you think you look like, Sergeant? I can live with dress down Friday, but today is Saturday, if you hadn't noticed, and I didn't think to bring my sunglasses in from the car. Come on: what's your excuse, or are you just reverting to the norm?'

'I'd have thought you could have worked it out for yourself, sir. Yesterday was my birthday, and it was a Friday, but it was also *Good* Friday and I didn't think it would be respectful, given what the day stands for. My mum was very particular about that sort of thing. Wasn't yours?'

'I can't say that I really remember,' replied Falconer, slightly stunned by his sergeant's Christian sensitivity, but silently saluting it as part of the man's general goodness of character.

The two detectives sat in silence for a few minutes, while Falconer gathered his thoughts about the coming day. 'We've got to get back to the village and start snooping around. I've requested that PC Green and PC Starr do a house-to-house, asking that they take a look in kitchen drawers, and show a photograph of the murder weapon, but rather them than me. It's got to be done, but I don't hold out much hope of a result.

'We've got a few key residents to interview. I want to speak to the vicar, the people in the post office and the local shop, and I want a long chat with that other teacher. We also need a word with that Borrowdale chap, and the couple at the Ring o' Bells. Between that lot, we ought to be able to uncover something useful. If something happened that drove someone to murder, someone must remember something about it. I just don't believe that this is the work of a wandering madman. There would have been other incidents.

'A mind that damaged, killing at random, would have committed other acts of mindless violence in the area. This is personal. And I think it's something from her past. It's just a gut feeling, but we need to dig back, and see who she's crossed:

and it's probably something from her professional life. From what the other members of staff have said, it wouldn't appear that she had any absorbing hobbies. The school seems to have been her whole life.'

'Are we going now, sir?'

'Can't think of a better time. Oh, and Carmichael ...'

'Yes, sir?'

'Put your coat on. We don't want you scaring the horses, do we?'

'Really, sir!'

They took Carmichael's motorised wheelie-bin, as Falconer's Boxster was (metaphorically speaking, at least) at the vet's, being de-loused and deep-cleaned after their little misadventure the day before. The inspector had taken care to wear clothes he was not too financially worried about, or sentimentally attached to.

'We'll start with the vicar. A man of the cloth – or his wife – is always a hot-bed of parish gossip, and then we'll see what takes our fancy.'

The vicar was at home, and, fortunately for them, free to see them, and he conducted them through to the sitting room, the double doors now firmly shut on the dining half of the long through-room.

As it happened, Septimus Lockwood had only been the present incumbent for about five years, and the only incident of note that had happened during his time in Shepford Stacey was the one involving the 'terrible twins', and this, he didn't consider, warranted murder as revenge. He had met them at a Christmas Eve nativity service, and the little horrors had stolen the baby Jesus (displayed early for the benefit of the little ones), and stashed him behind a pile of mouldering out-of-date service books.

At this point in his narrative, they were interrupted by the entry of a whirlwind into the room, which resolved itself into his wife Ruth, holding a willow-pattern plate with a look of puzzlement on her face. 'Nobody will own up to owning this plate. It arrived with all the others from the school with, I think, a Victoria sponge on it, but everyone who contributed denies all knowledge of it. I've heard of anonymous letters, but never anonymous Victoria sponges.'

'I shouldn't worry about it, my dear. Someone will remember it eventually.'

'Well, I don't know who. I've just had a complete phone round.'

'Ruth – the phone bill!'

'Don't fuss so, Septimus. It was as good an excuse as any to check that everyone's all right, after poor Mrs Finch-Matthews' unfortunate accident – I mean 'incident'.'

'You mean her murder.' Falconer liked to call a spade a spade.

'Horrible man!' she retorted, flashing him a little smile. 'I thought if I used the plate as an excuse, it would save you hours and hours calling round to see everybody, and having to drink endless cups of tea and coffee, and be driven mad by the inane chatter that goes with them, Sep.'

'Clever girl!' exclaimed the vicar. 'Worth every penny of the bill, and you are worth your weight in rubies, my dear. Now, where was I,' he resumed, as his wife left the room somewhat more slowly than she had entered it, still staring at the plate with a puzzled expression on her face and muttering,

'Well, it must belong to somebody,' finally calling over her shoulder as she exited, 'Did you tell them about that weird woman who said she'd just been involved in some other murders, and wouldn't stay here another minute?'

'No, she'd completely slipped my mind.'

Falconer merely glanced at him in an enquiring manner, and he continued, 'It was someone who came to the bake sale – a couple – and as soon as the murder was mentioned, she went all peculiar, and said something about being involved in murders before. I'm sure it means nothing whatsoever with regard to our own unfortunate circumstances, but it does seem worthy of mention. Whoever it was was staying at the holiday cottages, but I can't remember her name. You'll just have to ask.'

'I'll do just that, thank you, sir. Make a note, Carmichael,' but he was too late. Carmichael had already noted it down, and licked his right index finger's top joint, and made a downward gesture with it in the air, to indicate that it was his house-point this time.

'Oh, yes: back to the twins from hell. While we were all searching for the little plaster figure, they got into the stable scene and took all the straw and strewed it around the whole of the altar area and the choir stalls. I won't repeat what they said when I admonished them, because it was unspeakably rude. I must admit, I was glad to see the back of the little terrors, and although their parents could see no wrong in them, I've since heard that they're boarders at their new school, so maybe mummy and daddy didn't have such bad eyesight after all.

'I'm sorry I can't be of more help to you, but I'm simply too much of a newcomer. The ladies in the post office have been here since the Flood waters receded, so you might strike lucky there, and Mrs Hammond at the shop loves nothing better than to have a good old shred of folks' characters, while she peddles her wares – sorry, I didn't mean that to sound quite so bitchy. She's got a good heart, and would help anyone in trouble. Well, good luck with your investigations.'

Carmichael slipped his notepad back into his mackintosh pocket and followed the inspector out of The Rectory. 'Where to now, sir?' he asked, wanting to know whether they'd be using the car, which they had left in the Temporary Sign's car park, or would continue on foot. It was a bright day, and the fresh air was very welcome.

'Shop first, I think, then the post office.'

Although Shepford Stacey's village shop stocked an amazing amount of diverse lines, it could nowhere near match the sheer diversity and multiplicity of items for sale in 'Allsorts', the general store in Castle Farthing. It did its best, however, and Falconer and Carmichael had to pick their way carefully between towering displays and teetering stacks of miscellaneous stock.

Anne Hammond was behind the counter drinking a cup of tea, into which she was enthusiastically dunking ginger nuts, slurping up the drooping results with an audibly liquid sound that might be written as something like 'schlup'.

'Enjoying those, are you?' asked Carmichael, before he could help himself.

'They're gorgeous, love. D'yer want one?' she offered, holding out the packet to him and smiling. 'If yer don't take one I'll have guzzled the lot meself between now and lunchtime.'

Carmichael smiled back and extracted a biscuit, looking sideways at the inspector to see what his reaction was to this somewhat informal introduction, but he didn't seem put out. In fact, he was secretly pleased that the woman wouldn't need opening up like an oyster. She was already receptive enough to questions, and he was proved right when their first enquiry netted them a mine of information.

'If I were you,' she advised them, looking to left and right, to check that they weren't being overheard, 'I'd take a close look at the Baldwin family. Don't get me wrong, they're all lovely people, but you've got to take into account what happened to their Stevie, haven't you?'

'Have you?' asked Falconer, bowled over by her speed of delivery, and trying to give Carmichael a chance with his notes, half-consumed ginger nut notwithstanding.

'Oh, yes. Accident like that must have been one in a million, with an outcome like that, that is.'

'What accident?'

'The one where Stevie lost her leg!'

'She's only got one leg?'

'Didn't you notice?'

'No.'

'She does cope well, doesn't she?'

'When did all this happen?' Falconer felt as if he were under attack from heavy artillery.

'It was years ago when she was at the village school. All the County schools were banning skipping ropes because some little tyke – oh, I can't even remember where it was now – some boy, had decided that he wanted a go at what is usually considered a girls' activity, got his feet tangled up in the rope.

'Boys have such bad co-ordination when it comes to things like skipping, unless they're boxers, don't you think?' Without giving them a chance either to agree or disagree, she ploughed on relentlessly. 'Anyway, this lad fell over and, as a consequence, broke his arm, and all the parents were up in arms. As a result, skipping got demonised, along with a lot of other innocent childhood activities – like conkers – mad, isn't it?'

'Hhhh.' Falconer drew breath, but was over-ruled again.

'Our parents said it was a daft thing to do, as it was something that had gone on ever since anyone could remember – like marbles: all games have their season in the school year. So the vicar at the time agreed, and so did the school staff.'

'Being?' He was more successful this time, and her faraway glazed eyes, lost in memory, suddenly became alert as she tuned into his one word question, and she shot him an admonitory glance.

'I was just getting to that bit!' Anne Hammond reacted like someone who wasn't used to being interrupted when she was in full flow. 'It was the same old birds as now, only they weren't quite so old then – Harriet Findlater and Audrey Finch-Matthews – may she rest in peace.' She was thrown right off her track now, and Falconer managed another question.

'There was an incident with a skipping rope, at the local school, I presume?'

'That's right!' Stevie – little Stephanie, as she was known then – got in a tangle and fell, breaking her leg. Well, that was the end of that, as far as the school was concerned, but it was only the beginning of a sorry tale of woe for the Baldwins.

'They took her to hospital, operated to set the bone, and she had to go into traction – I don't know enough to describe exactly what happened; I could've got that bit wrong after all this time, but the up and down of it was that she got an infection, and gangrene set in. If they hadn't taken her leg off, she would have died.

'She coped awfully well, poor kid; but I shouldn't say that. She's made a marvellous job of just getting on with her life, and never moaning about it or blaming anyone other than herself, for being so clumsy.'

'But you think that there may be resentment harboured in the Baldwin household?'

Ooh-er, thought the inspector. Was that really Carmichael asking that question? It sounded as if he had been reading the 'Improve Your Vocabulary' section in the Readers' Digest, but Anne Hammond didn't notice the rather formal wording of the question, merely carrying on where she had left off.

'Patsy and Frank were heartbroken. She was their little princess, and now she looked more like Hopalong Cassidy – no offence meant. Patsy cried for months and had a bit of a breakdown because of it, if truth be told. Frank just disappeared inside himself, the way men do, but he spent a lot more time in the pub in those first few months after the accident.

'His mother lived with them even back then, and he probably wanted a bit of relief from the weeping and wailing after he got home from work of an evening after a hard day's graft. That all stopped when Stevie was finally allowed home, but they had a big, black pit to crawl out of, and I knew they weren't happy when Stevie applied for her job at the school, after she had little Spike.'

'So, in your opinion, how do they all feel now?' Falconer asked, feeling a little left out. After all, he was the senior officer here, and it must be his turn now.

'That grandmother, her opinion's absolutely wicked, and I'll only tell you if you promise not to tell anyone else I said it. You can confirm it yourself when you talk to her, though.'

This sounded interesting, and both detectives pricked up their ears for a juicy titbit, and Anne didn't disappoint. 'You know she's got that little boy, Spike, that I just mentioned?

Both detectives nodded in silence, now actually wanting her to continue in full flow.

'And you know he was born out of wedlock?'

They did now, and nodded in unison again, like a couple of toy dogs on the back shelf of a car.

'Old Elsie told me once, in confidence, that she reckoned Stevie only went to bed with someone so that she could prove she could attract the lads, even with only one leg. And what's more, she reckoned that someone took advantage of her because she was a cripple, and deserved – what? Pity? Contempt? I don't know which, but it's an absolutely horrible thing to think about your own flesh and blood, and I don't want this to go any further than these four walls, and I hope I've made myself very clear.'

She had, and the two nodding dogs obliged for a third time.

'Stevie was a pretty child, and she's grown into a pretty young woman. I reckon if she didn't marry the father, it was because she didn't want to. At one point Patsy accused her of not knowing who the father was, but I doubt that. Stevie's not that sort of person. She travels her own road, and anyone who says otherwise is talking rubbish.'

Falconer picked up on the reference to Patsy Baldwin, and decided to press for more information. 'How do her parents feel now, so long after the event? Have they finally come to terms with what happened?'

'I don't really think so. Most of the time they seem just like everyone else, but now and again, you can see it in their eyes – that sort of agony at not being able to change things, and incomprehension at why it should have happened to their daughter, and their family.'

'Thank you very much, Mrs Hammond. You've been most informative,' Falconer thanked her as they prepared to make their exit, Carmichael chewing appreciatively at a ginger nut, another three clasped possessively in his right paw, and a look in his eyes that challenged anyone to try to take them off him.

'Carmichael, you're shameless,' the inspector opined, his ear catching the sound of enthusiastic crunching.

'No. I'm not, sir. I'm an opportunist, and I'm hungry,' was the brief reply, through a mouthful of fragrant crumbs.

The sisters in the post office were also inclined to gossip, and it began to feel like it was going to be a fruitful visit. Vera and Letty had been mulling things over since the murder, and had reached a conclusion as to the identity of the killer.

'It's usually very quiet at this time of day, Inspector. Why don't you and the sergeant come into our little back parlour, while I make us a nice pot of tea, and I'll put up my 'please ring' sign by the bell,' Vera invited, definitely mistress of her own post office.

'We don't want to interfere with the smooth running of Her Majesty's postal service,' replied Falconer.

'But we'd love a cuppa,' added Carmichael, whose mouth was dry after his handful of biscuits.

The post office was behind a bay window, probably Georgian, and consisted of what must have been the front room, with a side room where the post was delivered. At the back of the actual post office was a cosy little snug where the two sisters could go for refreshment breaks, without having to go upstairs.

In front of a cast-iron fireplace, a gas fire hissed gently, although it was not cold outside. Two 1930s armchairs sat at each side of it, and to the left front of the room was a tiny dining table and two chairs. A corner at the other end of the room boasted a miniature sink, and equally minute work surface adjacent to a power point, where hot drinks could be prepared during opening hours. Between the two armchairs was a worn Turkey rug, over old brown linoleum, and a bouquet of everlasting flowers sat in a glass vase in the exact centre of the table.

While Letty busied herself at the sink, Carmichael admired the ornaments on the mantle-piece. 'My gran used to have a pair of dogs like that,' he commented, indicating the Staffordshire spaniels, one at each end. Got 'em from her mum,' he informed the room at large.

'Those belonged to our grandmother,' Vera said, entering the room, apparently satisfied that the post office would not be burgled during the next half hour. 'Has she still got them?' she asked, referring to Carmichael's own grandmother.

'Nope! She sold 'em to a 'knocker' at the door for twenty quid, a few years ago,' he replied, ruefully. 'I loved 'em,' he added. 'I gave them names, and thought about where I'd put them in my house when I had one.'

'I know they've gone down in value in recent years, but I'd say that was daylight robbery, young man. Did she get the man's name?'

'No, and she was furious when she found out she'd been done, but the next week she won a hundred pounds on the bingo, and just forget all about the dogs, saying that Fate had seen her right in the end.'

There was no polite answer to that, so Letty took up the conversational reins with, 'We've got a theory, Inspector.'

'Yes, a theory about who the murderer is, but the roots of it go back a long time. Shall we tell you who we think it is, or shall we start at the beginning, and tell it like a story?'

'Story, please.' Carmichael answered for the inspector. He loved stories, even if he did have to take notes.

'Let's take it in turns,' suggested Letty, almost treating the situation as a game. 'You go first, Vera, dear.'

'Thank you Letty. Now, let me see: where shall I start? I suppose we'll have to go back about thirty years to find the beginning.' Carmichael smiled, and started to scribble. This was the bit he liked about an investigation, when all the threads of a case turned out to be little vignettes, and when they had them all together, they could be woven into a tapestry that showed a clear picture – a bit like a jigsaw puzzle, but with less cardboard, and with no box with a helpful picture on it.

'It was the two of them together that caused most of the trouble, although they were bad enough separately. I'm talking about David Darling and Seth Borrowdale. From the moment they met at school, they became a pair of little devils, each one egging the other on to worse things.

'Audrey and Harriet did what they could. They disciplined them as far as they were allowed to, and spoke to the parents, but nothing curbed their behaviour.'

'And, of course, as they got older, their mischiefs grew into actual criminal acts,' Letty took over, without missing a beat. 'Things that had been 'borrowed' at school, such as dinner money, or sweeties from a coat pocket, or a satchel, could be sorted out internally, but as they grew older, it progressed to shoplifting.

'Anne Hammond's parents ran the village shop back then, and they showed no mercy where shoplifters were concerned. They'd spotted that small stuff was going missing, and they had a fair idea who was responsible, so they kept an eagle eye on them, and caught them at it, the pair of them. First thing they did was call the police: none of this 'speak to the parents' first. They knew the little devils were out of control, even at that age, and the police were the beginning of a story that's still going on to this day, certainly in the case of David Darling, and, more than likely, in the case of Seth Borrowdale.'

'Are you sure about that?' Falconer asked.

'Well, David Darling's in prison, just been sentenced to four years, and that Seth Borrowdale's been in trouble with the police a couple of times. That was quite a while ago now, but that's probably just because he's being more careful these days. The man's so naturally crooked you could open a bottle of wine with him.' It was Vera's turn again, and she believed in 'telling it like it is'.

'If you're looking for a suspect, you could do worse than to consider him,' Letty chimed in, 'or that Margaret and Ernie Darling. Their David was a spoiled and pampered only child, and they never could see any wrong in him – especially her. Since he's been inside again, she's taken to the bottle with a will. Perhaps she staggered over there in a state of fugue, and gave Audrey Finch-Matthews one in the eye for her little darling David. Ha ha!'

So like each other had they become, living and working together over the years, that Falconer was finding it difficult to tell them apart. They both dyed their greying hair an improbable shade of chestnut; both tended towards plumpness, they dressed in similar late-middle-age clothes, and both wore glasses. It was these latter that gave Falconer the only clue as to which was which. Vera's glasses had red frames, whereas Letty's were black.

They sat opposite each other, the armchairs hauled round so that they could face the dining room chairs in which the detectives were seated. 'I suppose, being of the same age group, in a small place like this, you'll probably miss Mrs Finch-Matthews?' asked Falconer, in a rather arrogant manner, in Carmichael's opinion, but the inspector had met his match in the Gorman sisters.

They both leaned forward in their chairs, taking on the quality of demon twins as their faces grew dark. 'Couldn't stand the woman!' they declared in unison, leaning back as if choreographed, each with an audible sigh.

'Why?' queried Falconer, surprised by their vehemence.

'There was an incident involving the dinner money, some time ago.' Letty began.

'It's all right, I'll tell it, sis. It was a mix up, that's all. Letty'd been given two different bags of dinner money, and mislaid one.'

'I'd just forgotten about it. There was only ever one bag, except for this week, when some of it came in late.'

'Let me tell it: you'll only go and get upset again.' A bell sounded in the room that housed the post office. 'You go and see to that customer, and I'll finish off the story here, Letty.'

As Letty left them, her face beginning to get flushed with emotion, Vera carried on with the story, to get it finished before her sister returned. 'That Finch-Matthews bitch only went and accused my own dear sister of thieving, and said she'd go to the head post office and complain, so that I'd have to give my own flesh and blood the sack.'

No love lost there, then. 'And where exactly was the money?' asked the inspector, surprised at the venom in the woman's voice.

'She'd put it under the counter instead of in the safe, because someone came in right after it was dropped off – it was a separate bag, left here a good two hours after the first one, and

Letty simply forgot, because she'd had a customer to deal with, and she'd already been to the safe with the first bag, earlier. It was an oversight anyone could have made, and it just got shoved behind some of the stamp books. We didn't find it until after closing time the next day. Letty was in a right old state by that time, and I've never forgiven the old biddy since.

'She said some horrible things, that still upset my sister to this day, and if I'm brutally honest, I'm glad she's dead, and I expect Letty is too. So there!' Vera Gorman had surpassed the evil twin look now, and looked positively deranged with hatred, and then her face just cleared, and the sweet old lady looked out of her eyes again.

'Still, what's happened can't be changed, and I think that's about all I can help you with, Inspector. Would you like a top-up of tea? No? Sergeant? Oh well, I'd better let you get on with your investigation, instead of listening to the reminiscences of a rambling old woman.' She smiled as she said this last, and Falconer wondered if he'd imagined the evil old hag who had hissed her hatred at him only a minute or so before.

'You've been very helpful, Miss Gorman, and your sister, too, of course. We're grateful you could spare the time to see us,' he thanked them, exchanging a look of profound puzzlement with Carmichael, as they rose from their hard wooden seats.

'What do you think, Carmichael?' he asked, when they were out in the open air again.

'Mad as a bag of ferrets,' Carmichael gave as his considered opinion on the post mistress. 'Where to now, sir?'

This constant traipsing around repeating questions over and over again could prove to be very tedious, but they'd had a fairly good hit rate so far, and Falconer had decided that they'd finish the morning with the properties in Forge Lane, grab something to eat, then work their way down Four Stiles, finishing in Cat Hanger Lane, which was near where they had left the car. That was about as much as they could fit in at the moment, and he hoped to be a bit closer to finding out who was responsible for the murder by the end of the day.

So far, Carmichael's garish outfit had raised no eyebrows, but he ran out of luck as they approached the front door of High Gates. What they assumed were Harriet Findlater's parents were stuffing suitcases into the boot of an elderly car, while Miss Findlater herself was wringing her hands, and whining, 'Are you sure I can't come with you? I'll be frightened after what happened last night, you know I will.'

'Don't be such a baby, Harriet. And nothing happened last night, except a bad case of over-active imagination on your part. You're fifty-seven years old. When are you going to grow up? You know the three of us will be too much for your gran, but I'll tell her you'll come and see her by yourself before the new term starts,' barked the elderly woman, her husband nodding his agreement as he got into the driver's seat.

'Mr Findlater? Mrs Findlater?' called Falconer, taking a punt. 'I wonder if I could have a word with you before you go away. I can see you're in a hurry, but would you be kind enough to spare me a minute?'

'You'd better make it quick, young man. I presume you're plain clothes policemen, here about the murder?'

'That's right, madam.'

'Well, do make it quick, will you? My husband doesn't like to drive fast, and we want to get to my mother's sometime before midnight.' It was only eighty miles, but Mrs Findlater liked to appear a long-suffering martyr.

God, she was prickly, Falconer thought, before launching into his opening gambit. 'I wonder if we could ask you a few questions about that tragic incident at the school on Thursday?'

The two detectives had just about come into focus for Mrs Findlater's elderly eyes and she let out a hoot of laughter as she nudged her husband and pointed at Carmichael. 'Going to a fancy dress party, son?' she chortled, her husband now out of the car again and wheezing with mirth at her side.

They had enough to do today without having to deal with George Burns and Gracie Allen, so Falconer decided they could wait until they came back. They'd probably get enough out of their daughter, who was much more in the thick of things. 'When are you coming back from your trip?' he asked, trying to keep his voice polite, and not glare at them for their rudeness.

'Monday,' the old man informed them, the first words he had spoken since they had laid eyes on him.

'We'll come back when you've returned home,' he informed them. 'Perhaps we can take this opportunity to have a word with your daughter?'

'Take it!' This was Mrs Findlater again. 'At least it'll give us the opportunity to get away without another bout of her whinging and whining about prowlers that only exist in her over-active imagination.'

What an evil old bag, he thought, as he smiled at Harriet, and motioned towards the front door.

'Bye, all!' the old couple called through the open windows of the car. No one answered them, the three figures already on their way into the hall of High Gates, all of them wishing the ghastly old people a really foul journey, and an even worse stay.

'I'm so sorry about that,' Harriet apologised, as she showed them into an over-furnished sitting room, fussy with patterned curtains, patterned carpet, and patterned upholstery, and far too many little tables covered in silver-framed photographs. The fact that most of the photographs were either pre-Second World War, or of a selection of dogs and cats, was a testament to the quality of her parents' relationship with Harriet – or lack of it.

'I'm afraid they've got rather cranky in their old age. Don't think they've singled you out. They're like that with everyone, except when they're down at the pub sinking a few sherbets. Drink seems to mellow them a bit, as far as other people are concerned, but nothing makes them any nicer to me.'

'That must be awful for you,' commented Carmichael, genuinely horrified.

'Oh, I've got used to it over the years. I never left home, you see, except to do my degree and my teacher training. I've got my bedroom upstairs, and a little sitting room, so we don't have to get under each other's feet very often.'

'And what happened last night? You mentioned something,

and your mother wasn't very nice about it.' Carmichael wanted to get to the bottom of that one. He was horrified that parents could show such coldness to their own flesh and blood, for his family was happy and close-knit.

Harriet gave a big sigh, and stared at him with a wry face. 'It was probably only my imagination, like Mummy said.'

'Tell me. Not everyone's like your mother.' Falconer was interested too now that Carmichael had brought up the subject.

Shrugging, she began to explain in an apologetic voice. 'They were out at the Ring o' Bells, and I was here alone. I thought I heard someone trying to turn the back door handle, and I also thought I heard someone moving about in the shrubs. We don't have any outside lighting, and the street lights don't really penetrate the trees.

'Neither of them has a mobile phone, and I was scared stiff, with what had happened to Audrey the day before – and in broad daylight.'

'I'm not surprised. So what did you do?' This one was definitely down to Carmichael. He had just the right touch with people who had been hurt, or were upset.

'I managed to get out of the house, and hared off to the pub. And when they saw me …' She broke off, and her eyes flooded with tears.

Carmichael moved over to sit beside her and put his arm round her shoulders, to show he was on her side. 'What happened when they saw you, Miss Findlater? We won't tell anyone anything you confide in us. Honest Injun!'

Harriet managed a watery smile, amused at the schoolboy still inside this giant of a man in his garish clothes. He made her think of the Pied Piper of Hamelin.

'Instead of smiling, or asking me what was wrong, they looked so horrified, and sort of disappointed. It was only for a second, but I saw it on their faces, and I wanted the ground to swallow me up, in case anyone else had seen it. I felt about as popular as a fart in a lift,' she finished, making Carmichael laugh out loud at the expression, which he had never heard before, and would certainly not have expected of so respectable-

91

looking a lady as this.

'You had every right to be scared, Miss Findlater,' interjected Falconer, now that she was back on a more or less even keel. 'There's a murderer on the loose out there, and who's to say there's not someone else on his list?'

'Inspector Falconer's right. If anything like that happens while your parents are away, dial 999 at once, lock yourself in somewhere with the lights out, and just wait for assistance.'

'Changing the subject,' Falconer began, 'Can you tell me what your relations were like with Audrey Finch-Matthews? Were you bosom buddies, just colleagues …?' He let the sentence trail off, giving her an opening to be absolutely straight with them, with no witnesses.

'We existed in what you might call a state of slightly uneasy truce.'

'And why was that?' The inspector had definitely taken over, and Carmichael had understood what was going on, and was already out of her sightline, over by the window, scribbling away in his notebook, with the very tip of his pink tongue sneaking out of the corner of his mouth, as if in search of air.

'It's no secret that I wanted to be given the chance of the headship when Audrey retired, which she would have done at the end of the Christmas term when she turned sixty. We'd both been at the school for decades, and, as usual in my life, I was always the bridesmaid, never the bride. I'm only a couple of years younger than her, and I thought she might have considered giving me a chance, just for a short time, for all the years I've supported her in the role.

'And she just said 'no'. Point blank! And when I asked her why …' The tears were threatening to return, and Carmichael stuck his notebook in his shirt pocket and moved over beside her again on the sofa.

'It's all right, Miss Findlater. You can tell us. Sometimes just telling someone else about something unpleasant that has happened takes the sting out of it, and makes us feel a bit better.'

Where did he get all this stuff from? thought Falconer. If

92

he'd been on his own with her, she'd probably be hysterical by now, with him wanting to grab her by the front of her sensible jumper and pull her up to eye-level, while he told her to just get on with it and stop acting like a five-year-old. He had to hand it to the younger man – he was good with emotion, whereas he, Falconer, was all at sea with it, and simply didn't know how to cope.

'Sh-she s-said I was useless with ch-children,' she gulped. 'She s-said I had n-no control, and that I ought t-to take early retirement when she w-went. I've n-never w-wanted anything m-more than a little while, to have m-my t-turn at the helm.'

'Well, she's dead now, and she can't queer your pitch, so surely that's something to look forward to, isn't it? County might put you in as a caretaker headmistress.' Falconer was trying his hand at bringing a smile to her face – but unsuccessfully it seemed. Miss Findlater burst into tears, and crushed her face into the material of Carmichael's shirt as if her world had come to an end. Carmichael put his arm round her shoulders again, and muttered 'there, there' quietly to her, while delivering a 'look what you've done, now' look, at his boss.

'I'm sorry if I've upset you, Miss Findlater, but I'm just not very good at feelings, and yours seem to be very hurt.' That was a better effort on Falconer's part, and she lifted her head and sat up straight, reaching into the pocket of her navy blue trousers for a handkerchief.

'I'm so sorry to make a fool of myself, but I have to keep everything buttoned up when Mummy and Daddy are at home. And Audrey and I used to be such friends. It was a knife through my heart when she suggested early retirement to me. I thought I was going to pass out with the shock of it.'

'Moving on, did you see or hear anything unusual on Thursday morning? I know we spoke about this the other day, but I wondered if you'd remembered anything in the meantime.'

'Not a thing, I'm afraid. It was just another day at school, and there was nothing out of the ordinary, except for people coming in throughout the morning and leaving their cakes for the bake sale, so that made it rather busier, but nothing unusual happened, to my knowledge.'

'Did you see anyone at the school that you didn't expect to see?' he asked.

Harriet had a fleeting memory of a face she thought she'd recognised, but that had been at the bake sale, and nothing to do with Audrey's murder. 'Just "the usual suspects,"' she answered, with a feeble attempt at a joke.

'That's fine, Miss Findlater. We'll come back when your parents return. Perhaps they may have noticed a stranger, or someone acting oddly.'

'I doubt it,' she replied. 'The only ones who act oddly around here are those two,' and at this feeble sally, she did manage the ghost of a smile. Maybe she was beginning to learn how to stand up for herself, after all these years.

When she'd waved them off the premises and closed the front door, Harriet went into the dining room to the sideboard to treat herself to a small sherry. There were going to be some changes around here, she thought, almost light-headed with rebellion.

It was lucky that she didn't know how drastic those changes were going to be, or how soon they would occur.

They could raise no answer to their rings and knocks at Laurel Lodge and a quick look through the small garage window revealed the absence of a car. They'd have to catch up with the Chadwicks some other time, as it looked as if they had taken advantage of the good weather to go out for the day. Maybe they'd even gone away for Easter, but Falconer thought that unlikely, as they hadn't let someone at the station know, and all those who had been spoken to on Thursday morning had been asked not to leave the area without informing the police.

They encountered the same lack of response at Copse View, the last house in Forge Lane, on the other side of the road, and just to the east of the holiday homes. Through the inadequately curtained windows was revealed a property that looked unloved and uninhabited, but they'd better check out who was supposed to be living there, or who the last inhabitant had been.

That left them with Blacksmith's Terrace to tackle before lunch, but that shouldn't take long, as all the residents were holidaymakers, only here for a week or two, and unlikely to be involved in what appeared to be a very local murder.

They started at the eastern end, so that they would slowly be working their way towards their lunch break, and approached number five to find the Graingers in a similar scenario as that in which they had come upon the Findlaters.

Virginia was putting soft holdalls into the boot, and Richard was placing cardboard boxes full of provisions on the back seat when they approached. As Virginia loaded, she maintained a quiet monologue, more to herself than to her husband.

'I'm not doing it again. I don't care what anyone thinks of me, I just can't face going through that sort of thing for a second time. It was the worst period of my life, and we came here to get a complete break, and try to exorcise it from our minds – or at least I did. It's not respectable, and it's frightening, and I'm not staying here to get mixed up in it again. Ooooh!' she cried, startled, as she noticed Falconer standing beside her, waiting for her to finish, so that he could speak.

'Who are you, and what do you want?' she asked abruptly.

'Steady, Ginny! Whoever he is, it's not his fault you're rattled, is it?' her husband said soothingly.

'No: you're right Richard, of course. Where are my manners? What can I do for you? We don't live here, if it's directions you want.'

Carmichael had arrived now, and stood beside Falconer, looming over her, looking as if he might to be about to say, 'Fee, fi, fo, fum ...' A little 'argh' of surprise escaped her lips as she surveyed the pair of them, put two and two together from her experiences of the year before, and stated, 'You're police, aren't you? About that ghastly business on Thursday? Well, I wanted to go home straight away, but Richard – my husband – made me stay another day to see if I could settle down. But it's simply not going to happen. I want to go home, although even that doesn't seem safe, now.'

She seemed to have entered into a world that existed only in her head, obviously a product of something that had happened to them before, and Richard Grainger gave her a look of exasperation, then turned to the detectives and held out his hand. 'Richard Grainger. Pleased to meet you. And this is my wife, Virginia. How can we be of assistance?'

'DI Falconer and DS Carmichael,' the inspector introduced them, nodding his head towards Desperate Dan beside him, dressed as if for a village fete fancy dress. 'I'm just checking on residents to see if they noticed any strangers or anything strange in the vicinity on Thursday morning. Of course, I appreciate that you're not permanent residents, but did anything odd catch your eye?'

'Nothing! Nothing! Nothing! We don't know anybody here, and we don't want to, now,' his wife answered for him, with a shudder.

'Go indoors, Ginny, and I'll speak to them. Don't upset yourself again: just go and make a cup of coffee,' he ordered, handing her a jar of granules from a box on the back seat.

As she walked back into the cottage he began a brief explanation for her – to someone who didn't know them – extraordinary behaviour. 'We got caught up in the events surrounding a double murder last year, in Little Marden, down on the coast. Ginny found herself in danger of her life on more than one occasion – I know it sounds rather melodramatic, but it's true.[2]

'Anyway, ever since then, she's been very nervy, and I thought a little break in the country might help her to relax a little, and come to terms with what happened. I must say, this murder at the school hasn't helped my plan one bit. It was all I could do to stop her bolting instantly, but I managed to get her calmed down enough to stay a bit longer.

'She found out what had happened at the bake sale, and she was nearly hysterical when we got back here. I managed to calm her down and reassure her that there was no way we could

<hr />

[2]For more on Richard and Virginia Grainger, see *Choral Mayhem*

become involved in this, but she's only managed another night, and she wants to get back home.'

'If you want to check us out, get in touch with Inspector Plover and Sergeant Ashberry of the Standchester Police, and they'll vouch for us,' he offered, as a sort of character reference.

'I'll do that, sir, if you don't mind. It'll dot another 'i' and cross another 't' for us, and we can take you off our list. Have a good journey home.'

'We will,' Richard assured him.

'Yes, but not today.' Virginia had come out of the cottage to join them again. 'That hysterical little jag I had just now made me realise what a fool I must look. Murders happen every day, and I don't get my knickers in a twist about them. Just because there's been one in the village we've chosen for a little break, doesn't mean I'm going to get involved in anything unpleasant.'

Richard looked at her, his mouth open in surprise. 'But I thought you were desperate to leave, Ginny.'

'Here's my business card, and I'll write my home number on the back, if that'll make you feel any safer, Mrs Grainger,' offered Falconer, anxious to keep everyone on the cast list still in the production, as it were.

'That would be marvellous, Inspector. Richard can look after that – I'm hopeless at remembering where things are. And I've simply got to get my head around the fact that we're on holiday. Just because something nasty's happened here doesn't mean we have to sit in the cottage and worry. We can go for days out, and just ignore what the police are up to. I gather there's a fantastic stone circle just a few miles away, and there are some monastery ruins just outside this very village.

'Then, there's a National Heritage place – Cranleigh Grange, I think it's called, on the way to a place called Stoney Cross; Ruth Lockwood recommended Castle Farthing as a very pretty place ...'

'I live there!' interrupted Carmichael. 'If you visit it, call in on my wife and she'll give you a cup of tea and a bit of history about the place. And you ought to take a look at Fallow Fold. It's a lovely winding little village with an absolutely great tea

97

shop – best vanilla slices in the county. And don't forget to call in at Fairmile Green – it's got a main street with some interesting shops, and a little stream running right down the middle of it,' Carmichael continued, always an ambassador for the area he loved so much, and knew so well.

'I'd love to call in on your wife, Sergeant Carmichael. You'll have to give me your address. And then there's a really queer old chapel in Steynham St Michael,' she continued, back in travelogue style. 'I read in a guide book for the area that there's a very old and interesting market cross in Market Darley, and there must be a museum of the countryside somewhere around here.' Virginia had, apparently, got her mojo back (*whatever that means!*) and had a small smile of genuine enthusiasm on her face.

'I've been too screwed-up for too long,' she continued. 'Let's get out and about, Richard, and make something of this holiday. The weather's great, and the countryside around here's just beautiful.'

'Anything you say, my love! Anything you say!' replied Richard, grinning and reaching into the car to remove the first of the boxes from the back seat. 'I'm sorry we can't help you, Inspector, but I think you should consider this as your good deed for the day.'

'I will, sir. Glad to have been of help,' replied Falconer, his eye already on number four: the next house in the terrace.

The door of number four was opened by a woman of about fifty, with a softly lined face and hair that showed a heavy smattering of grey. She was tall, and remarkably thin, but her face lit up when she smiled, which it did in welcome. 'How may I help you?' she enquired, and stood patiently while Falconer went through the inevitable introductions.

She showed no signs of inviting them inside, merely informing them that she had never been to the village before, but had fancied a change of scenery over Easter. She had seen and heard nothing, and knew nothing about what had happened on Thursday, and they were very soon on their way to number three.

98

Number three didn't appear to have anyone staying in it at the moment. A quick peer through the net curtain-less windows showed no signs of recent life, and Carmichael made a note to check this with the owners. That left only two more properties before lunch, and Carmichael hoped they wouldn't take long. The ginger biscuits had worn off by now, and his stomach, which needed a lot of stoking to keep such a big frame upright and vigorous, was making loud plumbing-like noises of anguish and emptiness.

'Was that you?' Falconer asked, after a particularly loud and resonant rumble.

'Sorry, sir. I need something to keep the wolf from the door, before I come over all woozy,' he replied with a hungry expression.

Falconer stepped a little to one side, hoping that the wolf was not Carmichael. He didn't fancy being bitten by a colleague, for he had no idea which forms he would have to fill out to report it. 'We'll be as quick as we can. If necessary, you can go ahead and order for us.'

The door of number two was opened by a young woman in a nightie, her make-up smudged and her hair in a state of disarray. She didn't look very pleased to see them. And when she had explained that she and her new husband were on honeymoon, they understood why, and withdrew tactfully, merely noting that their names were Alison and Dick (*tee-hee-hee!*) Clifton.

'And don't you dare say a word about the husband's first name and honeymoons.' Falconer warned Carmichael off, before the wheels in his brain could finish turning, and provide him with a smart but obscene observation.

An elderly man who introduced himself as George Smithers opened the door to them at number one. He and his wife, Kathy, had come to Shepford Stacey because they had lived there many years ago, and had fancied a trip down memory lane. They had bumped into quite a few people they remembered from the old days, some they'd spoken to, and some whose names they could not remember, but whose faces they knew.

They were having a grand time, and wished them luck with their investigation, before closing the door on them to get ready for a pub lunch, pub as yet un-chosen.

It was a great pity that Falconer questioned him no further as to who exactly they had seen, in the light of what was to follow.

Chapter Six

Saturday 2nd April – lunchtime and afternoon

They settled for the Temporary Sign for their lunch, for no better reason than that the car was parked at the rear, in its car park. Robbie Greenslade immediately left his post behind the bar to welcome them, his antennae aquiver, having instantly identified them for who they were.

'What can I get you two gentlemen? Something to drink, or will you be eating as well?' He looked like nothing more than a shrew, scenting the air with its whiffling long nose – which his own organ of scent somewhat resembled.

'A couple of halves of lager,' intoned Falconer, receiving a nod of agreement from his sergeant, 'and a look at the menu, if you have such a thing.'

'I'll get you the menus now, and I'll be back in a jiffy with the drinks,' he chirped.

They were served within ten minutes with their food, Carmichael choosing fish, chips, and mushy peas, with an extra three slices of bread and butter and a big bottle of ketchup. Looking up from his plate, after he had beeped the proverbial wolf on the snout with a metaphorical newspaper, he asked Falconer what he was eating.

'Gesiers salad,' he replied, 'done nice and crispy, the way I like it.'

'What's "jesseeay", sir?' and then wished he hadn't asked. The very thought of what the inspector was putting into his mouth made his complexion turn slightly green, and he re-invested his attention in the good old British fare on his own plate.

After a good few minutes of steady gastronomic enjoyment on the part of both diners, Carmichael felt comfortable enough with his calorific intake to attempt a little light conversation. 'I went to a school just like the one here, when I was little. But the seniors' was a nightmare.'

'Why was that?' Falconer was beginning to feel well-fed and contented as well, and thought he might as well join in.

'My family, as you know, sir, live in Market Darley, and the comp there was full of thugs and villains – and that was just the girls!'

'Oh, nice one, Carmichael! However did a delicate little flower like you survive in such a harsh environment?'

'I'm a big lad, if you hadn't noticed, sir, and I had brothers already at the school, so no one messed with me. They didn't want the Carmichael brothers on their backs. We look like a bunch of giants, as you found out at the wedding.'

'True. I'd forgotten how many of you there were.'

After a silence of perhaps half a minute, Carmichael chanced a personal question. 'Where did you go to school, sir? I know you've been in the army, but I don't really know anything about you,' crossing his fingers that this impertinence wouldn't earn him a verbal bollocking.

'Quick version, Carmichael. There's no need for me to go into any great detail: prep school as a weekly border from the age of seven, then on to a school not too distant from here as a full boarder. Then I did my degree – it doesn't matter where, or what in – then ten years in the army.

'I had a bellyful of that, came out with a bit of a pension, and joined the police force as a graduate on fast-track promotion. The next thing I knew, I was being introduced to you, and a much more colourful daily life, if you don't mind me saying so.'

'Thank you, sir.' Carmichael felt honoured that the inspector hadn't just choked him off and told him to mind his own bloody business. Falconer never mentioned his private life, unless it was something amusing to do with his cats, and Carmichael sometimes found it frustrating working for a cypher. What little he had learned seemed like a treasure chest, after his previous total ignorance of the man's past. Maybe Falconer was learning to trust him.

When their plates and glasses were empty, and Robbie Greenslade had returned to their table three times to see if everything was all right (snooping, in other words), Falconer suggested that they adjourn to the Ring o' Bells to see if they could rustle up an after-luncheon coffee. They needed to speak to the Darlings, and it would kill two birds with one stone, as it were. The Temporary Sign hadn't contained anyone of interest to them, so there was no reason to delay their departure any more than was necessary.

The Ring o' Bells boasted quite a crowd of lunchtime customers, many of whom looked like regulars who saw this place as a second home. They spotted Mr and Mrs Smithers in the middle of the pub, working their way through fish and chips. Carmichael waved to them, like a child saluting an aunt and uncle.

'Stop it, Carmichael! They're suspects, not long-lost relatives.'

'Sorry, sir. Just being friendly.'

'Well don't be. You're a detective, not a tour guide, although I'd have been pressed to spot that fact about an hour ago.'

Carmichael took this admonishment like a man, still thrilled with what he had learnt about the inspector, and they approached the bar to see if they could obtain coffee.

Ernie Darling suppressed a little sneer as he took their order, obviously putting them down as a right couple of sissies, coming into a pub and only ordering coffee, but business was business, and having checked whether they wanted white or black, disappeared off into the kitchen behind the bar, leaving his wife Margaret temporarily in charge.

Margaret Darling, spotting unknown faces, summed up who they were in an instant. Before she noticed them, she had been necking a large gin and tonic, but as her eyes alighted on them, she gave a little splutter, and turned away to face in the opposite

103

direction, suddenly developing an interest in a conversation that was being conducted between two men sitting on bar stools.

'You don't get off the hook that easily, my lady,' Falconer muttered under his breath, as Ernie Darling returned and handed them two cups of coffee, with little packets of sugar in the saucers, slowly soaking up the coffee he had slopped in them as he carried them through to the bar.

'Mr Darling?' he enquired politely, before the publican could slither away, for he had a knowing look in his eye too, now.

'That's right. Who wants to know?' he asked, already looking shifty.

'Detective Inspector Falconer and Detective Sergeant Carmichael of the Market Darley CID,' he announced, starkly and to the point. 'We need to have a word with you and your wife, and if it's not convenient during opening hours, we're quite happy to return at a more convenient time. Perhaps we could come to some arrangement now.'

It was nearly two o'clock, and they still had three more visits to make, so an agreement was eventually reached that they would return to the bar at five o'clock or thereabouts, when the doors were closed for a break between lunchtime opening and the evening shift.

As Ernie sidled away towards his wife, Falconer took a sip of his coffee and grimaced. 'Don't bother, Carmichael. Not only is it instant, but it's cheap instant. Tastes more like floor sweepings than coffee.'

'I'm not as fussy as you, sir,' declared Carmichael, downing his in one, then making a face that would not have disgraced a gargoyle. 'You're right, sir, it does! I'll take your advice in the future.'

As it was such a lovely day they decided to walk to their afternoon destinations, and set off at a leisurely pace down Four Stiles and past The Rectory to Forsythia Cottage, to meet the members of the Baldwin clan that they had not yet encountered.

With no car to give away their presence on the tarmacked

drive, they found themselves privy to an argument that was raging, the sound streaming from the open windows of the ground floor of the property.

It was Stevie Baldwin's voice that they recognised, and Falconer concluded that she must have the weekends off, as he had not noticed her in the Temporary Sign. 'I don't know how you can say such a beastly thing, Gran. I had no axe to grind, and I don't see why you should've. How can you say you're glad? None of it was her fault: it was just bad luck.'

Another voice said something indistinguishable, at a lower volume, and whatever had been said only helped heap coals on the fire of Stevie's rage. 'And you can shut your mouth, too, Mum. If that's what you think of me, I don't know if I can stay here any longer.'

'Now, now, Stevie, darling,' the other voice rose in pitch, adopting a whining tone. 'I admit that I spoke in haste just now. You know how much I love you, and little Spike, as does your father, and your gran here. We're just a bit up in the air, with all the memories it's brought back. And you can't blame us if we see it as just desserts.'

'I think you're all twisted. I'm happy with my life, even if you don't approve of some aspects of it. Why can't you just leave me be? Things could be a lot worse, but you don't see that, do you? Always harping on about the negative, and never the positive ...'

At this point in proceedings Falconer rang the doorbell and silenced any further exchanges. He knew it was only like the bell at the end of a round of boxing, and things would continue when they left, but they couldn't stand out here all afternoon and wait for them to finish.

Stevie opened the door, her face flushed with anger, and it was with considerable effort that she summoned up the ghost of a social smile. 'Yes?' she asked, somewhat abruptly, but was obviously still trying to get her temper under control. When she understood who they were and why they were here, she indicated that they should enter, not trusting herself to speak at the moment.

As they entered a large through-lounge, she announced them with a bad grace, and flung herself into an armchair by the door into the hall, with a mutinous expression on her face.

'Did you get a good ear-wig?' she asked with a glower.

'Stevie! Don't be so rude. They're only doing their job,' snapped the woman who introduced herself as Patsy Baldwin. 'We're all at sixes and sevens at the moment, with Mrs Finch-Matthews being murdered like that.'

'No, we're not, Mum. You, Dad, and Gran are. I'm not of the same mind as you three.'

'Is this to do with the loss of your leg?' Falconer took a flyer, thinking that the gods love a chancer, and this time it paid off. He didn't get ripped to ribbons for his impertinence. Neither did he get his face chewed off, nor get ejected with a boot up his backside. The presence of the police seemed to have introduced a calming element, and given them all breathing space. Even Stevie's face was losing its high colour as she stared at him, in disbelief at his directness and sheer brass neck.

There was a silent hiatus, as the faces of the three older Baldwins became blank, the silence finally broken by Stevie, who had seemed the most agitated. 'They're all glad that Mrs Finch-Matthews is dead. They say it's a judgement because of what happened to me, but that a load of bollocks – please excuse my French.

'What happened to me was an accident, pure and simple, and nothing whatsoever to do with Mrs Finch-Matthews' decision to allow skipping ropes to be brought into school. What happened could just as easily have happened when I was at a friend's house, or in the garden here.

'It was a series of bad luck and coincidences, and the chances of them all happening to the same person were probably one in a million. If I can accept it, why shouldn't they?' she asked the two detectives, but without the expectation of an answer.

'And they still can't accept that I got pregnant, and simply didn't want to marry the father. He would have been totally unsuitable. We'd have been divorced within the first two years, and that would have been much more harmful to Spike than being brought up here, with three generations of his family on hand to help with his upbringing.'

Falconer signalled with his eyebrows to Carmichael to keep schtum. This stuff was a gold mine, and had come from completely out of the blue.

'But we all love little Spike,' protested Mrs Baldwin, her husband and his mother nodding their heads in silent agreement.

'Sure you do – NOW!' Stevie shouted this last word, making her mother and grandmother jump. 'But you were pretty hateful about his very existence when I was pregnant, and when he was first born, weren't you?'

'We didn't know him then, Stevie. Give us a break. We're all doing our best here, and it wasn't our fault that that woman got herself murdered, now was it?' Frank Baldwin had finally entered the conversation, and there was a clear note in his voice that begged for mercy from his only daughter. 'We've only ever done what we thought was best for you. You know that.'

'Maybe you have, but you've never really asked me what I think is best for me, have you? You're all so puffed up with hatred, that it wouldn't surprise me in the least if one of you spiked Audrey in the eye, just for the sake of what you considered 'unfinished business'.'

'That's a horrible thing to say, Stevie, and you just take that back!' Frank had raised his voice, and his face was suffusing with colour again.

'I'm sorry, Dad. I just get so het up about the whole thing. What happened, happened, and none of us can do anything about it. Now, the woman you hold responsible has gone too, so can we just forget about the whole thing, and try to get on with our lives with a bit of love and harmony again.

'I know it's always been simmering somewhere in the background, but, on the surface, we'd all come to terms with it, and until Thursday last life was pretty good. Can we get back to that, please?' she begged. 'I mean, what happened to me wasn't as bad, or as final, as what happened to that little girl a few years before I started school, was it? What was her name? I can't remember.'

'Let me think a minute,' said Patsy. 'It was a long time ago … Got it! Carole Nicholson.'

'And what happened to her?' asked Falconer. 'No one else has mentioned anything about this.'

'I doubt they would,' said Elsie, who had been very quiet until then. 'It must be thirty years ago now. A lot of people weren't here all that time ago, and those that were have probably erased it from their minds. They remember Stevie's accident because she's still here to remind them, but poor little Carole Nicholson is as dead as a doornail, and if you ask me, that was all that silly woman's fault, too. I mean, that Audrey's own husband had even died in a car accident, you'd think she'd have been more careful of the kiddies.'

'Mum!' interrupted Mrs Baldwin junior. 'Let me tell it. You put such a negative spin on it because you've got an axe to grind.' Turning to the two detectives, she commenced her tale.

'It was when Stevie was just a baby. There was a girl at the school called Carole Nicholson – very pretty little lass she was. Anyway, one day – November, I think, because it was all because of the fog. It seems that Carole had fallen over in the playground – heaven knows why they didn't keep them indoors in that kind of weather – and she tried to tell one of the grown-ups, but they wouldn't listen. They were too busy trying to get the children back indoors after the bell had been rung, so little Carole decides to go off home and tell her mum that she'd fallen and hurt herself.'

Patsy Baldwin paused here, a faraway look in her eyes. 'She'd only got as far as the main road when a car ran right into her. They hadn't even noticed she was missing at the school; it was all so quick. They got an ambulance, of course, and fetched her mother, but she died the next day. The only thing her mum could do for her was to kiss her poor knee better, and then she was gone. And she was an only child.' Here, she gave a heart-felt sigh. 'Stevie's right. At least we've still got her. Things could be a lot worse, couldn't they?' She turned to stare at her family as she asked this.

With an embarrassed murmur of assent from the other three members of the family, the previous mood of resentment seemed to be broken, and they became aware again that they were not alone. Falconer was, at last, able to begin his questioning, although he was not destined to learn any more than he already had.

As he was leaving, he heard Stevie say to her mother and grandmother, 'I didn't know you'd made stuff for the bake sale. You should've said something. When Ruth Lockwood handed me two plates and said thanks for the flapjacks and jam tarts, I stood there like an idiot, wondering what on earth she was talking about.'

Making a mental note of this snippet of seemingly irrelevant information, he decided that his unintentional eavesdropping, and the ensuing emotional scrimmage as they had arrived, had been more than enough to be going on with. It had been like manna from heaven, and he'd learnt more from that than he would have done from hours and hours of patient questioning.

It would appear that quite a few people had had quite sizeable bones to pick with Audrey Finch-Matthews, including a few he hadn't yet had the chance to speak to. This was only round one, and he was being showered with players in that age-old game, 'Grass Thy Neighbour'.

Paddock View was a fine-looking property that occupied the corner of Four Stiles and Leaze Hollow. It was the home of India and Hartley Bywaters-Flemyng and their son Sholto. The family also owned the large paddock, of which the house had a fine view, the stables built thereon, and the row of six holiday cottages, and obviously did very well for themselves.

India opened the door to them, listened to their polite introductions, ushered them into a huge room, richly furnished and appointed, and introduced them to her husband Hartley, who shook hands and smiled, but did not speak. Their son had been interrupted in a game of some sort with his father, and suddenly flung a ball of some sort towards Hartley.

Unfortunately, Carmichael had chosen that very moment to cross the room to a chair, at a gesture from Mummy, and was caught somewhere just south of his middle, sinking to the floor with a cry of, 'He got me right in the scrofulas!'

Both Falconer and India Bywaters-Flemyng rushed to his aid. He was curled up on the floor in a foetal position, his hands doing temporary duty as a makeshift cricket box, and he moaned loudly and piteously. 'He got me right in the tentacles, right on me Little Davey! If I can't have kids, I'm gonna sue for loss of fertilisation!'

'Calm down, Carmichael. It was an accident – nobody's fault,' then to India, 'Have you got anything cold? A packet of frozen peas would do; just something to dull the pain and prevent too much swelling.' India's face collapsed into a mask of disgust as she thought of eating peas that, in their packet, had cradled Carmichael's 'gentleman's parts', and wondered if she would be considered eccentric if she returned them to the freezer using tongs, but the victim assured her that that wasn't necessary, and a little sit down was all he needed.

They helped him up and guided him to the chair which had been his original destination, a John Wayne missing his horse, and he sat there, cradled forward over his lap, a little green around the gills, and asked for a glass of water. As he waited for this to be fetched he keened miserably to himself, 'I'm never gonna be a dad now. What's Kerry gonna say?'

'She'll probably kiss them better for you when you get home. Now, show a bit of backbone and let's get on with what we came here to do,' Falconer hissed, already weary of the drama. For this, he received a glare and a small moan of self-pity, but Carmichael got the message, drank his water, and took out his notebook, still crouched protectively over the root of his male pride.

'I'm trying to find out if anyone saw a stranger in the vicinity of the school on Thursday morning, or saw someone they didn't expect to see there?' Falconer's question was posed to both of them, but it was India that answered.

'I'm afraid I can't help you there, Inspector. Everything was

110

just as normal. I took Sholto to school, then came back here to check out the bookings for this week and the next with Hartley, then he went off to the cottages to make sure that the empty one was ready for the next visitors.'

'And did you see anyone or anything unusual, either on the way there or back, or while you were there?' This question was addressed specifically to Hartley.

It was India, however, who answered for him. 'I'm sure he would have mentioned it to me, if that were so.'

'I was asking your husband, Mrs Bywaters-Flemyng, and I'd be grateful if he was the one who answered me.' Falconer had been caught like this before.

Hartley's face went completely blank, and his colour began to rise. He looked like a boiler building up pressure, and there was a look of despair in his eyes. For a moment Falconer got his hopes up. Here was a man hiding something, if ever he'd seen one. What was about to be confessed? And then the man spoke. 'Aye-aye-aye-aye-aye ...' he began, and it seemed almost an impossibility that he wouldn't follow this up with 'like you ve-ry much'.

'I d-d-d-didn't s-s-see any-w-w-w-w-one out of the aw-aw-aw-ordinary,' he informed them, his face now a deep crimson colour with embarrassment. He hated, more than anything else in the world, having to talk to strangers, because it made his problem so much worse.

'Well, thank you very much, Inspector. I suppose you realise that he's not going to be able to speak properly, even to me, for the rest of the day?'

'My apologies, Mrs Bywaters-Flemyng – and to you Mr Bywaters-Flemyng, but I'm sure you'll understand that I have to ask.'

'And before you make matters even worse, it was that bitch at the school that caused his speech impediment. He was perfectly all right before he went there, but he was cripplingly shy.' Hartley nodded in confirmation of this information, and his wife continued with her explanation, which she felt was necessary in the circumstances.

111

'She saw it as helping him to gain confidence in front of others, and she used to make him read out loud to everyone. Even before he could read, she'd have him up to the front of the class on a Monday morning, when she used to choose a few of the children to tell the class what they'd done at the weekend.'

'B-b-b-b ...' Hartley spluttered.

'It's all right, Hartley; I know what you're trying to say. That vicious old cow got to enjoy seeing him fight it: she could see the dread in his eyes, and she enjoyed the feeling of power it gave her. And Hartley is the end result of her cruelty. I wonder if she ever looked on her work, and found that it was good?' She was steaming mad when she finished the explanation, and Sholto came over to her and put his arms around her legs.

'Are you OK, Mummy? Don't get mad, please. It makes me feel all funny in my tummy, when you get mad.'

'I'm not mad, darling. I've just been a little bit cross, and now I'm better, 'kay?'

''Kay,' he agreed, and went over to give his father's legs a hug too, so that he wouldn't feel left out.

Falconer volunteered to fetch the car for his wounded sergeant, and left Carmichael still sitting hunched forward, a look of pained indignation on his face as he mulled over the odds of permanent damage having been done.

On the short drive to the Borrowdales' residence in Cat Hanger Lane, Carmichael was still sitting in an unnatural position, when he turned to Falconer, who was driving, to spare his sergeant the pain of operating the pedals, and asked, 'You said earlier that you were going to find somewhere we could use as an incident room. Whatever happened to that idea?' He was obviously still feeling ropey, because he forgot to address Falconer as 'sir', something he was usually most meticulous about.

'Cuts, Carmichael; cuts, and the lack of any available space suitable for that purpose. Normally we would have asked to use the school, as all the children are on holiday, but that's not been possible as they've had to cancel the decorators and declare it a crime scene. And I don't know if you've noticed, but there doesn't seem to be anyplace in the village for public gatherings other than the church. Even the bake sale had to be held in The Rectory, and we can hardly ask if we can move our activities there.

'Not only would it be unprofessional, but it would leave all our notes and information open to public view when we weren't there. There's no way we could trust a locked door to stay locked, when unattended, in a private dwelling. There's simply no money in the budget for a Portakabin, so we're stuck with the drive every day. I'm sure if we could summon up a mass murderer, the money would suddenly become available; but for one little death – no chance. And by the way, Carmichael, the words are *scrotum* and *testicles*, should you ever need to use them again. And I don't think I want to hear another word, for the rest of my life, about your "Little Davey"!'

They parked the car outside Creepers, not wanting to give any advance warning of their presence to Seth Borrowdale next door at The Vines, in case he decided to be unexpectedly unavailable, by legging it out of the back door and over the hedge into Back Lane. Fortunately, the drive was not gravel, as they had noticed it was at the holiday cottages, but was tarmacked like the Baldwins', and they were able to approach a front door, once more, without any indication of their approach to anyone inside.

In fact, it was Seth Borrowdale himself, who answered the door, as he'd been expecting Cameron MacPherson, from whom he had requested the use of an electric drill, not possessing one himself, and Martha having acquired a small shelf that she wanted fixed to the kitchen wall to hold her recipe books. Seth saw no point in buying either DIY or gardening tools, when he lived next door to a perfectly well-equipped neighbour, who was always willing to lend him things. Presuming on the kindness of others was just one tiny part of his *laissez faire* attitude to life.

His wife came bustling out of the kitchen drying her hands

on a tea cloth when she heard voices, and wriggled her way past her husband to take charge of whatever was going on. When Falconer asked if they could speak to them individually, she made it clear that she knew all about her husband's past, and insisted that the interview be a joint one.

This was not at all what Falconer had planned, but he let it pass, and they followed her into a living room furnished, surprisingly, with antique furniture, the only seats available being upright and horse-hair stuffed, and not at all comfortable. Presumably Borrowdale had a den somewhere with a more accommodating chair, and his wife, maybe a recliner or something of that sort, in another room. Neither of them looked as if they would enjoy sitting in there in the evenings, and in fact, there was no sign of a television set.

Martha noticed them looking round and, surmising their thoughts, promptly provided them with an explanation. 'This is for 'best',' she explained. We've got a kitchen diner, so we keep the middle room for lounging about in. It doesn't matter if Lorcan makes a mess in there with his toys, and the cats can sleep where they please, without Seth yelling at them to get off this, or get off that, and asking them if they knew how much so and so was worth.'

Her husband cast her a glare as he heard this, but made no comment himself. In fact, he looked rather like a 'no comment' man for life in general, and he sat perched on a particularly stern sofa, waiting for someone other than himself to start the conversational ball rolling.

Falconer took the cue, and asked Martha the now tedious questions about whether she had seen anything or anyone unusual on the last day of term, and got the usual reply. He could have just photocopied one statement and given it to all the people to whom they had spoken to sign.

Fortunately for him, the smell of cake beginning to burn wafted in through the door, and Martha left the room in rather a hurry. Here was his opportunity. 'I don't know what you're up to, Seth Borrowdale, but I do know you're up to something, and I'm going to find out what it is, and charge you with it. That

114

aside, what do you know about the murder at the school? We've been reliably informed that you hated Mrs Finch-Matthews, and have done since you were taught by her. Did she find out something about what you're up to and threaten to expose you?'

'No comment,' said Seth Borrowdale.

'You've got two kids at the school, haven't you? Isaac and Jacob? Did one of them let something slip?'

'No comment,' said Seth Borrowdale.

'Did one of the staff overhear something, or were they told something that allowed them to put two and two together about what you're up to? Because I know you're involved in something dodgy, so don't bother to deny it.'

'No comment,' said Seth Borrowdale.

'This is a complete waste of police time,' Falconer decided. 'We're leaving now, but I want you down at the station in Market Darley, with your solicitor present, if you want him, at nine o'clock on Monday – no, scrub that, Monday's a Bank Holiday – on Tuesday morning, and I don't want any feeble excuses about why you can't be there. If necessary, I'll send a car for you. Have you got that?' The confusion with the days had rather taken the sting out of the tail of his diatribe, but he felt he had got his message across.

'No comment,' said Seth Borrowdale.

They left the house without catching sight of Martha again, but they could hear the hum of the vacuum cleaner from the room behind the one they had sat in, so she had obviously dealt with the little matter of a scorched cake.

On the way out, Falconer had noticed that every surface gleamed from regular polishing, and that everything was clean, tidy, and cared for. That Borrowdale chap had landed himself a good little wife, and definitely didn't deserve her. Perhaps keeping everything in apple-pie order was her way of shutting out his rather coarse and criminal nature.

Back in the car Carmichael felt recovered enough from his knock in the nuts to take over the driving again, and asked if they could make a triangle of the return trip to Market Darley so

115

that they could stop in Castle Farthing. There was something he wanted to show the inspector of which he'd be glad of an opinion.

Falconer had no beef with the suggestion but, as it was just after five o'clock, and they had promised to return to the Ring o' Bells to talk to the Darlings. 'Duty before pleasure, Carmichael,' he intoned in a sepulchral voice, while his sergeant mimed throwing-up over the sill of the open window.

Ernie Darling answered the quite energetic knocking on the door after a long two or three minutes, which Falconer suspected was deliberate, rather than him being out of earshot. Ernie's eyes were a little like underdone fried eggs as he gazed up at Carmichael's impressive height, and bade them enter.

'Breast-fed, were you?' he enquired in a sarcastic tone and, not waiting for an answer, transferred his gaze to Falconer, with the comment, 'That's a National Dried baby if I ever saw one. Spot the difference a mile off, no trouble. Now,' he turned in their direction as if his previous remarks had not been uttered aloud, made a failed attempt at a smile, and asked them to be seated while he roused Margaret, who had gone upstairs for her afternoon nap.

Ernie disappeared behind the bar and through a door at the right hand end, from where they could hear him calling , 'Margaret! Get up, you lazy bitch! The filth are 'ere! Get yer lazy, fat arse down here so that they can 'ave a good go at yer.' This second demonstration of Ernie's contempt for the police went straight over Carmichael's head, but it was beginning to irritate Falconer, who had little respect for those who sided against the law just because they had a delinquent friend or relative.

'Do feel you can take as much time as you want, Mr Darling. We can sit here all day, being paid in taxpayers' money from the public purse. You probably make enough here not to have to worry about your tax bill at the end of the year. Just wander on in here at your leisure, and we'll put our feet up and have a nice little PAID break.' In fact Falconer suspected that they were standing just the other side of the door from the

116

bar, to see how long they dared spin out their absence.

This brought results, and the couple soon joined them: a fact that did not escape Falconer's notice, and only went to prove, in his opinion, that the pair had been waiting to see for how long they could take the piss, as Ernie had done when they had knocked (*and knocked, and knocked*) on the door for admittance.

Finally seated round a table – no admittance to a private lounge here – Falconer glanced at Carmichael with his 'notebook' look, and commenced questioning them about their son, David.

Mrs Darling didn't look capable of answering many questions at all. Her eyes were bloodshot, hung with impressive bags, her colouring was faintly grey, and she was either under the influence of a monster hangover, or suffering from some mortal disease.

The former proved to be the case, and it wasn't long before she excused herself and went off to quaff a glass of water, returning to the table with a glass of clear liquid, which she excused as 'the hair of the dog that bit me'.

Ernie was sullen in his replies to questions about David's incarceration, muttering about his son either being framed by the police, or taking the fall for someone else. About his son's earlier life, he was a little more forthcoming, and it seemed that the young David had been the apple of his father's eye, and could do no wrong.

Mr Darling Senior had managed to continue in this vein, keeping his blind eye firmly turned to the wall, until the police started to arrive on the scene, which made things rather difficult for him with his version of his lily-white boy. Slowly, it would seem, his illusions had been peeled away, layer by painful layer over the years.

In point of fact, even now, he was inclined to blame others for David's 'little misfortunes', and opined that when the lad, (*He was a lad no more, existing as such only in his father's eyes*) came home, he could work in the pub with a view to taking it over when he and Margaret were transferred to that

Great Bar in the sky. They were just working here for a decent retirement and to be able to build up a nice little inheritance for their boy.

Bollocks! thought Falconer, turning sideways and winking at his sergeant, with a most unexpected result. Although Carmichael took impeccable notes, he wasn't always 'listening' as it were, to what he was writing, and Falconer's wink seemed to have no context, and made him shy in his chair like a compromised virgin, thereafter glaring suspiciously towards his inspector.

'At ease, Carmichael! You missed something there, that I'll have to explain after we've finished here.'

To say that Margaret Darling did not stand up well to questioning would be a gross understatement. She did not stand up to it at all, and just burst into tears, keeping her fluid level up by constant little nips at her glass of gin.

Going for blunt rather than gold, Falconer asked her baldly, 'Do you always drink this much, or has your consumption increased since your son was imprisoned?'

This elicited another outburst of sobbing and the draining of the glass of spirit from her, but her husband was more informative. 'She's been on the sauce for a good while, but not like this. This only started when our David were sentenced. Half the time she's awake she's senseless, and half the time she's supposed to be asleep, she's wandering around looking for him, imagining he's a little boy again and they're playin' 'ide an' seek. Get this! I even found 'er out in the street in 'er nightie one night, sleepwalkin' for Britain. She was only on her way to the school to collect little 'un, thinkin' he were still six or seven years old. Didn't remember a thing about it in the morning. An' all this to-do in the village isn't helping 'er. She's drinkin' even more since that old dame got 'erself killed.'

'Very interesting,' Falconer thought, as he asked, 'Can you tell me where you were when Mrs Finch-Edwards was fatally attacked?' Might as well ask. Not a lot of point, but might as well, just for form's sake.

'I were in 'ere, servin' me customers as always, and as for

118

madam 'ere, well, I think she was getting over one of her 'special' migraines, weren't you, dear?'

'Oh, probably. I usually am,' his wife confirmed, walking carefully towards the bar to refill her glass.

Back in the car once more, the confusion of Falconer's wink explained, but neither of them any the wiser for their visit to the pub, Carmichael took the wheel again, and it was only a short while later that the car skirted the end of Castle Farthing's village green and pulled up outside Jasmine Cottage. As they got out of the car, Falconer asked after the two puppies that Carmichael had recently acquired; one for each of his stepsons.

'They've really grown, sir. You won't recognise them. They eat their heads off, and rough and tumble like a couple of little clowns. The boys just love them, and they're starting to train them now they're old enough – the puppies, that is, not the boys. They're going to take them to proper classes soon, then I said they could enter them in the local pet competitions at some of the village fetes this summer.'

As they entered the living room from the tiny box of a hall, two little boys flung themselves at Carmichael, delighted at his unexpected appearance, and two furry little bundles attached themselves, one to each of Falconer's trouser legs, and began to climb him, making tiny growling noises in their throats as they scaled the perilous heights of his lower half. He managed to resist the urge to swat the pair of them off, and was very relieved when Carmichael's wife, Kerry, came to his rescue, plucking them off him and rubbing them against her face, making little cooing noises as she did so.

'I thought you said they'd grown, Carmichael. They're still microscopic,' Falconer commented, to save himself from swearing with annoyance. He could see a pulled thread on one of his trouser legs, and they had not been cheap.

'They're nearly twice the weight they were when you last saw them, sir.'

'What? Four ounces each instead of two?' For Carmichael, tower of a man that he was, had chosen to buy a Chihuahua and a tiny Yorkshire terrier, both of which were still puppies, but which would never look like fully-grown dogs, however old they got.

'Ha ha, sir! Should've gone to Lens-Savers: they're getting huge!'

Falconer wondered what the tiny scraps thought of the head of the household, but was not feeling mean enough to ask. Carmichael had forgotten all about his 'doo-berries' in his exuberance at being with his family.

'What is it you want to show me, Carmichael. I've got to hook up with Green and Starr when we got back, to see how they got on with their game of 'hunt the skewer'.

'It's this dresser, sir, over on the far wall.'

Falconer took at glance over at it, and saw what appeared to be a very trendy dresser, with the latest distressed paintwork look. 'Very nice, Carmichael! I bet that cost you a pretty penny.'

'Not even one penny!' Carmichael beamed with pride as he embarked on the story of the dresser. It was sweet, really, for him to think his boss would be interested, but he was that sort of person: the sort that wants to show how happy things make them, and what things make them happy.

'The dresser was part of the stuff we kept from Crabtree Cottage,' he began.[3] 'The paint was an unused pot from the shed. I painted it, then distressed it myself. Do you like it?'

'It's lovely, Carmichael.'

'They call the style "sub-lux",' he announced with pride.

'I think you'll find that they call it "shabby chic", Sergeant. Shall we go?' Falconer was feeling quite distressed himself, with Carmichael's cavalier misuse of language so far that day. PC Green and PC Starr were already back at the station, such as it was, writing up their notes. 'Any luck?' asked Falconer, before going upstairs to his own makeshift office.

PC Starr sighed, and said, 'Yes! In just about every kitchen, in the houses that had someone over fifty living in them. The

---

[3] See *Death of an Old Git*

older half of the group had bought them when they first got married, the younger half had got them from their mothers or their grans. I never want to see another skewer as long as I live.'

'You want to hope you never see one as up-close as Audrey Finch-Matthews did,' was the inspector's wry comment, and it made PC Green look up, annoyed at the man's flippancy in front of a woman, commenting, 'Hey!'

'Green!' answered Falconer, acknowledging his presence. 'Would you like to tell me why you're sporting a rather spectacular black eye?'

Green lowered his gaze again, saying nothing; a pale imitation of Seth Borrowdale.

'It was all my fault,' offered PC Starr, blushing with embarrassment.

'Tell me!'

'We went for a drink together at lunchtime, down at the Coach and Horses. You know. that old dive with the low ceilings, that still stinks of tobacco after all this time? It's sort of been taken over as the coppers' pub, since we've moved here, and there was a student from the Poly working weekends behind the bar.'

'French,' interjected Green, lifting his head and leering. 'Lovely bit o' skirt.'

'Anyway, Merv doesn't know any French, so I told him a sentence to say to her, if he wanted to get to know her better,' admitted Starr, becoming even redder.

'And was the word *coucher* contained in this sentence, Starr?' asked Falconer, trying to stop his mouth twitching.

'Yes, sir,' she mumbled. 'And he said it to her, and she landed him one right in the eye, even though he was in uniform. She just didn't care, and gave him a fourpenny one, as my gran would've called it. I have apologised – to both parties,' she said, a woeful expression on her face.

It was Carmichael who started laughing first, and Falconer left the three of them to it, as his sergeant launched into the tale of his own mishap that afternoon, without even knowing whether it had bruised or not, and causing further hilarity when

121

he offered to show them.

It was good that they'd shared a laugh together, for the mood was to turn much more sombre before the weekend was out. Maybe they were feeling fey.

Back at his desk Falconer looked up the number, and made a call to Detective Inspector Plover of the Standchester Police. He wouldn't have felt comfortable if he hadn't followed up on the Graingers' story. At the mention of their name, the disembodied voice that was Plover sighed deeply, and just said, 'Don't get involved with her. She seems to have an A-Level in getting herself into dangerous situations.'

'I don't think there'll be any of that sort of thing on this case, Plover. She's only on holiday in Shepford Stacey for a few days.'

'Don't trust her. Don't trust her an inch. If there's anything dangerous going on, that's where you'll find her – right in the middle of it. She led me a right merry dance last year, keeping information to herself, and going off sleuthing without telling me first.'

'I get the idea, Inspector, and thanks for the warning, but there'll be nothing like that up here. She's planning to spend the rest of her time here sightseeing, so I doubt I'll come across her again.'

'Oh, you will, Falconer; you mark my words. You will!'

Falconer terminated the call, having formed the opinion that the Standchester inspector sounded like a man who has waited all his life for something to happen, only to find that it has been accidentally left off the agenda, to be replaced by a meddling member of the public, currently staying in Shepford Stacey.

With a smile at the lugubrious predictions of his colleague from the coast, Falconer set to, to list his suspects: there certainly seemed to be plenty of them. Getting something down on paper always helped him to get things into perspective, and gain a better understanding of what had actually happened. There were plenty of characters to choose from, and he was at his desk until seven o'clock, scratching away with his pen, with occasional pauses for thought.

122

Chapter Seven

Sunday 3rd April

If he was not in the office, or out and about on a case, Sunday was a day that Falconer found difficult to fill. A free Saturday could be passed with food shopping, a little window shopping, and changing one's library books, but Sunday, even though all the shops were open now, and it was supposed to be the same as any other day, simply was not: it was different, and curiously empty on occasion.

Before he started on his planned work, however, he remembered that he wanted to know about the empty house next to Blacksmith's Terrace, and dialled The Rectory's number with little hope of success, as this was Easter Day. To his surprise, Ruth Lockwood answered the summons after only three rings.

'Yes,' she confirmed. 'I do remember who lived there. It was an elderly lady called Fanny – short for Frances: Fanny Anstruther, if my memory serves me correctly – who went into a nursing home ... probably, at least: I don't know for sure. But the place has been empty for quite a while now, and we assume it will go up for sale either when she dies, or the funds from it were needed to pay her fees. I'm afraid I've no idea of next-of-kin, but it's hardly going to impinge on your investigation, is it?'

It wouldn't. Falconer just liked to know just who and what he was dealing with, and he couldn't discount the occupier, or previous occupier of Copse View, until he knew who that person was, or had been. This information meant one person less for him to chase up, question, and consider as a killer, and that was OK by him.

This Sunday he had brought all the case notes home, and was going through the reports and interviews, making notes, correlating and condensing, to give him a definitive suspect list, and there sure were a lot of people who harboured some sort of grudge against Audrey Finch-Matthews.

His pen raced across sheet after sheet of paper, with an occasional pause to screw up a piece, and toss it towards the waste paper bin. After a couple of hours, he had more or less what he wanted on paper, and fetched a cork board from the garage. Although they used boards at the office, he liked to have one of his own at home, where he might be able to see things from a different angle, without any interruptions from other officers or the telephone.

Opening the top right hand drawer of his desk, he extracted a packet of plain postcards, uncharacteristically tore the plastic packaging off using his teeth, and began to fill them in with details of all those he had decided had a reason for making off with the head mistress, no matter how weak or unconvincing the motive seemed to him. Emotions were strange things, and what might seem trivial to one person could prove to be entrail-chewingly important to someone else.

Scrutinising the school staff, he started with a card for Harriet Findlater, noting that she was a spinster who lived at home with her parents and, in his opinion, had always existed in Audrey's shadow. She was an ineffectual woman who was easily cowed, even by the boisterousness of children, and was quietly furious with Audrey for refusing to recommend her to take over the school when she retired.

To someone of Harriet's meagre achievements in life, this might be enough to enrage her to commit murder. In times gone by, she might have been described as being 'at a funny age'. Audrey's retirement really was her last chance to achieve her life's goal, and the woman had casually shrugged off the idea as if it were too ridiculous to contemplate. It would only have taken her a couple of minutes – easily explained by a bathroom break – and she could have poked her colleague one, and reappeared in the classroom as if nothing had happened. Unlikely, but her rage may have infused her with sufficient courage and motivation.

Saul Catchpole had actually been dismissed from his post as caretaker at one point in his rather chequered career, and was no fan of the woman. He'd had a nice little scam running with the milk money, and it must have been a severe blow to his wallet to lose not just his scam, but his job as well. It was possible that his resentment could have simmered over the years, and he'd pictured her retiring shortly with a very comfy pension, thank you very much, and compared this with what he had to survive on, including his meagre wage. Resentment and jealousy were powerful motives for acts of pure spite, and what was more spiteful than murdering someone?

He paused now, with fresh cards in his hand, and considered the Baldwin family. What a nest of hatred existed there! With the accumulated resentment of Mrs Baldwin senior and Frank and Patsy, Audrey was held responsible for the accident after which Stevie lost her leg. It had been down to Audrey that skipping was allowed to continue, in their eyes, and the bitterness just got worse after that. Add an unplanned pregnancy into the list, and 'bingo'.

It had appeared to him that they all three believed that if Stevie had not been disabled, she would not have 'got herself into trouble'. That her disability made her, somehow, worth less than an able-bodied person, which was not only deeply insulting, but incredibly bigoted towards the disabled, thinking of them as some sort of second-class citizens. He had been disgusted with what he had heard from them, and wondered how Stevie and Spike put up with it. He could only presume that they kept it low-profile, and the murder had brought it all to the surface again, like a boil coming to a head. The poison had to escape somehow.

And how come Mum and Gran had gone to the school separately with contributions to the bake sale, and neither of them had bumped into Stevie? Or found her, to say 'hello'? Why had they never mentioned that they'd been there? Was it simply forgetfulness, in the light of what had happened, or something more sinister? Did each even know the other had gone? And was it just luck that no one had apparently seen them? So many questions, he thought, and not enough answers.

He used three cards for this family, omitting Stevie, and added the cards to his board, with the others he had already pinned in place. If he worked his way methodically through everyone on his list, he could re-pin them in a variety of configurations, and maybe see something that he hadn't noticed before. Also, it filled an otherwise empty Sunday for him.

Seth Borrowdale may need more than one card, now Falconer had received notice of his previous convictions, and his holiday at Her Majesty's pleasure as a youth. He'd spoken to a few others with this particular gentleman in their sights, and it looked like his balloon would soon go up. Computer frauds – and all sorts of electronic scams – were up-and-coming, crimes that allowed one the luxury of not dirtying one's hands or revealing one's voice or features, and they had proved very popular of late. Seth was just on trend.

But Audrey had heard something from the man's own son, and interpreted it correctly – out of the mouth of a babe he was betrayed. Falconer hoped that retribution would be swift, and that little Isaac didn't suffer because of something he didn't even realise he'd done. When parents speak openly, they should be more aware of little ears. They may not understand, but they can transfer what they heard to little mouths, and other people's ears might find it easier to interpret what had originally been heard.

Moving on to the Bywaters-Flemyng household, he removed another two cards. Whatever Audrey had done to inspire such fear in Hartley had been horrifyingly effective: she'd done a real job of work on him, and, although Falconer knew the man could speak in a totally uninhibited way in front of his family, he was almost incoherent before strangers.

It must have a very limiting effect on their social life, and was probably a deciding factor when they decided what to do with their lives. Hartley's jobs were, in the main, solitary:

taking care of the maintenance at the holiday cottages and the stables, and making sure that everything was in apple-pie order for new holidaymakers in the properties. He must resent the way his life had been curtailed from such an early age, and so must India.

India was an outgoing young woman, strong and handsome, and yet here she was, buried in this not very interesting village. Yes, she got to meet people when the properties were let out; she got to get to know people who came for regular riding lessons, and she met those who hired horses or ponies for trekking, but it wasn't what you could describe as any sort of a social life. Perhaps she was full of resentment at the hand that had been dealt to her husband.

That gave him eight cards covered with small, tight writing on his board, and that only represented those who had a direct connection to the school. There were others in Shepford Stacey that he needed to consider.

He decided to start with Ernie and Margaret Darling. Their son David had been to school with Seth Borrowdale, and it sounded like they had been a couple of bad lads at that early age, and had not really changed over the years. Seth was still up to his eyebrows in scams, and David Darling was actually in prison starting a four-year sentence – which would probably put him back on the streets in less than two, but it was still a long time to his mother.

Margaret Darling had been hitting the bottle lately, he had learnt. Now, that could be because she was mourning the loss of her son's freedom, but it could also be guilt at having murdered the person she probably blamed for ratting on him when he was a child: or it could be a combination of the two, he considered. If she'd been necking rather a lot of booze, she might have lost her inhibitions to the point of doing something totally out of character. Drunken people could carry out acts that they would never have considered consciously, but had a subconscious urge to commit.

Ernie, too, had appeared rather furtive, and not inclined to chat, when they had gone to the Ring o' Bells for the after-lunch coffee. He must have been proud of his son once, even if it was only when he was very young. Did he feel that life had cheated him out of the opportunity to have a son he could boast about, and showcase to his friends and customers? It must be galling for him to work in the public arena, and know that everyone knew his business. It wasn't as if he worked office hours, and could retire behind a solid front door at the end of the day.

The other couple in the village that had an axe to grind were the 'weird sisters' at the post office, who were just short of qualifying for jobs in Royston Vasey. Vera had seemed very concerned about what Letty should hear when they had been there, and he had learnt that it was the younger sister, Vera, who was postmistress. She was obviously very protective of her sister, who had been accused of misappropriating some of the school dinner money.

It had all been a storm in a teacup in the general scheme of things. But to those sisters, it was a huge slight against Letty's character, and a slur on her intelligence, that she couldn't even remember what she had done with the unexpected extra bag. Letty did seem to be viewed as a little simple, and maybe she was, and had only survived thus far with Vera's protection. Neither of them had ever married, and they seemed to share an unusually strong sibling bond, considering that there was a gap of three years between them.

He halted here, with the thought that he had covered everyone he could think of, when he heard a sound outside, and rose slightly out of his chair to see who was visiting whom.

The noise hit him first, a mixture of children's voices shrilly raised in excitement, a booming, and the sound of more than one creature yapping. Halfway to his feet he recognised Carmichael's car outside his house (he had sensibly filled the drive with his own vehicle), the whole family gathering to launch an assault on his castle.

His eyes took in, in an instant, his porcelain, glassware, cream carpet, and white leather, and his body was galvanised into action. In a complicated slither, like a human eel, he was away from his desk and beneath his white baby grand piano. There was plenty of room underneath, and the sofa sheltered him from any prying eyes at the window. He knew this was a good plan, as he had hidden here before, and knew he would be impossible to spot.

He could hear them, now, at the windows, the miniature dogs yapping their heads off. With a slight blush, Falconer realised that they could probably smell him, and could not understand why he was not letting them in and feeding them delicious little treats, and he thanked God that humans did not have the olfactory organs of canines.

Carmichael knocked on the window with a knuckle, and called out to his boss, and Kerry rattled the letter-box, calling out his name, in case he was on the lavatory and suffering from an acute case of sudden deafness. Movements then relocated to the side and rear of his home, and he began to feel personally invaded, and acutely so when he heard the rattle of the cat-flap and Carmichael's voice booming through it, in case his boss had his head in the freezer, or other such domestic appliance, and failed to hear their knocking and shouting.

Grabbing a cushion from the top of the sofa, he got himself comfortable, lying in a foetal position, and waited for the invading hordes to give up, and go off to irritate someone else on their free Sunday afternoon: let them go and wreck and plunder some other Englishman's castle. He'd have been willing, at this particular point in time, to hand-dig a moat, if he could repel such unwelcome invaders.

He awoke two hours later, having unaccountably fallen asleep while waiting for the sound of the Skoda starting up with its trademark cough and whine. Every joint in his body ached, and the cheek that had rested on the cushion had a nice flowery pattern on it in red. It would seem that Carmichael didn't even have to enter the house to do him over.

As he crawled out from under the piano, his elbow caught a small crystal glass on a bookcase, and tipped it on to the floor, where it promptly turned into a see-through jigsaw. He sighed.

His sergeant could also inflict physical damage on his possessions while not even in the house. A vigorous stretch, however, left him staring at the piano, a question in his eyes.

One's first encounter with sexual chemistry, the kind that makes you shake like a jelly and unable to speak – a real chemical reaction, whether one is fourteen or forty – is always deeply disturbing, if not downright frightening. Falconer's first time 'in the barrel', as it were, had been the previous year[4], and he had been so affected by it that he had abandoned many of his previously much-enjoyed leisure activities, instead adopting the less productive pastime that is usually referred to as 'mooning around' in an aimless manner.

Still with his eye on his usually treasured white baby grand, he extracted a copy of 'Over the Rainbow' from the piano stool: one of those settings that has so many flats in its key signature that you just know it's going to need an elevator. He sat down at the piano, staring at the dots and lines and the battalion of flat signs, lifted his hands, and played.

His laughter rolled round the room, as he sight-read with great inaccuracy, but equal enjoyment, the clashing chords his hands were making causing his heart to sing, and in his pleasure, he knew that he was cured, and ready for whatever life had in store for him. Singing along in a light baritone, he decided that he ought to return, too, to his Greek studies – modern, of course – and decided (causing a ten finger pile-up on the keyboard) that he would probably have to go right back to the Mr Men books. Boy, did those kids know some difficult words!

In Shepford Stacey, Ruth Lockwood was sitting with a cup of coffee and a biscuit, slumped in an armchair with her feet up on the sofa when the phone rang. It was eleven o'clock on Sunday morning, and her husband was caught up in a sea of 'Allelujah, He is risen, He is risen, indeed.' Their daughter was in the Sunday school class, absorbing the Easter story for the

---

[4] See *Choked Off*

umpteenth time.

Ruth had gone to early communion at seven o'clock, and had bagged this time as a precious oasis in her busy life, when she knew that not only her family, but her husband's parishioners too, were imprisoned in the church, and could not interrupt her with their petty domestic disputes and family problems.

That was probably her sister phoning, for she had told Olivia that they would be able to have a conversation in absolute peace, and not the usual chaos she usually had to put up with when she phoned her younger sister.

They had been talking for the best part of an hour, when Ruth heard the back door, and a noise in the kitchen. 'I've got to go,' she informed Olivia. 'I can hear them in the kitchen: the service must be over. I'll speak to you again in a week or so. Take care; love you; goodbye,' and she headed for the kitchen, calling, 'Hello. Do you want coffee, or are you awash already?'

From the kitchen there sounded the scuffle of feet and a little 'yip' that could have been interpreted as a greeting, and she fully expected to find her husband and daughter in there raiding the biscuit barrel, because they were always hungry, Sep, because he had a fast metabolism, Dove, because she was a child, and had a lot of growing to do.

But the kitchen was empty when she entered it, the back door open and swinging in the slight breeze that had sprung up overnight. She walked outside to the corner of the building, and looked down the side, but there was no one visible, and she went back in, perplexed and puzzled.

As she stood, lost in thought, Septimus and Dove burst into the house via the front door and headed straight for the kitchen. 'Biscuits, Mummy! We need biscuits! Daddy's been saving souls, and I've been acting in an angelic way, and we both need biscuits!'

'Good service?' Ruth asked, as she passed the biscuit tin to her small daughter.

'Not bad: the usual twice-a-year souls that come for Christmas communion as well, and the usual faithful band.

131

What about you? Nice bit of peace and quiet?'

'Yeah, I suppose so,' she answered. 'Tell me, Sep, did you see anyone leaving here as you came home. Someone perhaps coming out of the front gate?'

'No, no one.'

'What, you didn't see anyone at all?'

'There was a figure in the distance, just turning into Forge Lane, but I couldn't say who it was. Not even whether it was a man or a woman. Why?'

'Oh, it doesn't matter. It's probably just me being silly,' she answered, dismissing the incident from her mind.

It wasn't until quite a while later, that she noticed that the rogue plate that hadn't been claimed after the bake sale, had disappeared from the work surface and was now nowhere to be found.

Harriet Findlater saw Virginia Grainger outside the holiday home as she approached her own drive. The woman from number four Blacksmith's Terrace had also just overtaken her, a stout canvas bag in her right hand, on her way back from some unknown errand. Feeling unusually sociable because it was a nice day, the Easter service had been very uplifting, and her parents were away, giving her free run of the house, she hailed them both with a 'Yoo-hoo!' and invited them in for a cup of coffee, or a rather daring sherry, as it was almost lunchtime.

Virginia agreed instantly, as they had decided not to go anywhere today, as most places would be shut, and when her neighbour declined, they both set about convincing her that she really wanted to join them, she just hadn't realised it yet.

She introduced herself, reluctantly, as Caroline Course, stating that it was her first visit to the area, and she'd come here for a bit of peace – a strong hint that she would not be staying long, whether she chose coffee or sherry.

'Are you sure?' asked Harriet, sounding very impertinent. 'You look very familiar.'

'I should be grateful if you would credit me with knowing whether I have been somewhere or not. I must resemble someone else you know, and you're getting muddled. You seem a muddled sort of person to me,' she replied, trading impertinence for impertinence without the trace of a blush.

'I'm so sorry,' Harriet apologised, 'but in my job I see so many faces that you're right: sometimes I do get muddled.'

As predicted, the small gathering suffered from a dearth of conversational topics. Harriet tried to stop the boat sinking by asking Mrs Course if she had any family. No, she had no children and her husband was dead. She asked about other relatives, where she came from, and finally, in desperation, if she had any pets, indicating the framed photos scattered about the room displaying past furry members of the family, gone but not forgotten, but Mrs Course stonewalled her on every topic.

The reluctant guest left after ten minutes, having swallowed her sherry in one gulp and handed her glass back, saying that she must get back across the road. Holding her bag against her chest, as if protecting it from some sort of attack, she walked across the road, without even turning to wave goodbye.

Virginia stayed on for another half an hour, mentioning that she had seen Mrs Course visiting at High Gates before her parents went away, and gave it as her opinion that it was odd that the other woman hadn't mentioned it. Harriet was rather short with her about this, for she was sure that, if it were true, her mother would surely have informed her with one of her superior smiles, implying she was more popular than her daughter.

With a small blush that this piece of information may be true, and withheld by her mother out of spite, Harriet consoled herself that she had had the rather charmless woman round for refreshments all on her own.

Virginia tried other conversational gambits, but finally gave up in sheer boredom, for Harriet talked about nothing other than the harsh and unsympathetic treatment she suffered at the hands of her parents. Making an excuse about Richard expecting her back to make the lunch, she gathered up her jacket and left, glad to get away, and not impressed in the least with the woman who was holidaying next door to her.

The rest of Easter Sunday passed without notable incident in the unremarkable village, and the sun went down in a blaze of glory, setting the clouds on fire with the splendour and richness of its colours.

Back at High Gates, Harriet Findlater dined off a piece of shop-bought quiche with a microwave-baked potato and salad, washed her few dishes, and settled down in front of the television set, in sole control of the remote. Yet even this unusual situation did not comfort her, for with the arrival of darkness she had become nervous again, remembering her fears of a prowler, and the fact that she was on her own.

It wasn't much of an advantage having her own choice of what to watch on the television, if someone came in and strangled or stabbed her. Rising from the most comfortable chair, usually her mother's perching place, she locked both the front and back doors, and the windows that she had had open earlier to air the house on such a fresh and relatively warm day. No one was going to catch her unawares tonight, if she could help it.

She was well-secured inside the house, and she would take a couple of her mother's sleeping tablets when she retired. The old biddy might give her a right verbal going over when she got back, but there'd be no way she could retrieve her two tablets, and Harriet would have had a good night's sleep – in fact, she got a rather longer sleep than she had intended, as it turned out.

Cursing both her mother and her late boss as singularly unsympathetic to her, Harriet Findlater's, wishes and desires, she stumped off upstairs to bed, wondering if maybe she would be put in temporary control at the school after the holidays. At least that would be a consolation, even if a very small one.

Chapter Eight

Sunday 3rd April – after dark

The first light became visible through the glass panel of the front door, flickering and jumping, desperate to grow up, and learn to roar. It was hungry, and needed urgently to feed, and there was little food here in the hall. Maybe the coats on the coat hooks would make a tasty little snack. Hunger! Hunger! Hunger! It had to eat, and it had to eat now, or die.

The first person to become aware of the light was a man from Leaze Hollow, out walking his dog, as he couldn't sleep. (*The dog was compliant, grateful even, of this unexpected late exercise.*) The man dragged his mobile phone out of his pocket to inform the appropriate authorities of what he was witness to, his dog whining at this unexplained halt, so far from home.

The first ring woke Falconer, and he reached automatically for the phone, his body well ahead of his brain. 'Whoozzit?' he asked, his normally immaculate hair spiked and askew, as if he had been asleep in a ghost train, when the telephone rang. 'Whaaa …?

Consciousness finally returned as he realised what he was being told, and he sat bolt upright, his brain racing now, its previous torpor shed like an old snake skin. 'Let Carmichael know,' he requested, 'Tell him I'll pick him up as soon as I can get there, and tell him not to expect to be back home much before breakfast.' As he terminated the call he was already halfway into his trousers, theories forming then evaporating in his brain.

He had not anticipated this, and realised that his previous opinion on who may be responsible for the murder might be a

135

bit off kilter. It could still be one of the people on his cork board, but there was also the possibility that there was someone out there who had managed to stay under his radar, and was very, very dangerous.

The light licked its way into the living room and started to make its way up the stairs, beginning to crackle now, like a chuckle of evil laughter. There was enough food here for it to grow to magnificence, to become a fire to remember; a fire to go down in village history. If it remained unchecked, it might even be the bringer of a village tragedy, and it produced as much smoke as its fuel would allow, trying to build up its strength so that it could roar its power through the house, destroying everything in its path, licking, as if to taste, new areas and objects it came upon.

The man with the dog, after making the emergency call, approached from the other side of the road, to see if there was anything he could do, but Harriet had made a good job of locking up. Having taken two sleeping tablets, she was determined not to be disturbed that night. Little did she know that she would never be disturbed again, but would have been comforted to know that she would not have to endure her mother's fury, and look suitably chastened under the fire of her contumely:

Harriet, how could you have been so stupid as to burn down the house? We were only gone a couple of days, and now we're homeless. Have you got no consideration for your poor old parents? Whatever were you thinking of to allow the house to be gutted like that? You really are a very careless and stupid girl, and I don't know why we put up with you.

Harriet slept on, oblivious to the oblivion into which she was about to be plunged, while the good Samaritan banged on double-glazed windows and shouted himself hoarse, the dog joining in with its sharp barking.

Across the road Virginia heard the unexpected noise, and came out of the front door of her holiday cottage to see what was happening. Surely there were not drunken street fights in such a peaceful little village? The only sounds they had heard

136

from the street outside since they had arrived had been that of the occasional car passing.

She looked with horror across the road to the flickering light behind the front door and downstairs windows of High Gates, spotted the man with his dog, and ran over to see if there was anything they could do. She called for Richard to come and join her as she ran, thinking of garden sheds with hoses in, but it was obvious as she approached the building that nothing as paltry as a hosepipe could deal with a situation like this. It was so out of hand now that only the fire brigade could be of assistance in vanquishing the monster that was an out-of-control fire.

Looking back briefly to whence she had come, she saw Richard dragging on a jacket as he made his way, at a run, to join her. At number four, next door to their cottage, she saw a figure in the doorway, silhouetted by the light behind it, and knew it was Caroline Course.

As the flames started to glow dully in the upstairs windows, showing that the fire was inexorably climbing the stairs towards the house's sole occupant, Virginia idly wondered why their neighbour didn't join them. There may be nothing they could do at this precise moment, but human nature dictated that people congregated when something disastrous was happening, and her very stillness seemed unnatural.

As if she were aware of Virginia's puzzled gaze, although this was impossible, given the darkness and the distance, Mrs Course closed her front door slowly, and pulled the curtains across her front window, as if she had seen as much as she needed to.

Inside the house, black smoke roiled lazily where it found pockets of clear air, filling them with the poisonous fumes emitted by old furnishings. Chairs and sofa showed the skeletons of their frames and springs, as if in x-ray, and the panes in the fronts of glass display cabinets began to explode, showering the downstairs rooms with a rain of deadly shards and arrows of glass.

As the fire reached the landing, it chuckled and laughed as it approached the bedrooms, knowing that behind one of these

137

doors was great fun, and was happy that the owners of the dwelling had been too miserly to install any smoke alarms. Undetected, it would graze more easily on what awaited its hungry maw.

It moved on, unchecked, as the sound of sirens approaching sounded quietly through the oh-so-secure, double glazed windows, and sauntered lazily towards Harriet's bedroom door in anticipation of a fine barbecue, with no interruptions, until it had finished feasting.

Two fire engines from Market Darley pulled up in Forge Lane, outside the blazing premises, and the leading fireman informed the few bystanders that there was another unit on its way from Carsfold. And suddenly the night was full of uniformed bodies, all made brightly visible by their luminous yellow over vests, shouted instructions and urgent activity.

One fireman grabbed Virginia by the shoulders and asked her if there was anyone inside, and she stutteringly told him that the couple who owned the house were away for the weekend, but that their middle-aged daughter was in there, presumably sleeping through all these disastrous events.

As he walked away from her to pass this information on to the rest of the team, she felt bemused that she had sat, only that morning, in Harriet's house drinking sherry, and wanting nothing more than to get away from the woman. For all she knew, Virginia might have been the last person she spoke to before this happened. By now, it seemed impossible that anyone could survive the conflagration, and she amended this thought to 'the last person she had spoken to in this life', with an involuntary shudder, that anyone might arrive at the Pearly Gates with only *her* voice ringing in their ears, in tones that declared without need for words, that she wanted to get away and back to her own comfortable life.

Shame flooded her, and she was overwhelmed with the childish notion that St Peter would have a right dressing down waiting for her when she finally popped her clogs: *Look at the disgraceful way you treated that poor woman, who had only a few hours to live. There's no point in saying that you didn't*

138

know that, for you wouldn't have treated her any better, and you know it. She had a meagre, mean little life, with very little joy in it, and you couldn't even be bothered to share her last drink with her and offer a little lively conversation and the hand of friendship, so that she could leave this world a happier soul.

Her cheeks flaming as much from guilt as from the heat, she ran towards Richard and flung herself into his arms, horrified at what was happening right before her eyes, and grateful that she was safe, and had a life to get on with on the morrow. As they walked, arms round each other, back across the road, so as not to hinder the fire team, he asked her what was the matter, as he could feel her shaking from head to toe.

'That poor woman in there! My mind's running the nastiest video possible in my head, at what might be happening to her. She's going to die, Richard, while we stand outside watching, and there's nothing whatsoever that we can do about it.'

'Don't torture yourself, Ginny. Most people in fires die from smoke inhalation, and know nothing about what happens to the body they've left behind.' His words of comfort fell on deaf ears, however.

'That's as might be, but someone's got to see what happened to her – what's left of her – and they're never going to forget it, are they?'

'Ginny, stop it! They're trained men who are hardened to this sort of thing. Just be grateful we have something like the fire service, to save us the horror of sorting through that for her remains. And professional medical staff who can deal with what's come out of there and pass it on to an undertaker.'

'I wonder if she ever considered being cremated when she died? And whatever is her mother going to say about the state of the house when her parents get back tomorrow? Oh, those poor people, having a kebab for a daughter,' Virginia rambled, with a high pitched hysterical giggle, then sobered up when she saw the woman at the upstairs window of number four.

The flames were now fierce enough for the light to illuminate the occupant's face, and she seemed to be smiling an exultant smile, but that couldn't be so. It must be her own hysteria getting the better of her, and she asked Richard to get her indoors where she could do something useful, like making tea for the hard-pressed firemen.

She had just disappeared indoors and shut the front door when a car drew up outside the empty house on the other side of the terrace, and Falconer and Carmichael emerged, their faces glowing an angry red as they neared the source of the heat. All available access to the inside was now open to the elements, and hoses sprayed through the openings in a vain attempt to bring the conflagration under control, and a couple of streams of water played in an apparently lazy fashion over the roof, in an effort to keep the flames damped down.

The fire was much stronger now. Fuel had given it strength and ambition, and it would not be content with just the interior of the house – and of course its sole resident, who was still burning merrily like a church candle. It was determined to aim for the stars, and chewed its way enthusiastically through the upstairs ceilings and into the attic, where it took very little effort to break through the tiles and into the cool night air, defeating without too much effort the pathetic streams of water being aimed at it.

It was strong and mighty, and would not be defeated by these pygmies with their little spouts of water. Exultantly, it reached upwards, casting an orange glow that could be seen for miles around. It knew it had brothers that had destroyed whole towns and forests, but there were also others who had been extinguished almost at birth, and it wanted to 'burn hay while the sun wasn't shining'. The opportunity deserved its best shot, so that it might achieve its place, if not in history, then at least in local memory.

Falconer had a quick word with the fire chief, and wandered back to Carmichael, his face a blank mask. 'Apparently Harriet Findlater is in there, and there's no way any of the fire service personnel have been able to get inside to look for her. It looks like she's a goner: there was nothing anyone could do about it.'

Carmichael's face crumpled with distaste, as he contemplated, involuntarily, what lay within, and asked when they might ascertain the cause of the blaze. Just because there had been murder done in the vicinity didn't mean that this couldn't be the result of an electrical fault.

'The passer-by who made the original phone call said he could smell petrol or paraffin when he went to the door. The tragedy is, if anyone could have got in there then, Harriet Findlater might have been standing with us now, but the house was locked up as tight as a drum – no windows open anywhere. If the man's right, it's a case of arson we're dealing with here – another murder, if you like – but it'll have to be officially confirmed by the fire investigation officer before we're allowed to treat it as such.'

At his shoulder a voice asked him if he would like a cup of tea, and he turned to find Virginia Grainger holding a large tray filled with mugs of the English liquid solution to every problem or situation, simultaneously noticing her husband Richard, moving between the fire fighters with a similar burden.

As the two of them helped themselves to mugs, Carmichael adding the inevitable six sugars to his mug, Falconer informed his ad hoc waitress that he had spoken to Inspector Plover about her.

'Why?' she asked, her mind not at all on what she was doing, fresh horrors arising with her renewed proximity to the burning house.

'To make sure you're not a mass murderer or a bank robber,' he answered in jest, only to find his little joke had back-fired, and that she had taken him seriously in her distraction.

'I can't believe you asked him that!' she stated, looking bewildered.

'Of course I didn't, Mrs Grainger. I was just trying a little levity to lighten the mood.'

'Well, don't!' she replied brusquely, her gaze straying across the road again, to her neighbour's upstairs window, where the face still stared out at the devastation taking place just a few yards from her holiday home.'

'Have you met her?' the inspector asked, inclining his head to the row of houses opposite.'

'I had sherry with her only this morning in this very house,' she answered absently. 'She doesn't seem a very sociable person. I can't understand why she's come to a small village like this for a holiday if she doesn't want to mix with any of the locals and get to know some of them. She might just as well have gone to a city, where there would at least be lots of museums and art galleries for her to walk around on her own, without having to socialise with anyone else.'

'That's a very acute observation, Mrs Grainger, if you don't mind me saying so. Now, you get off with the rest of those mugs of tea, and make some very thirsty firemen happy.'

With another glance at the face at the upstairs window, Virginia did as she was told, but her mind was busy going over what she had just said to Falconer. It was odd that the woman had chosen Shepford Stacey for her solitary break, and she wondered that she had not just stayed at home behind closed doors. To pay good money to stay somewhere where she was just going to stay inside was mad, absolutely mad, and Virginia could not fathom where the enjoyment that usually was part and parcel of a holiday was, in this reclusive plan.

After her departure Falconer had another word with the chief fire officer, who confirmed that he was of the same opinion as the passer-by, who had left his name, address, and telephone number, and could be more conveniently interviewed in the morning. The seat of the fire would have appeared to be in the hall. If there had been the whiff of an accelerant, then it would definitely turn out to be arson, with someone having poured flammable liquid through the letter box, followed by a lit rag.

It would have been easy to have avoided being seen, he added, with a nod to the high hedge that fronted the house, and the lack of a porch light, which had been noted when they arrived. 'A very petty economy,' he had added,' especially when it came to scaring off burglars, or at least making them visible if they decided to use the light to help them open the door.'

Falconer agreed with him wholeheartedly. There had also been no mention of the piercing bleep of smoke alarms. He

142

simply could not understand the mentality of a householder who would install expensive double glazing throughout, then save a pound or two by not having any security lighting or smoke alarms. It was almost an invitation to be boiled alive in their own juices, should there be a fire, and they were overcome with smoke.

He took the piece of paper with the passer-by's details, wandered across to Carmichael again, and suggested that there was nothing useful they could do here now, so they might as well go and try to get some sleep. Tomorrow would be a busy day, and they'd need at least some rest before tackling it.

He dropped Carmichael off at about two o'clock, and by a quarter to three was in his own home, freshly showered, and just climbing into bed with a mug of hot chocolate to help him sleep and calm his seething brain. He'd need that organ to be fresh and ready for action tomorrow, too. There was something here he didn't understand. Lots of little things kept nibbling at his subconscious, like a school of tiny fish, but as soon as he turned his attention to what they were trying to tell him, they turned and flashed away, impossible to focus on.

Carmichael too was in bed, having scooped up the dogs and carried them up with him to his room, for extra comfort. There were some things that were too ghastly to imagine, and the warmth and snuffling from these two tiny creatures, together with the ladylike little snores of his wife Kerry, should distract him sufficiently to be able to drop off. Any nightmares were just a risk he would have to take.

Chapter Nine

Monday 4th April

The day after Easter Day may be Bank Holiday Monday to some, but to those who work in the emergency services it is just another day on the calendar. In fact, with those who have to continue to toil to keep our household supplied with electricity, gas, live radio and television broadcasts and newspapers (*there are even newspapers available now on Good Friday!*), and shops opening seven days a week, twenty-four hours a day in some cases, there are precious few in the population who can take the day as a period of leisure – with the exception of teachers, and those ancillary to school services.

The deadbeats, indigents, and long-term unemployed who usually hung out in the street outside the temporary police station had, however, taken their possession of a Bank Holiday seriously, and appeared to be enjoying a lie-in, as the street outside the ex-Mr Bankrupt was curiously empty of those who habitually waited to taunt the police whenever they entered or exited the building.

Despite their experience of the night before, Falconer had made some time to have a quick fiddle with his post cards on the corkboard, adding information from the night before, and occasionally shuffling them around, to see if the different date positions would stimulate his deductive processes, but nothing leapt out at him.

Even after the truncated sleep they had had to endure, both Falconer and Carmichael were in the office early, clean, and fresh, and with a greater determination to solve this case before anyone else lost their lives. It had been confirmed that the fire was no unfortunate accident, but the result of deliberate arson, and was now being treated as a case of murder, the second in this self-effacing and unprepossessing village within a week.

They surveyed each other in exasperation at the lack of progress, and the only consolation that Falconer could think of was to state that the Graingers were definitely out of the frame, because they didn't smell of petrol or paraffin, or anything else flammable, when they had so kindly arrived bearing tea and sympathy.

'But we never really thought they were involved, did we?' Carmichael asked listlessly.

'No,' the inspector replied, with no enthusiasm whatsoever. 'Plover declared them to be of spotless character when I spoke to him, so there wasn't really any possibility that they were involved, was there?'

'No, sir,' replied the sergeant, scratching his head as he thought.

At that moment, the telephone on Falconer's desk rang, and he grasped it, as a drowning man grasps at a straw. Maybe this would be a breakthrough for them. Maybe this call would provide the answer to all their questions.

It was Rev. Lockwood, and Falconer's 'expectation-ometer' plunged to zero. 'Sorry to bother you, given the recent tragic events, but something slightly out of kilter happened yesterday while I was out doing the morning service, and I've read in books that anything out of the ordinary, in a situation like this, could prove important.'

'Absolutely correct, sir,' the inspector agreed, suppressing a yawn, a peculiar habit he had formed when in conversation with men of the cloth. 'Fire away.'

'It was something that happened just before Dove and I got home from church, and Ruth was on the phone to her sister. I'm sure it's got nothing whatsoever to do with what's been happening in the village, but here it is, for what it's worth. Ruth had arranged the time of the phone call so they could have a good old sisterly chin-wag, while the house was empty.' There was a slight hesitation.

146

'Go on, Vicar,' Falconer prompted him.

'Sorry, I was just wondering what it could mean, if it means anything.'

'What what could mean, Vicar?' Falconer was beginning to feel his usual exasperation with what seemed the habitually woolly thought processes of priests and vicars everywhere.

'Well, it would appear that Ruth heard the back door open, and some noises, as if we'd come home, so she called out that she was just coming. The next think she heard was a small squeak of what she has now convinced herself was alarm from a possible intruder. Not realising this at the time, however, she just went through to the kitchen expecting to find the two of use raiding the biscuit barrel, and found the back door swinging open – it hadn't been locked as she would be in – and later, she noticed that the unclaimed plate from the bake sale was missing.'

'Do you think the owner had come back to collect it, and was surprised to find the house occupied?'

'I suppose so,' agreed Septimus.

'I wonder why they didn't call out and make themselves known,' Falconer wondered out loud.

'I've no idea on that one.'

'How many people knew that Ruth would not be at the service,' asked Falconer. This could be useful information after all.

'Just about everybody. Since we moved here, she's always gone to early communion on both Christmas and Easter days, so that she can get on with ordering our celebration days in uninterrupted peace.'

'Did she manage to see anyone leaving the garden, or perhaps on their way out from The Rectory?'

'No. She didn't realise there was any hurry, as she thought it was us, and, although she heard the gate go, she couldn't see anyone once she'd turned the corner of the house. I'm sorry about that, Inspector. She just didn't realise that it could be important. Well, you don't do you? Hindsight is a wonderful thing.'

147

'And foresight can be even better,' added Falconer, but he said it to himself, and silently, for every piece of unsolicited information was precious, and could prove to be the key to a case. 'I'm just about to leave for Shepford Stacey. Shall I call in when I arrive?'

'Please feel free. I've been out on a few parish visits this morning, so I can give you the mood of the locals, and their reactions to this tragedy, before you call round to find out for yourself. They might have been a bit more candid with me, as I'm not a stranger and they know it's not my nature to gossip.'

'Mine neither, Vicar.' There was a gasp of surprise and embarrassment on the other end of the line. 'No need to apologise, Vicar. My colleague and I will be with you as soon as we can,' he informed his caller, and got up to get his jacket, with a glance at Carmichael, to urge him to do likewise.

As they exited the blessedly un-picketed doors of the building, the phone on Falconer's desk began to shrill. After what seemed like an eternity it stopped, and the phone in his house began to ring its urgent summons, but this attempt to contact him also went unanswered. His mobile number must have been unknown to the unsuccessful caller, for it remained stubbornly silent. Which was a pity really.

It was raining feebly but steadily, the fair weather of the previous two days being thoroughly quenched with low cloud and the constant light but persistent drizzle that manages to soak to the skin, while being mostly unnoticed by those who don't wear glasses.

The remains of High Gates consisted of a blackened shell boasting no windows, doors, or roof, and would need to be demolished, for there was no way even to make it safe, let alone refurbish. A skeleton crew of fire officers were in attendance to damp down the last of the smouldering debris, and in case one of these smouldering areas tried to re-ignite the fire.

Smoke drifted lazily up from the wreckage, to be met by the fine veil of water that was falling from the sky, combining with it, and producing what should probably be referred to as a cross between fog and smog.

There was definitely fog, because the temperature had dropped a number of degrees since the sunshine of the day before, and the ground, still wet from the rains of a few days ago, and with the overnight dew fall, had produced a fog that seemed to rise from the ground in wraiths and tendrils, as if there were an underground fire that was rising, in an effort to meet its brother from the night before.

There was also definitely smog, as the acrid wisps from the smouldering ruin commingled, to produce a cloud that made anyone who came into contact with it cough, as the firemen were doing now, as they moved closer to the front wall of the destroyed house to investigate a brief flash of colour somewhere inside.

The Graingers, in Number Five, Blacksmith's Terrace, woke late. After last night's emergency and tragedy, they had retired late, and spent hours tossing and turning, their minds preoccupied with what had happened and what was happening. Sleep had been elusive, impossible in fact, until about four o'clock, when they both achieved a state of unconsciousness within five minutes of each other.

Virginia rose now, tired because her body clock was slightly out of whack, and descended the open treads of the staircase to the kitchen to put the kettle on. As she stood at the sink while this vessel filled, she looked through the window and across the road, confirming that it hadn't been just an extremely vivid nightmare which had disturbed her so. The house was really gone, and Harriet was undoubtedly dead.

Whatever would Harriet's parents say, she thought, when they got back from visiting her grandmother? Events weren't supposed to occur in that order, children dying before their parents and, in this case, even their grandmother. Life was a fair cow sometimes, and there was absolutely nothing you could do, but accept what was thrown at you, and get on with it. Her mother would have said, 'play the hand you're dealt', but then her mother was full of silly little sayings for every eventuality, and she could be a real pain in the arse.

149

As the water boiled, she gave Richard a token shout, then assembled the necessary crockery for morning tea. If he didn't come down, she'd take it up on a tray. It was when she was pouring the water into the pot, the sound of the kettle heating now extinguished, that she first heard the noise. From the kitchen, it sounded vague, unidentifiable, but not a happy sound.

Moving to the living room at the rear of the house, the sound resolved itself into a muffled sobbing, coming from the other side of the wall. For a moment she stood, doubting her own senses, wondering if she was imagining something summoned from the distress of last night, but in the end, she realised that the sound was real, and its only source could be Caroline Course.

The woman had not seemed at all moved the night before, as she had stood at her bedroom window, a strange expression on her face, given the circumstances. Maybe she had been hit by the reality of what had happened before her very eyes, during the night – maybe one disturbed by nightmares – and there she was, in a strange place, and all on her own.

Virginia's neighbour and very good friend in Little Marden was called Caroline, and this only contributed to the softening of her heart, and the part of her that was a natural comforter.

On the journey down to Shepford Stacey, Falconer gradually became aware of a strange crackling and popping noise coming from the seat beside him, but did not dare take his eyes off the twisting, turning, narrow country lanes to investigate visually. It sounded vaguely like the crackling and popping of the timbers of the burning house, and he hoped he wasn't having an aural hallucination.

Pulling into a convenient farm gateway, he asked, 'Can you hear that crackling noise, Carmichael, or am I going mad?'

'Wh-*crack*-at *pop* w-*sizzle*-as th-*crackle*-at, s-*snapppp*-ir?' asked the sergeant, the volume of the mysterious noise increasing as he opened his mouth to speak.

Turning towards his colleague, Falconer noticed a pink froth on Carmichael's lower lip, and gave a high-pitched shriek. Surely his sergeant hadn't contracted rabies? He knew it was a rural area, but rabies was supposed to be safely contained across the Channel. Though he wouldn't put anything past Carmichael – even going to the trouble of taking a quick daytrip to France so that he could be bitten by a rabid animal, just for the hell of it.

'What the hell is that?' he asked, pointing, but with the back of his hand resting on his throat, just under his chin, so that his digit would not have to get any closer to his passenger than was absolutely necessary.

'*Whizz*-Sp-*pop*-ace D-*crackle*-ust, s-*crack*-ir,' answered Carmichael with a convulsive swallow and a sigh of appreciation, which filled the car with the strong scent of artificial strawberry flavouring.

'What in the name of God is Space Dust, Sergeant?' asked Falconer, annoyed now that he knew the answer, and realising that he had acted like a bit of a 'wuss' before.

'It's crackling candy, sir,' Carmichael answered, as if even an idiot ought to know about that particular line of confectionery. 'When you put it in your mouth and it gets wet, it starts to fizz and explode – quite loudly. I used to love it when I was a kid, and now they've re-issued it. I got some for the boys, but I couldn't resist taking a couple of packets for myself, for old times' sake. Would you like some?' he asked, holding out a small paper packet with rockets and cratered planets printed on it.

'No thank you, Sergeant, and I'd be very grateful if you didn't eat it in my car again. It's very distracting when I'm driving, and besides, there are some things best done behind closed doors, and I, personally, consider that the consumption of this 'Space Dust' is one of them. Do I make myself clear?'

'Y-*pop*-es, sir,' Carmichael replied. 'Sorry, sir. A bit got stuck to the roof of my mouth. It won't happen again, I promise you.'

'Not if I can help it, it won't,' was Falconer's final pronouncement on the matter, and he pulled on to the road again, their journey continuing in total silence.

At Shepford Stacey, Falconer steered the car once more into the car park of the Temporary Sign, but did not undo his seatbelt, or get out of the car. His head bowed in thought, he asked Carmichael, 'Who do you fancy for this one, Sergeant? Have you got any favourites running?'

'Not sure, sir. The only one I would consider to have a motive for the here-and-now is Seth Borrowdale, but I don't get the feeling that he's a physically violent or vindictive man. I think he's all mouth, but just can't be arsed to do anything. Every other motive seems to stem from so long ago. How could anyone keep up that level of hatred over that amount of time?'

'I don't know, Carmichael, but I've got a feeling in my water,' (There was a quiet 'Yuk!' from Carmichael) 'that the solution to this case lies in the past, and, as far as I'm concerned, the household with the most motive is the Baldwins'. Every member of that family had an axe to grind with our Mrs Finch-Matthews, and who's to know how that has simmered and grown over the years?'

'I suppose there are four of them; and at least three of them seem to have hated Mrs F-M's guts. Maybe they blamed both women: Audrey for not having banned skipping earlier, and Miss Findlater for being a wet hen and not challenging her decision.'

'Exactly! Frank Baldwin says he was at work last Thursday, but he's surely capable of slipping out and doing a little freelance murdering, isn't he?' Falconer wasn't feeling quite as facetious as he sounded. 'Stevie's had her activities curtailed for life. Her mother thinks that her disability is to blame for her having an illegitimate child. And, for all we know, Granny might be away with the fairies, and at this very minute may be burying her box of matches from last night, and casting about for her next victim.'

'Don't be silly, sir. I hardly think that's likely,' replied Carmichael, thinking that the inspector's remarks had been in rather bad taste. (*15-love to Carmichael.*)

'Stop being such a sissy, Sergeant, and give me a hand here.' (*Falconer had just evened the score to 15-all*) 'I can't solve this all by myself.' (*Oh yes I can. 30-15. Falconer loved Wimbledon.*)

'Look, what about the Borrowdales? I know I said it wasn't likely, but do you want to go round there to see if we can find out where the head of the household was last night?'

'And the mistress of the house, sir. Women are just as capable of setting a fire as a man,' commented Carmichael, with a slight smirk. (*30-all.*)

'But more likely to need to be there, after the children go to bed, in case one of them wakes up. They're more likely to want Mummy, aren't they?' (*40-30 to Falconer.*)

'But there are two boys, and only one girl. Maybe they'd prefer Daddy?' suggested Carmichael, prolonging the rally. (*Deuce! – or as Carmichael may have scored it, 'juice'.*)

'Well, I don't give a flying fig about which parent they prefer,' (*Advantage Falconer.*) 'I'm the inspector, and I've decided we'll go there and speak to both of them about where they were yesterday evening.' (*Game to Falconer.*)

Carmichael grinned, not knowing exactly how he had got his own way, but nevertheless pleased that he had, and corkscrewed his body out of Falconer's dinky little Boxster, like a 'slinky' getting out of its box of a morning in Toyland.

The sobbing sound continued, occasionally interspersed with little moans, and words which were not decipherable through a wall, no matter how thin. Virginia was really starting to get worried about her neighbour now. What could possibly have triggered this storm of weeping?

Walking back to the kitchen, she made her decision. Adding a plate of chocolate fingers to the tray, she managed to open and close the front door, carrying her burden on her hip, finally approaching the front door of number four, and ringing the doorbell with her nose. The woman was obviously very distressed about something, and, whatever her shortcomings socially, was probably in need of a good absorbent shoulder to cry on.

Being of a nosy nature, her plan felt like a very satisfying one, and she looked forward to listening to her neighbour unburden herself. With only Richard to talk to for most of the time on this holiday, she felt starved of gossip and general female chatter. Her little excursion of mercy this morning, transporting nourishment and comfort, would do her the world of good.

She had to use her nose on the bell again, being careful not to tilt the tray and spill the tea, before she was heard, and her summons answered. Caroline Course was still dressed in the same clothes as she had worn the day before, but she must have been out of doors sometime since the fire had started, as she smelled vaguely of soot and smoke, and there was a black smudge on her forehead near the hairline, where a smut must have landed and not been noticed.

Her eyes were red and swollen, the whites of them muddied with tiny red veins. Her nostrils were red, her lips, puffy, and, all things considered, with her hair all over the place, she looked a complete mess. Although Virginia had no children of her own, the sheer state of the woman instantly triggered in her a maternal response.

'You poor thing! Whatever has upset you so much?' she asked, trying to manoeuvre her way past Mrs Course with her awkward burden. 'If you'll just let me by, I've got tea and chocolate biscuits with me, and we can sit down and have a nice little chat, then perhaps you may feel up to telling me what's wrong. Remember: a trouble shared is a trouble halved, and there is a lot of truth in that. Just talking about something sometimes makes it seem a lot better than you thought.'

Mrs Course looked at her as if she were speaking Mandarin. 'Whatever are you talking about?' she asked, apparently forgetting that she resembled what Virginia's mother would have called 'The Wreck of the Hesperus'.

'I heard you crying. Through the wall,' Virginia explained. 'The walls are very thin, you know, and I thought I'd come round and see if I could be of any help.'

'I don't need any help, thank you very much,' replied Mrs Course in a clipped voice, then spoilt everything by letting a tear trickle down one cheek.

'Don't be so silly,' said Virginia, as bossy as a school teacher. 'Let me in.' She finally managed to 'hip' her way past the woman and into the living room which, being an opposite design to her own, next door, had the kitchen at the back.

She headed straight for a coffee table, placed conveniently in front of a sofa, with an armchair at either end of it, placed her tray on it, and started to pour tea. 'If you want sugar, I'm afraid you'll have to use your own, but the cups already have milk in, and the pot's still hot. Can I tempt you to a biscuit?' she asked, holding out the plate to her bemused neighbour.

Mrs Course stared dumbly and incredulously at her, sinking slowly into a chair, and shaking her head at the offer of the plate. Putting down the biscuits and stirring an already poured cup of tea, Virginia came over and actually took the other woman's hands, so that she could place the cup and saucer securely in them, then sat down herself on the sofa, drawing her dressing gown tightly around her body, as the house was quite chilly. At least she had on her fluffy bunny slippers, and her feet would be kept warm.

'I'd like you to go, please,' Caroline requested. 'I'm perfectly all right, and I don't need to talk, or to be babysat.'

'Nonsense! There's nothing that can't be put in a better light by a good old kicking-around verbally.' Spotting a small photograph in a silver frame on a side table, Virginia reached over and picked it up, asking casually if it was her reluctant hostess's daughter.

'I thought I'd already told you I had no children,' she intoned in a flat voice.

'Are you sure?' Virginia asked, sounding rather like Harriet Findlater, only the previous morning, asking if Mrs Course was sure that she had never visited Shepford Stacey before.

'I think I can be trusted to know whether I have any children or not, Mrs Grainger. Now I'd really like you to go.' Her voice was now cold and distant, but Virginia was absorbed in the photograph. 'This is a school photo, isn't it?' she continued to probe.

'My niece, I expect. Now would you excuse me a moment while I get my pill from the kitchen?' she asked, a shrill note creeping into her voice.

Virginia gave a snort of surprise at something she had noticed in a corner of the picture, and finally returned to the here-and-now, glancing, as she did so, towards the door into the kitchen.

It wasn't a pill at all, that Mrs Course had gone in there to get – it was a bloody great knife, and she was just securing her right hand around it and tucking the long, sharp blade between her arm and the side of her body, pointing it in such a way that, if – no, when – she used it, it would be with an efficient downward stabbing motion.

After maybe a second or two of indecision and surprise, Virginia galvanised her body into action, preparing for flight, for she could not hope to win a fight, not against a weapon like that.

Chapter Ten

Monday 4th April – still morning

Falconer and Carmichael had put themselves in the line of fire again in the Borrowdale household, but both parents seemed to have cast-iron alibis, with witnesses as corroboration. Seth had been ale-swigging in the Ring o' Bells until after closing time, staying on after lock-up, to have a few more drinks with Ernie and one of his other publican mates.

Martha had had a couple of school friends round for a reunion, after many a year of absence, and they had drunk and giggled into the early hours, oblivious of the fire, in the raucousness of their joy at seeing each other again.

In answer to questions from Falconer, yes, Seth could confirm, as could others, that he never left the pub until two o'clock, and that when he got home Martha's friends were still jawing, so he gave them the old heave-ho and told them not to go anywhere near the fire, as their breath would probably ignite, and he didn't fancy having to identify their manky bodies the next day. He really should have sued the charm school!

Virginia fled through the open door, trying to escape into her own cottage, but she had closed the door behind her and didn't have the keys, as she was still in her night clothes. She knocked like a mad woman, but not for long, as she heard Caroline exiting her own cottage, and Virginia knew what she would have clasped in her hand, and what she intended to do with it.

'Richard! Richard!' she yelled, wishing that she had taken him a cup of tea before embarking on this foolish, and now dangerous, errand, but there was no turning of the door handle, no answering call to confirm that he had heard her, and was on his way. How could he sleep through her knocking and shouting?

Fleeing once more, from what had seemed like safety to her a minute ago, she ran into the garden of Copse View, an overgrown tangle of vegetation wreathed in mist, and the smog created by the still-smouldering fire site. She plunged into a forest of shrubbery at the other side of the garden, beyond the conservatory and towards the back, then became as still as a statue as she could manage, and concentrated all her hearing on identifying the whereabouts of her pursuer.

For one horrified moment she thought she had been discovered immediately, then realised that the clicking and clacking she could hear was coming from the pampas grass behind which she sat. She had forgotten how it chattered to itself the whole time, like a crowd of ghosts whispering to each other.

When she was a child, her parents had buried two of the family cats in the centre of a triple crown of such grass in their front garden, and she had imagined that the continual chit-chat was the two cats gossiping, keeping themselves up to date with family news. But this wasn't the right time for such reminiscences ... or maybe it was.

On examination, there proved to be four crowns, planted as if there were one in each corner of a square. This was probably why she had not identified the plants in the decreased visibility – because there was so much of it. If she could only wriggle herself into the middle, she might be safe, but she had to alert Richard somehow, or she'd eventually be dead meat.

She could hear the dreadful Mrs C, still at the boundary of the property, probably relishing the thought that she had her prey cornered. Taking a huge risk, Virginia pushed her way to the back of the garden where there were some sturdy brambles, and shouted Richard's name at the top of her voice, while ruining the skin on her hands by waving stalks of the prickly brambles around wildly to indicate that this was where she had gone to ground.

The diversion appeared to have worked, for she was able to use the noisy progress of her hunter through the tangle, to cover the noise of her own return to the pampas grass, and the rather tight squeeze between its four clumps.

She settled as quickly as she could, becoming as silent as it was possible for her to be, trying to identify the sounds of the other woman's search for her, through the constant clicking and chittering of the grass. It wasn't easy to discern one noise through the other, but she realised that Caroline Course sounded as if she was getting fed up with the brambles, and began to shout at the top of her voice, 'Nosy! Nosy Parker! Come out! I'm waiting!'

This ought to have frightened Virginia to the very marrow of her bones, but she realised almost immediately that the shouting was actually to her advantage. It told her where her pursuer was, confirming that she wasn't, say, just a few feet away, and toying with her, *and* it might alert someone to the fact that there was something very wrong going on. It might even rouse Richard, but she somehow doubted this last.

And then the calling stopped, the noise of the grass interfered with her ability to pinpoint her pursuer, and she got really frightened.

On leaving The Vines, the two detectives decided to collect the car and make the other calls on their agenda using the vehicle. It was a very unpleasant day weather-wise, the temperature having dropped quite a bit, and with the smell of smoke and burning still on the air. The car might shield them from smelling like they'd spent the day tending a bonfire, rather than about official police business.

The Baldwins proved to be at home, all four adults and little Spike. This being a Bank Holiday, Frank was present, as he had been on their last visit here, and it was he who opened the door to them, sighing, 'Not you lot again. Haven't you stirred up enough shit from the past already?'

'Not quite, sir,' answered Falconer, in his official voice. 'I have a few more questions to ask, and I should be grateful if you would invite us in, so that we may continue with our investigation of what, you have no doubt gathered, is a double murder – yes, it was arson,' he confirmed, as Frank raised an interrogatory eyebrow at him, 'and not just some unfortunate electrical fault that caused the fire at High Gates.'

Frank stepped aside and cocked his head towards the living room in resignation, calling out to the rest of his family, 'It's the police, to give us the third degree again – or should that be the fourth degree, considering this is the second time you've called here and disturbed our Easter weekend?'

'Two women have died, Mr Baldwin. Don't you feel you owe them a few minutes of your time to help find their murderer?' That was a killer blow, and Frank merely sat down in an armchair without another word, as first Stevie, then Patsy entered the room, the latter guiding Elsie, Frank's mother, by the elbow, towards her special high-seated armchair.

Carmichael removed himself to a high-backed wooden chair, which stood at the front of the room as emergency seating, in the event of a plethora of visitors, and extracted his notebook. Falconer repeated the information he had relayed to the head of the household on arrival, and when he spoke the word 'arson' there were audible gasps from all three women.

'You mean that fire was started on purpose?' Patsy asked, unable to grasp the fact that there had been a second murder in this boring little backwater. 'Harriet was killed on *purpose*? Who on earth in their right mind would want to kill *two* harmless old women from the local primary school?' This was not exactly what she had said on his last visit, but it nevertheless showed a softening of attitudes, post-mortem.

Falconer's universe suddenly shuddered on its axle. 'Would you mind repeating what you've just said, Mrs Baldwin?' he asked, still computing what her questions had caused to slot into place in his mind.

'I asked who on earth would want to kill two harmless old women who taught at the primary school,' she obliged him. For a moment, he sat without speech, introspective: staring at nothing, and combing his memory.

At last he broke the silence, as the piece of jigsaw fell into place, for he had known all along that the explanation for what had been happening here had its roots in the past. 'When we were here on Saturday,' he stared at Carmichael, hoping to jog him into looking back in his notebook, 'you told us about a child who was killed. Could you elaborate on what you said then?' A second furtive glance in Carmichael's direction confirmed that he had, indeed, found his notes from their previous visit, and was busy scanning them.

'It was thirty years ago, and there's not much to tell, now. A little girl from the school fell over in the playground on a foggy day. Nobody took any notice of her when she tried to get some sympathy and a plaster, so she decided to go home. Only she never got there. She was hit by a car and died later in hospital.'

'Tell me the name of the little girl, please?'

'Carole Nicholson,' supplied Elsie. 'Pretty little thing she was, too. Her mother never got over it.'

'Have you any idea what happened to her parents after the death of their daughter?' He was on to something now, and he knew it.

Frank, Patsy, and Stevie shook their heads, five year old Spike shaking his in imitation, but Elsie answered in the positive. 'Yes, Inspector, I can tell you at least part of the story, if not all of it.' All eyes in the room swivelled to look at her.

'Don't look at me like that, Patsy. I knew her mother from the Mothers' Union meetings, and you were too busy with being newly married, and trying to carve a career for yourself at the council. I didn't always live with you. I did used to have a life of my own,' she explained to her daughter, with a rather dirty look.

'She had a nervous breakdown, you know, the mother: never got over it. Then her husband upped sticks and left her, because he couldn't stand her constant weeping and wailing. He just took off in search of a life out of mourning, and she became even worse after that. I think they put her in a special hospital or a home after that. She stopped washing or doing her hair, or the housework. Damned near stopped eating altogether as well, before someone alerted the doctor, and he went round and eventually called in a second opinion, so that they could section her.'

'And to your knowledge, has anyone not local, but familiar, been spotted round here recently?' he asked. This was a very long shot, but he had to take it, although without hope of getting a bite from such meagre bait.

'Well, yes,' answered Stevie, making Falconer almost jump out of his chair with surprise.

'Who? When? Where?' he asked, urgently now.

'At the bake sale. I was in The Rectory washing up, because nearly all the cups had been used, and Harriet Findlater came and sat with me for a while, and we had a little chat.' Never had she received such rapt attention. 'She only went back into the sale because she said she saw someone she thought she recognised.'

'And who could you see? Anyone that might have been in her line of vision?'

'I wasn't facing the door, so I couldn't see. The last people in the kitchen, though, were that couple from the holiday cottages. Someone did tell me their name – now what was it …? That's it! Grainger.

'Hang on a minute, though, I'd just been asking her who she thought might have done that to Audrey Finch-Matthews, and whether it could have been anyone with a grudge from long ago, and for a few minutes she got completely immersed in things that had happened donkey's years ago.'

A nod was as good as a wink to the inspector, and he recalled that the Graingers had been involved in a murder investigation before, and that Inspector Plover had referred to Virginia as a damned nuisance, or something along those lines. What if she was more than that? He knew she'd declared her intention of going home after Audrey's murder, but there she still was, and now Harriet Findlater was nothing but crackling, with Virginia bloody Grainger just over the road from her.

'Come on, Carmichael,' he ordered, abruptly rising to his feet, and directing a, 'Thank you very much for your time. I

162

hope it won't be necessary to disturb you again in regard to this matter,' to the Baldwins, he marched out of the house and unlocked the car, his next destination firmly fixed in his mind, Carmichael scampering along at his heels like an overgrown hunting dog.

Virginia continued to crouch as quietly as possible in the shelter of the pampas grass, but the acrid smoke mixed in with the fog was tickling her nose and her throat, threatening to make her either sneeze or cough, and memories of a previous experience of being pursued in a heavy bout of mist made her want to scream from a combination of remembered fear and present terror.

It was, however, an unexpected cramp in her right calf that forced her to give away her position, for, as it closed its talons on her leg muscle, she gave an involuntary cry of pain, and changed her position to drive it away. This had been heard from over by the conservatory, and a low syrupy voice began to coo her name.

'Vir-gin-ia. Vir-gin-ia. Come on out, Ginny, I know you're in there, and there's no escape. Come to Caroline, and let me send you to join Audrey and Harriet. I'm sure you'll all get on very well together.'

Virginia's buttocks clenched, lest her bowels evacuate from fear, and settled in silence once more, hoping that the fog would disorientate the woman with the knife, and make her lose her way.

'Virginia! Where are you?' The voice was now an impatient hiss, rather like that of an enraged cobra deprived of its prey. It was fog that had been partly responsible for her darling daughter's death, and its presence now was sending her further down the path of insanity. She would dispose of this woman, but she had no idea of what was beyond that. Maybe she'd use the knife on herself, and they wouldn't know who had killed whom. She'd just have to be careful that she had the strength to throw the knife in the direction of Virginia's body, after she had stabbed herself.

The pampas grass continued its sibilant whisper of incomprehensible conversation, and Virginia felt a little better, having placed the direction of the hiss as slightly further away than had been the cooing entreaty.

Suddenly, another voice joined the cast of today's melodrama, and she heard Richard calling her name, and blundering into the situation, with no idea of what he was up against. He must have heard her calling before she had sought shelter, but his voice did not reassure her. He was putting himself in danger too, and he didn't know it. He probably thought she had gone exploring, and done what all female leads do in old films: fallen over and sprained her ankle.

What on earth should she do? Should she stay hidden, and let him blunder innocently into the path of a maniac, or should she call back to him, thus giving her position away, and putting herself back in the spotlight. Coming to a sudden decision, she stood up recklessly, and shouted, 'Richard! Help! Somebody help! She's mad!' as loud as she was able.

Falconer's car was flagged down as it was passing The Rectory, the vicar shooting out on to the road to apprehend him. He had the stark choice of mowing down a man of the cloth, or continuing on to where he thought a killer dwelt. It was a tough choice, for he was no lover of the clergy.

Executing an emergency stop in his frustration, he lowered the passenger window, and shouted across Carmichael, an action that not many people would have got away with scot free. 'What do you want, Vicar? We're in rather a hurry, so I can't stop unless it's absolutely necessary.' He crossed his fingers out of sight, and hoped the vicar would fall for this one.

He didn't. 'I managed to get a number for the Findlaters senior, and I gave them a call. They're in The Rectory right now, having a cup of tea, and expressing the wish to speak to the senior investigating officer. Ruth and I would be grateful if you could spare them a couple of minutes.' The man's eyes told the whole truth. Please come and talk to them so that I can get rid of them, was what he would have asked, if he had been completely truthful.

With no intimation of the life-and-death drama that was being played out just down Forge Lane, Falconer had no choice but to oblige, and he nosed the car on to The Rectory's drive, and they both got out of the vehicle, to deal with this irritating interruption of the due process of taking a murderer into custody. Maybe!

And it was this 'maybe' that allowed the inspector the luxury of the time to stop. He knew he was on to something, but he wasn't convinced that 'Virginia Grainger' was the answer. He just knew that he was headed in the right direction, and that he'd know what he was looking for when he got there.

Inside The Rectory they found Edith and Bill Findlater, stony-faced, sitting bolt upright in the north-facing and rather bleak living room. Even before the niceties of social greeting could be served, Edith, metaphorically, rose like a snake to the attack.

'What's this I hear about our house being burnt down, and us only gone a couple of days? There's just no police presence in rural areas these days. Whatever is the force thinking about, leaving helpless communities like this at the mercy of any maniac who happens to be passing through? Thank God we're insured, but heaven knows how long this is going to take to sort out. Paperwork seems to take forever these days.

'Computers promised us paperless offices, and yet everything takes twice as long as it used to before they were even invented. I simply don't know what the world is coming to. Well, I hope you're going to do something about it. We can't afford to stay in a hotel or anything like that. We're old age pensioners you know. I suppose we shall have to go back to mother's and stay in that dreary old dungeon of a house of hers, until this is all over.'

'I'm very sorry about your daughter, Mrs Findlater,' Falconer interrupted, unable to believe what his ears were hearing, given what had actually happened, and wanting to give them a chance to compute the apparent lack of emotion from her parents, about their Harriet's horrible end.

165

'Oh, she's not much of a loss. Always whining and grumbling about something, and hanging round the house at the weekends like a bad smell. We had no peace from her. At least we can get on with our plans to move abroad now – nice little apartment we fancy. In Portugal. Better weather than here, and hopefully no nosy neighbours who can eavesdrop on us, because they can't understand what we're saying. Ernie and Margaret were friends of ours as well as Harriet's. They can have some nice little holidays with us when we're settled, and we can all have a gin and tonic on the balcony and watch the sun go down.'

He tried again. 'It was a very fierce fire, Mrs Findlater.' (Bill Findlater just sat with a blank face, apparently tuned to a different station to the others in the room.) 'I'm afraid your daughter will have to be identified from dental records.' That ought to bring the old bag up short.

Apparently not. 'Well, her teeth always were rotten – forever complaining about them, she was – so there'll be plenty of fillings for the dentist to work from. Shouldn't be too much difficulty with that.'

Bill Findlater finally looked in Falconer's direction, and the inspector thought that, at last, he was going to hear some words of grief and appreciation for the poor woman who had just lost her life in an arson attack.

Wrong again! 'We had an insurance policy on her, you know – a life one. I said it would be a good idea, in case anything happened to her, and she wasn't around to look after us when we got frail and needed taking care of. Never fancied one of those nursing homes, myself.'

'Well remembered, Bill. I'd completely forgotten that, with all the rush to get back here. It means we can look at those better-class, more spacious apartments closer to the beach now, and not be too cramped: retire with a bit more style than I thought we would be able to.'

'Would you like to view the remains?' asked Falconer. This was an outrageous question, never likely to be agreed to by the powers-that-be given the state of what was left of Harriet, but

166

he asked it all the same, just to see what reaction he got.

'She wasn't much to look at when she was alive. I don't expect she's any prettier now, but thanks for asking.'

Luckily for all present, the telephone rang at that moment, Septimus Lockwood left the room to answer it, as it was in his study, and the ensuing silence gave them all pause for thought, and for the two detectives to gain control of their tempers, and try to reintroduce their finer feelings to the proceedings.

Finding this an impossibility, and aware of the expression on Carmichael's face, Falconer was just about to announce their imminent departure when Septimus came flying into the room, his cassock flapping round his ankles. 'That was Richard Grainger on his mobile, trying to get in touch with you, or summon help from any quarter available – me, I suppose, at a pinch.'

'Get to the point, man, and don't start rambling, or we'll be here all day.' As he said this, Falconer felt a frisson of apprehension at what he was about to hear, and adrenalin flooded his system with that jittery 'fight or flight' sensation.

'Apparently the woman next door has gone mad. She's chased Virginia into the grounds of the empty house next to the holiday cottages, and has hold of her, with a knife at her throat. You've got go to there now, before the woman does something irreversible.'

Only a vicar would have expressed the danger Virginia was in using the word 'irreversible'.

Virginia, having revealed her position, was struggling to free herself from the middle of the dense growth of the pampas grass when, in her peripheral vision, she was aware of a figure hurtling towards her, one hand raised in threat, and holding what she knew was a knife, but could not actually distinguish at such an angle and in the misty gloom of the morning.

She could hear Richard's cries suddenly cease, and was almost free of the vegetation when she was aware of being grabbed from behind, something cold and sharp being held against her throat, while a singsong voice in her ear crooned,

167

'Bed-time, Vir-gin-ia. Time to go to sleep.' Her throat was as dry as sandpaper, and she could not have screamed had she wanted to.

Letting her body go limp, so that her captor would have more of a struggle to keep her upright, she prayed hard that Richard was doing something useful during his sudden silence. As Course struggled with the sudden extra weight of her burden, there was a loud crashing through the overgrown garden, as Richard headed in their direction, calling Virginia's name over and over again, out of sheer fright for her safety.

'Stop right where you are!' The voice wasn't singsong any more; it was hard, and cold as the grave. 'If you don't stop right there, I'll cut her throat this minute,' she threatened.

The sound of movement ceased, but Virginia could tell, even through the rushing panic in her ears, that he was much nearer than he had been before.

'I've stopped. I've stopped. What do you want me to do?' he shouted, his voice hoarse with panic.

'Absolutely nothing, my dear.' A playful zephyr disturbed the smoggy atmosphere for a couple of seconds, and he could see their neighbour, her face a crazed mask, standing with Virginia firmly in her grasp, a long, gleaming knife held to her throat.

'Don't hurt her,' he croaked, as loud as his dry mouth would allow. 'Please don't hurt her. For God's sake don't kill her.'

'Oh, I don't think I can promise not to do that. I'll do what I want with her, in my own time, and be advised: you'll be next.'

'Why?' It wasn't so much a question that escaped his lips, but a one word prayer.

'Because somebody has to pay.' The mad voice was loud and coarse now, and as evil as the devil's own.

'Pay for what? If you're going to kill my wife and then me, at least let us know what we're supposed to be paying for.' Richard was playing for time, hoping to inch forward to Virginia's rescue, but their tormentor was all too aware of what he was up to.

'My daughter's death,' she screamed. 'And stay where you

168

are. I can hear you moving.'

Virginia gave a little yip of pain, as the tip of the blade was pressed further into her skin. 'Do what she says, Richard! For God's sake do what she says!

Chapter Eleven

Monday 4th April – morning

Falconer and Carmichael had made a dash for the door, alerting the elderly Findlaters that they may be about to miss something, and they had risen too, intent on following the action wherever it went.

The Boxster shot out of The Rectory's drive, and turned right into Forge Lane with a squeal of tyres. Neither of its occupants had any idea of whether they would be called upon to use negotiating skills, or brute force, or whether the outcome would be another death, or just an arrest. Everything had sorted itself out in Falconer's mind now, and all he lacked was the fine print. No doubt Mrs Grainger would be able to provide that, should she survive her ordeal.

The Findlaters followed hard on the wheels of the front car, wanting to be spectators at the end game, and curious to see what was left of their house. Mrs Findlater had even begun to view the fire as a blessing, as they would not have to wait for years to sell the place. The insurance should pay up, and the site could be cleared for demolition and rebuilding. It was all very simple in her mind, the only obstacle to their plans for year round sunshine gone now, along with the house.

Both cars screeched to a halt almost simultaneously, and spouted figures that rushed in two separate directions, the Findlaters to what was left of High Gates, and the detectives towards the rear garden of Copse View, not stopping their headlong rush until they were beside Richard Grainger, who was breathing hard with emotion.

A yell of fury from Virginia's captor was drowned by

shrieking and yelling sounds coming from the other side of the house, and Falconer took pause to comprehend that the reality of the situation had suddenly hit Harriet's parents, with their first view of their erstwhile home, and gave a wry smile at their distress, the heartless bastards.

Caroline Course was momentarily distracted, her head shooting round in surprise at the sudden sound. Virginia wriggled and struggled in her grasp, trying to kick her in the ankles, and Carmichael suddenly burst into voice.

'Oh my God!' he shouted at the top of his voice, pointing just over Course's right shoulder, his face a mask of utter horror.

'What?' asked Falconer. But Carmichael was no longer there, the space where he had stood, empty and uninhabited. Instead, he saw the sergeant actually in the air, in the middle of a rugby tackle. Course had fallen for his distraction, even in her crazed state of mind, and she had looked where he had been pointing, giving him just enough time to launch himself in her direction.

Virginia finally managed to free an arm that had been held tightly by Course's left arm, and elbowed her in the ribs. Carmichael caught her round the legs, as Virginia executed a final twist, and managed to distance her throat from the blade of the knife.

At that point Falconer caught on, and joined the melee, Richard hard on his heels. Between the four of them, they separated Course from the knife, and got handcuffs on her, although it took the efforts of all of them to subdue her. Richard's first action was to ask Virginia if she was all right, Falconer's to ask the same of Carmichael, worried that he might have been injured in his free-fall attack.

'Not so good, sir,' he replied, curled over into a ball now that the action was over.

'Was it the knife?' Falconer asked with concern, worried that his sergeant may have suffered a stab wound in reward for his heroics, and surprised at the level of concern he was feeling. He didn't want to lose his partner; he was finally getting used to him, and would be at a loss without him. They were developing a style, between them, that seemed to work very well, impossible as this might have seemed, only the previous summer.

'No, sir. Just a knee in me nadgers. I'm coming into work tomorrow with my old cricket box on. If I don't take more care of myself, I'll never be able to produce little Carmichaels.'

'Good idea!' Falconer agreed, imagining his partner in the afore-mentioned piece of sports protection equipment and shuddering, but quietly considering that if the gods hadn't been on Carmichael's side a few minutes ago, Kerry might have been a widow, and Carmichael wouldn't even have had the chance to be a husband any longer. And he'd have had to get used to a new partner, which was now quite an alarming thought.

Back-up had been summoned, and Caroline Course, now subdued, a husk of the woman she once was, was removed from the scene to Market Darley to await questioning, then assessment by a mental health professional (*or a 'shrink', as we used to refer to them*), and Falconer and Carmichael helped Richard and Virginia back to their holiday cottage. They were both weak, and shaking with shock at what might have been, and the first thing Carmichael did when they got into the house was to put on the kettle.

'I said we should go home,' stated Virginia, a little huffily. 'I said on Friday morning that I didn't want to stay another night in a place where there had been murder done.'

'I know you did, Ginny.'

'And then you persuaded me to stay on.'

'Sorry, Ginny.'

'You assured me that lightning couldn't strike twice, and I believed you.'

'I didn't think it could. You're like a magnet for murder. Oh, Ginny, I could've lost you back there.' Richard finished on a wail, his face crumpling, and Virginia went over and put her arms around him, the two of them now standing in the middle of the little room in a tight embrace.

As Carmichael approached from the kitchen, Falconer cleared his throat, and they took the hint and separated. 'I can't seem to find a tray,' he stated.

'Oh my God, it's next door!' Ginny ejaculated, and her face clouded.

'Don't worry, I'll get it,' volunteered the inspector, and went off on his small domestic quest.

When he returned, he was carrying a framed photograph as well as the tray, still laden with its tea things from earlier, and handing this latter to Carmichael, who took it in one hand, and set to with the other, to make the chocolate fingers disappear – presto magico!

'There are some more in the wall cupboard near the sink,' Virginia called helpfully, noticing his enthusiastic consumption, as Falconer handed her the photograph.

'Do you know who this is?' he asked. 'Because I think I do, but I'd like to hear what you know first.'

'She said it was her niece, when I asked her, but she said she'd never had anything to do with Shepford Stacey before and I recognised the school building in the photograph. I'd say it was taken in the playground. She also said that she had no children, but that didn't ring true. Then, when she saw me looking at the photograph, I suppose she must have seen the recognition in my eyes. That's when she went off to get the knife, and I twigged who it really was in the photograph.'

Falconer took over at this juncture. 'It's her daughter, Carole. Carole Nicholson, she was, and she was killed here in Shepford Stacey. I've just been told the whole story at the Baldwin household.'

'She told me in the garden, but in not quite such comfortable circumstances,' Virginia said, in a small, frightened voice, on the brink of tears but, with a stout hug from Richard, she pulled herself together and continued, 'And Caroline – I suppose Course must have been her maiden name, because she told Harriet and me that she was a childless widow – never got over the loss. Oh, poor Harriet. She wouldn't have harmed a soul!'

'Did she tell you anything else while you were … together?'

he asked, before she could dissolve into tears.

'She blamed both those women for what happened. She said that neither of them took any notice of her poor little girl, and that's why she tried to make her way home, simply so that someone could kiss her knee better, and give her a hug. What an awful way for a child to lose its life – just because she needed a hug.'

Shock and emotion were now flooding Virginia's mind and body, and she burst into inconsolable tears, her whole body wracked with weeping, and shaking uncontrollably. Richard put his arms back round her, but didn't know what to say in the light of the fact that he might have lost her – again – at the hands of a killer. This was their second brush with murder, and his wife seemed to be becoming a magnet for such evil.

He knew he couldn't wrap her in cotton wool, but he'd keep a closer eye on what she was doing in the future, and make sure he listened to every word she said, in case she was unwittingly putting herself at risk again, unlikely as this might seem amid the ordinary, everyday course of their lives.

Falconer drank his tea and made a face at Carmichael (who appeared to be trying to look down the waistband of his trousers in order to assess the damage to his crown jewels), to indicate that they ought to go. The sergeant tucked in the front of his shirt as unobtrusively as can a man of six-feet-five-and-a-half inches, although Richard was so concerned with his wife, that neither of them would have noticed even if he had mooned at them. Thus, Falconer and his superhero sidekick made their goodbyes, leaving the two alone together, to come to terms with the morning's events.

But more was to follow, and when Falconer received a phone call informing them that the forces of law and order were moving in on Seth Borrowdale, and that he would be taken in for questioning within the hour, he shared this information with his partner with an unusual level of satisfaction. It was about time that the tide began to turn in favour of the police. Criminals had so many rights and processes to hide behind now, that the chances of a conviction in any one crime were almost as

175

poor as the odds on a three-legged donkey entered in the Derby.

Caroline Course had been booked into custody in Market Darley, a lockable office serving as a holding cell, and a psychiatrist summoned to assess her mental condition. A few phone calls and a small amount of time on the computer revealed that the woman had spent the accumulation of years between her daughter's death and now in and out of mental health units. Her stays had been sporadic at first, but with the desertion of her husband, she had become a more or less permanent resident, in one establishment after another, as these were closed down, and Care in the Community became Don't Care in the Community.

She had absconded from a halfway house about ten days ago, but had been absent for half a day a couple of months before. Presumably this was when she had booked her little 'holiday' in Shepford Stacey, and decided that revenge was a dish better served stone-cold than not at all. Grief had robbed her of her wits and her ability to know right from wrong, and she had stated that she was just extracting the price for the women robbing her of her little girl, and all the intervening years that they had not shared together.

Falconer had a very long chat with the psychiatrist before she left the premises, not only extracting what information he could, but prolonging the interview because he wanted to continue to look at the person who bore this designated title.

She was tall and Nubian-like, her skin like polished mahogany, and her features almost European. Her hair was woven in cornrows close into her head, and short, and her eyes were like polished amber. In a low and almost impossibly seductive voice, she introduced herself as Hortense Dubois, then invited him to call her 'Honey', as everyone else did.

When she finally left, the inspector found himself making little buzzing noises, and wishing, ridiculously, that he were a bee.

Removing a prisoner's shoelaces, neck-tie or scarf, and belt – in fact anything with which harm can be done to the person – isn't really as thorough as it seems. Hanging one's self is only one option. Another is to bang one's head against a wall as often and as hard as one can. This may only result in unconsciousness and stitches, but a lucky 'wham' might cause a fracture of the skull, and might end a life quite effectively.

Caroline Course was a resourceful woman, cunning in her madness, and would never have considered this last option, it being (a) painful, (b) messy, and (c) not very likely to succeed. She had thought of something much more sure-fire and original, and intended to see it through to her eventual extinction. It was nothing lingering and painful, such as a hunger strike – quite the opposite really, and something that no one would think she needed to be protected from, for they would never guess that someone would attempt to take their own life in such a way.

Carole was dead – had been dead for many years – and she had managed to take the lives of the two women she felt responsible for her loss. The car driver she didn't even consider. How could he help it if, in a narrow street on a foggy day, a small girl darted out in front of his vehicle? He had not been going fast, and his vehicle was merely the instrument of her death, not the root of it.

She was checked at thirty-minute intervals, due to her mental state, but she was acting calmly and rationally, merely sitting in the room serving as her cell. This room had once been the office of the previous business in the building, and conveniently had a re-enforced door, and a thick safety glass window with integral wire mesh, thus making half-hourly checks easier to accomplish, in complete safety, for the officer concerned.

She was checked when her evening meal was brought to her, the custody officer signalling through the glass panel that she was to move to the back of the room, while he placed her food on the floor just inside the door, telling her, as he set it down, that she could collect it when the door was relocked.

The re-enforced door to the room made the room almost completely soundproof, as indicated by the custody officer

177

having to mime moving away from the door to deliver her food. This was a real advantage as far as her plan was concerned, and she moved into a corner where she could not be seen from the door. There was the noise of a sharp intake of breath, followed by a short choking sound, then a fit of coughing.

In the corridor outside the room there was absolute silence. The sequence of sounds was repeated inside the room, and Caroline summoned her courage yet again. This was not an easy way to voluntarily take one's life, and she had known it wouldn't be easy, but with half hourly checks, had still had plenty of time, and plenty of ammunition left on her plate. The inhalation sound was repeated, but the sound of choking went on for longer, with no hint of a cough. Slowly the choking noises died away, and movement from the body on the floor gradually ceased, a lifeless silence now filling the dreary little space.

The next check revealed a worrying scenario to Sergeant Constable. (*Don't mention his name to him, as a smack in the mouth often offends.*) The woman was stretched out on the floor where she had fallen forward in her last choking seconds, and was now visible through the window, her tray near the left side wall, the food only slightly disturbed, and her body appeared to be utterly still and without life.

Calling for immediate help, as this could be a ruse to 'jump' him, and effect an attempt at escape, he unlocked the door when Bob Bryant arrived (*yes, you've guessed it – he's still desk sergeant*), and the two of them entered cautiously. Bryant knelt down beside the stricken form and felt for a pulse, while Constable checked the tray.

'Get a doctor,' said Bryant, in a voice that also confirmed that there was no rush.

'She can't be dead. She was fine when I was here, just half an hour ago.' Constable seemed quite indignant at losing a prisoner on his watch. 'What was it, do you think? Heart attack?'

Bob Bryant got to his feet slowly, his face a mask of disbelief. 'She's only gone and choked to death, hasn't she?

And we'll never know now whether it was intentional, or a tragic accident.'

Having recovered a little from the initial shock, Constable added callously, 'Well, they did say she was as mad as a vestful of ferrets. You pays yer money and yer takes your chance; that's what I say, anyway,' after which meaningless drivel, he went off to summon someone medical who could certify that life was extinct.

In the insect world, wasps attack bees, and the same can be said for the human world. If Falconer had harboured, for a few mad seconds, a desire to be a bee, then Superintendent 'Jelly' Chivers was definitely a wasp, and his words stung Falconer with the expected venom.

'Well now, I hope you don't have any ambitions to join the Canadian Mounties, Inspector.'

'No, sir.'

'Because a Mountie always gets his man, doesn't he, Falconer?'

'Yes, sir.'

'And, gender aside, where's your man, Inspector? She's dead, isn't she, Inspector?'

'Yes, sir.'

'She managed to commit suicide using a plate of sausage and chips, didn't she, Inspector?'

'Yes, sir.' Falconer's face was now as red as a stoplight.

'You fumbled it, didn't you, Inspector?'

'Yes, sir.' (*Even if this was unfair, there was no other answer.*)

'And this isn't the first guilty party you have failed to deliver to the justice system, is it, Falconer?'

'No, sir.'

'In fact you've got a rather poor record where that's concerned, haven't you, Inspector?'

'Yes, sir.'

'And saved the British taxpayer quite a bit of money along the way, haven't you, Falconer?'

179

'Yes, sir.' This answer was given with a certain amount of surprise.

'Well done, Inspector.' The wasp suddenly withdrew its sting. 'And tell that young shaver Carmichael well done from me, too. I know he was slightly injured in the course of duty, so tell him if he'd like Dr Christmas to have a look at things, I'll arrange it myself.'

'Yes, sir.' Carmichael would probably rather die than expose his 'Little Davey' to someone who would no doubt have a good laugh about it with his police colleagues.

'Dismissed, Inspector.'

'Yes, sir. Thank you, sir.'

As Falconer returned to his own makeshift office, he made a few quiet buzzing noises, and smiled to himself. 'And is there honey still for tea?' he enquired in a barely audible voice, his smile broadening slightly. Life wasn't too bad at all at the moment, he thought, for the first time in months.

Epilogue

On the cusp of summer – site of refurbished police station.

DCI Falconer and DS Carmichael stood and surveyed the broad expanses of white walls and ceiling. The windows that would now be of the opening variety, instead of that well-known type of window, 'I shouldn't bother, it's all painted up', from which they had suffered before. The flooring was of hard-wearing tiles, the skirting-boards and doors, newly painted.

A little judicious knocking-through had produced an acceptably large room, now labelled the CID suite, which boasted fancy see-through boards for them to assemble cases on, instead of the clapped-out old whiteboards they had struggled with before.

The final-fix electricity was nearly completed, the furniture would be moved in at the end of the following week, and then they would move back into their 'made-over' and extended premises.

Falconer took a good look round, wandering through what had been a dingy and warren-like workplace, with a plethora of over-small offices and scuffed and dark paintwork. It was unrecognisable, and he gave a little whistle of approval.

Carmichael was also taking it all in; forming his own judgement on what difference this might make on the standard of policing in the area.

'So, what do you think, sir? It's all bright and shiny and new. Do you think we'll be any happier here?'

'I think the impression the make-over will have on most of the members of the public who visit us will be a good one. If they enter a building that looks well cared for and smart, they

181

will assume that those who work here will provide a shiny, bright and new service for them. No doubt they'll think it makes us appear smarter and more efficient.

'Then there'll be those who will curl their lip, and ask what the point is in making those tiny rural stations now only open during office hours, cut and rearrange staffing levels, if a load of money was going to be squandered – and they will use the word squandered – on a complete re-fit and a knock through to the old, empty offices next door? They weren't just donated to the force, those offices: they had to be paid for by someone, and that someone is, as usual, Joe Public, via the funding for the police force, so they'll have a point.'

'But it'll still just be us, sir. The same people as before, with a few additions from those other stations. It's not as if we'll be different people because we've got posh offices.'

'Precisely, Carmichael! Just like you shouldn't judge a book by its cover, neither should you judge the efficiency or dedication of the police by the newness or trendiness of their offices. A police force is people, not buildings.'

'So, no change really then, sir?'

'No change, Carmichael.'

Market Darley High Street

A wicked little wind blew erratically down the road, swirling small pieces of litter into little eddies, and making airborne, for a few seconds, empty crisp packets and chocolate bar wrappers.

The nomadic, dispossessed individuals outside the temporary police station pulled up their collars or put up their hoods against the sudden spiteful chill of the little gusts, aimlessly kicking at discarded soft drink cans and empty cigarette packets in a desultory way.

Inside the building, a number of boxes were being distributed, so that the staff could begin the packing of non-essential records and equipment, ready for the move, and there was a low buzz of excited conversation at the thought of what surroundings lay ahead of them.

'I wonder what my new reception desk will look like,' contemplating his new 'station' in the new station. 'It should be a lot less battered than the old one – all new and shiny, I hope.'

'It'll be a desk, Bob. It doesn't really matter what it looks like, does it?' asked PC Green.

'It does to me.'

'Will it make you work any better, then?'

'Course it will. Stands to reason, don't it?'

'Bollocks, Bob! You can put lipstick on a Rottweiler, but it doesn't change its character, just because it looks different, does it?' Merv persisted.

'So, you've met the wife have you?'

This was Bob's last word on the subject.

THE END

Battered to Death

A Falconer Files Brief Case: #3

Andrea Frazer

Battered to Death

A Falconer Files Brief Case: #3

186

PORTION ONE

Friday 16th April

It was after ten o'clock on a mild evening, and the rather pathetically-named shop unit called Chish and Fips was doing its usual roaring trade for a Friday night. The shop was packed with customers being served and waiting to be served, with even one or two customers standing outside, waiting for the queue to get a little shorter, so that they could join it on the other side of the door.

The heat in the little unit was furnace-like, the faces of the customers nearest to the counter a bright red as the fryers belched out heat and clouds of steam. From outside, the little unit was a beacon of smeared colours, like a work of abstract art, behind its condensation-clouded and dripping plate-glass window. The face behind the counter, trying to cope on its own, was of a similar hue to that of its closest customers, but with the features down-turned and cross. The owner, Frank Carrington, had promised to come in at half-past nine to give her a hand, and had still not shown up.

'Who's next?' queried the cross-faced figure, Sylvia Beeton by name, trying to serve, wrap orders, rescue cooked food from the fryers, take money, give change, and put fresh food on to fry, all at the same time, and getting mighty fed-up with the gargantuan effort she was putting in for what was just a smidgen over the minimum wage.

As a voice shouted out for two cod and chips, and to make it quick, she shouted back, without diverting her gaze in the voice's direction, 'You wait your turn like everyone else,

187

Sanjeev Khan. Just because your dad's on the council doesn't give you priority over anyone else.'

'Two cod and chips, one double battered sausage and chips, and one meat and potato pie and chips,' the next customer called out, while she was still adding up two burgers and chips, two pickled onions, a pineapple fritter, and a portion of chicken with extra chips.

'I'll be with you as soon as I can. I've only got one pair of hands, and I've not taken for this lot yet, she called out, handing over a bulging carrier bag and taking, in exchange, a high denomination note. 'Haven't you got anything smaller, sir?' she asked. 'Oh, well, can't be helped.' She sighed, then raised her voice to the rest of the gaggle in the shop, 'Correct money if you can, or as near as possible. I'm not a bank, and I've nearly run out of change. If you can't, I may have to refuse to serve you.'

As she got on with serving the next order, throwing an extra load of chips into the fryer and pulling a dozen pieces of fish out of the batter tray and throwing them into another receptacle of boiling fat (for everything was fried in lard in this establishment, in the old-fashioned way), there was a muttering amongst the customers, and some, who knew each other, got wallets out and rummaged around in pockets to see if they had the exact money, or could help out friends, who looked woebegone, when they flashed a twenty-pound note at them, and felt devastated at possibly having to forego their supper just because of lack of change.

The queue shortened slowly, as the lull before 'chucking-out' time at the pubs arrived and from the flat upstairs there suddenly boomed an almighty racket of drum and bass music, shaking the fluorescent light fitting on the ceiling and causing some customers to cover their ears.

'It's all right,' Sylvia shouted. 'I'll just go up and give them a blasting. I can't take orders with this racket going on,' and with that, she was off, through a door at the back, and could be heard thumping up a flight of stairs to the first floor. There was then a roar that rose even above the music, the deafening racket was turned down to a reasonable volume, and Sylvia returned, a look of triumph on her face.

'That's sorted *them* out!' she said, with satisfaction, rubbing her plump hands together with satisfaction. 'Now, who's next? Curry Khan, you put that can of drink back in the fridge where it belongs. If I know you, you'll high-tail off with it before I get to your order. You can take one then, and not before.'

'But I'm thirsty, Mrs Beeton.'

'Then squeeze to the front and put the exact money on the counter, and I'll let you take it now, and then you can wait for your order like everybody else here. But no pay, no drink. Got it?'

'Got it, Ma,' agreed Curry, the son of the owner of the local Indian restaurant, and leaned through and put a pound piece on the serving bar. 'I'll get my change when I order,' he shouted to Sylvia, then removed his cold drink and began to gulp at the contents.

'Who's two haddock and chips?' Sylvia shouted above the sizzling and bubbling of yet another load of fish fresh into the fryer, and a cloud of steam enveloped her for a second or two, making her invisible.

'Over here! And I've got the right money,' called a voice from the other side of the counter, and an arm extended, hand clasping a pile of change, and the paper wrapped packet was given in exchange.

She had almost dealt with this deluge of customers, and there were only three people waiting to be served, when Frank Carrington strolled in. 'I thought I'd come in and give you a hand during the rush,' he announced, as if he were doing her a favour, rather than working in his own business to line his pocket, not hers.

'You know damned well we have a rush at ten, then

189

another one just after eleven. Where were you at ten o'clock? I was in here getting broiled and working my guts out, just so as you can go on a nice holiday in the summer then swank about how well your business is doing.'

'Well, if you're not up to it anymore, Sylvia ...' he said, and left the sentence hanging.

'Don't you threaten me! You wouldn't get a fraction of the work out of a young 'un as you get out of me, and you know it. I'm more than value for money, and don't you forget it.'

'Only pulling your leg, Sylv. Don't get all hot and bothered about it.'

'Don't get all hot and bothered? Just look at the colour of my face, and my hair's dripping under this hat. You wouldn't know hot and bothered unless it had a sauna attached to it, you wouldn't.'

'Look, I'm here now, so let's not argue about it. The after-hours rush will be here any minute now, so make sure you've got enough chips ready, and plenty of batter. We can get on with some of the frying before they get here, so that at least we can serve the first dozen or so customers with what we pre-fry, then the next lot will be ready for the queue behind.'

'Makes sense to me. Get your coat and hat on then, and we'll get started for the first wave,' replied Sylvia, scooping the last of the chips out of the fat and adding a new batch.

The next wave arrived just a few minutes after eleven. and was the most difficult to deal with, because it consisted of those who had been in the pub just that little bit longer.

The queue was, unsurprisingly, not so well-behaved with the new batch of customers, and there was a fair amount of shoving and barging for position, and quite a few angry words exchanged as they waited.

Sylvia let fly. 'Get yourselves into a proper queue and act like civilised human beings. I don't care how much you've

190

had to drink! If you want your chips from here, you can bloody well behave, or I'll chuck you out myself!'

She received some unexpected support from Frank Carrington, who raised his voice above the hubbub, and shouted, 'You'd better to listen to our Sylvia, because she means it, and I'm here to re-enforce her decisions.'

'Bloody little Hitler!' came from the middle of the queue, and Sylvia was on to it immediately. 'Dogger Ferguson, you get out of here this minute. I won't have talk like that in this chip shop, and you're barred.'

'You can't bar me! This is a chip shop, not a pub,' he replied, not really bothered by her threat.

'No, but *I* can!' This was Frank Carrington's voice, 'and *I'm* barring you. Get out now, and go quietly, or I'll call the police. I will not have insults like that bandied about in my chip shop. And if any of you think that's unfair, you can go too!'

'So where am I supposed to get my chips then,' the youth shouted back, now not looking so sure of himself.

'You'll just have to go into the town centre, won't you? Come back in six months, and I'll see if you've learnt any manners. Until then, don't come back!' This was from Sylvia, who was usually the one to restore order, if trouble seemed to be about to break out.

'Chalky White, you come back here this minute! Not only have you short-changed me, but one of the fifty pees is an old Irish one. You get back here, or I'll tell your mother!'

A dark-skinned youth wove his way back to the counter and corrected the transaction. 'God, I'm glad you're not my mother,' he said, as he left the counter.

'So am I!' called back Sylvia, giving as good as she got, 'Because if you were mine, I'd have drowned you at birth!'

'Old bitch!'

'I heard that!'

The rest of the evening was unusually aggressive, and by the

191

time they had cleared up, prepped for the next day which, being Saturday, was a busy one, both she and Frank were exhausted.

'Where do they get it from? That's what I want to know,' said Sylvia, pulling on the old coat she always wore to work because she didn't want to smell like the lady from the chip shop wherever she went. This way, she didn't have to have any of her other coats sullied by the tell-tale smell of where she worked.

'The telly?' offered Frank. 'School?'

'More like the fact that their mums were only just out of school when they had 'em, and don't know a thing about bringing up a child to have good manners,' was Sylvia's considered opinion, and on this thought, Frank locked up. Sylvia got her bike out of the back hall and made her way home, another Friday evening over and done with. And good riddance to it, too, she thought, puffing and blowing her way back.

PORTION TWO

Saturday 17th April – morning

Detective Inspector Harry Falconer of the Market Darley CID was having a well-earned day off. Apart from other crimes, he had already dealt with three murder cases since his explosive entry to the New Year, courtesy of Carmichael's pantomime-themed wedding, and more booze than he'd ever indulged in in his life before, and that included his time in the army. He really needed a day away from the office and work, and had decided to indulge himself in one of his lazy days.

He'd not risen until half-past eight, a veritable lie-in for him, then treated himself to a fried breakfast, sharing the last rasher of bacon between his three cats, Mycroft, Tar Baby, and Ruby, who had all begged very nicely to share his unaccustomed treat.

After that, he'd spread the main body of his Saturday newspaper on the floor, laid down at the bottom of it, and begun to read. He was usually much more grown-up about this activity, but occasionally indulged in this sort of lounge on the floor because he enjoyed it, and holding up the paper (which was a broadsheet) made his arms ache, and, folding it, his temper ache.

He knew he wouldn't be able to stay in this position for long, because the cats so loved to play with the corners of the pages, stalking and pouncing on them, then chewing them a bit, and eventually, clawing them. He reckoned he had a good half an hour of shooing them off before he had to

193

transfer the newspaper to the dining table. After that, he intended to watch an old black and white movie he had recorded weeks ago, and hadn't yet had the time to look at. And after that? Who knows? He might even go for a walk, or take a trip to the local garden centre.

In Castle Farthing, Detective Sergeant 'Davey' Carmichael was also enjoying a day off, and spending it with his wife, Kerry, and her two sons, Kyle and Dean. In his opinion, there was no better way to spend his leisure time than with these three dearest of people. They had also, recently, become the proud owners of two tiny dogs that the boys had named: a Chihuahua called Fang, and a miniature Yorkshire terrier called Mr Knuckles.

After an enormous breakfast – for, if Carmichael were a car, he'd be a gas guzzler, given his size and fuel consumption – he suggested that they all go out on to the village green and throw a stick and a ball around for the dogs. They had managed to find a very small ball in the pet shop that the young dogs could get their jaws round, and a twig sufficed, in their case, as a stick.

The boys were very enthusiastic, as were the dogs, for they loved getting out of the house and having a mad run around with the big man, and the green was so big to them. Kerry, however, pleaded household duties and, after closing the door on them gratefully, put on the washing machine, and sat down in her favourite armchair with a magazine and a cup of coffee. She already had a stew cooking away for their evening meal in the slow cooker, and felt that this was about as much as she wanted to do this morning.

Through the open window, it being such a fair day, she could hear the high-pitched yips of the dogs' excitement, and the voices of the boys calling after their pets. Occasionally her husband's voice boomed out with an instruction, but more often with laughter so, it seemed to her, that they were all having a jolly nice time, including herself in this thought.

Harry Falconer had finished with his newspaper for the time being, and was having a pre-luncheon doze on the sofa, covered in three furry bodies, joining him in this unexpected opportunity to use his body heat, when the phone rang. He started awake and sat up immediately, scattering cats as he got to his feet. This had better be a cold call. And if it was work, it'd better be good, disturbing him on the first day off he'd had for a fortnight.

'Falconer. What?' he answered, peremptorily.

'Harry, I'm so sorry to disturb you,' said the voice of Bob Bryant from the station, 'but there's been a very nasty death in Upper Darley. I think you need to get out there. And Carmichael.'

'What's happened? And why can't someone else handle it for a change?'

'I've spoken to Superintendent Chivers, and *he* wants you out there.'

'Sadistic bastard! Right! Where is it, and what happened?'

'It's at the chip shop on the Riverside Parade, in Upper Darley, and it's a nasty one. I don't even want to describe it. It turns my stomach.'

'And yet you want me to go out and *look* at it?'

'Sorry, Harry, but it is your job. Get yourself out there, and I'll send Carmichael to join you.'

'I'm on my way,' sighed Falconer. It was half-past twelve, and he now wouldn't have time for any lunch. And on his day off, too! Maybe he could snaffle a bag of chips when he got there.

The two little dogs, now exhausted, were having a nap on Kerry's lap when the phone rang in Jasmine Cottage, in Castle Farthing's High Street. Sliding them carefully off her, she rose to answer the phone. 'Hello, Bob,' she greeted the sergeant. 'Surely you're not going to disturb Davey on his day off? He hasn't had one for a couple of weeks, and he's out on the green, now, playing football with the boys.'

'Sorry, Mrs Carmichael. I wouldn't have called if the super hadn't insisted. Can you call him in, so that I can have a word?' asked Bryant, apologetically.

'Of course I can, and call me Kerry. Everyone else does. Hang on a moment,' she said, and put the receiver down on the little table where the phone base lived.

Opening the cottage door, she put her hands to her mouth, to create an improvised loud-hailer, and called, 'Davey – phone. Urgent!' and watched as he said a few words to the boys and sprinted back to the cottage, the boys trailing in his wake, evidently disappointed that their fun had been cut short on their day with Daddy Davey.

'Carmichael here,' said the sergeant, picking up the phone, wondering what could be so urgent on his day off.

'Davey, it's Bob from the station. There's been a nasty death at the chip shop, on that parade of shops at Upper Darley. Do you know the one? Good! The super want you to meet Harry out there. You'll find out the details when you arrive.'

'But, what's hap ...' Carmichael started to ask, but Bob Bryant had cut him off, without a shred of detail. He'd just have to get himself over there as quickly as he could, and find out what had happened when he got there.

Falconer, living on the outskirts of Market Darley, was the first one to arrive on the scene, and found a crowd of would-be customers, now turned rubber-neckers, outside the plate glass window. Crime-scene tape had already been stretched across the front of the shop, and PC Merv Green was on duty at the door to keep sight-seers away, as far as was humanly possible. There was always an audience at the site of any public death. It was simple human nature, but not a nice side of it.

Pushing his way through the people gawking for a look through the window, he held out his warrant card and pushed his way through to where PC Green stood guard. 'Know what's happened in there?' he asked, before entering.

'Very nasty one, sir,' replied Green, his face in agreement with his name. 'I'm not usually squeamish, but this is a very unpleasant one. I think you'd better go inside and see for yourself. I don't want to think about it, let alone talk about it. Sorry, sir.'

This was unlike Green, and Bob Bryant had been reluctant to give any details either. Falconer's insides gave a little flip of apprehension as these two thoughts collided. These were both experienced policemen. Whatever could have given *them* such a fit of the heebie-jeebies? Wondering if Dr Christmas had already arrived, or was still on his way, he pushed open the glass door and went inside the chip shop, preparing for the worst.

'Hello, Harry,' said a familiar voice, and Falconer became aware of Dr Phillip Christmas and another man, standing at the back of the shop, well away from the fryers. 'May I introduce you to Frank Carrington, the owner of this establishment?'

Falconer approached and shook the man's hand, taking the opportunity to introduce himself at the same time. 'So, what have we got here?' he asked, and was surprised when the owner just pointed at the counter of the shop. After staring at this for a few seconds, Mr Carrington finally spoke, his voice a hoarse whisper. 'It's behind there!' he croaked. 'At the chip fryer.'

Christmas gave Falconer a look, and added, 'I hope you haven't already had your lunch, Harry. It's gruesome!'

'I haven't, as a matter of fact,' Falconer informed them, and then, finally reaching the other side of the counter, stopped dead, his mouth opening in surprise and horror, his

197

eyes involuntarily closing to shut out what was in front of them.

Turning back to look at the other two men present, he opened his eyes again, and said, 'I think I might give lunch a miss today. Who the hell did this? It's iniquitous! What a bloody awful way to die!'

'Sorry, Harry. Wish I could have spared you this one,' sympathised Christmas. 'Maybe it'd be better if I told you what happened, rather than you poke around for yourself.'

'I think that's a very good idea. I don't fancy going any nearer to 'that' than I have to, and the thought of 'poking around', makes me positively queasy,' replied Falconer, joining them at the other end of the shop, well away from the fryers, where a couple of grotty tables and a few mismatched chairs were placed for anyone who wanted to dine-in.

'Take a seat, first, Harry. In fact, let's all sit down. It's not a nice subject for discussion, and I think we'd be better off seated once I start going into details.'

'Do I have to stay?' asked Carrington. 'After all, I found her, and I feel as sick as a dog.'

'Make a note of your name and address, and leave it on the counter, and I'll be in touch later,' Falconer told him, then waited until he'd complied before turning back to Dr Christmas. 'Come on, out with it. You know you've got to tell me sometime,' he said, looking apprehensive. 'Who? How? And when? And why, for God's sake. That's sick, and it took some doing. We'll work out who is responsible, when we've got something more to go on.'

Christmas drew a deep breath, and commenced his grisly tale. '"Who" is easy. The victim is a Mrs Sylvia Beeton, who had worked part-time here for years. I got her address from Mr Carrington, so you don't need to worry about that.

'"When' isn't too difficult, either, as she was supposed to arrive at work to get everything started at about eleven-thirty this morning, and open up at noon. Mr Carrington arrived

198

just after opening time, and found customers waiting outside, unable to get in – she'd have locked the door while she did her preparation, and then not unlocked it again until opening time.

'That seems straightforward enough, so far,' Falconer interrupted the doctor, in a vain effort to delay what he knew would follow next.

'Oh, it is, but it's the 'how' that's the stomach-churner.' Here it came then. Falconer steeled himself for the grisly details. 'From what I could glean from an examination of the scene, when I arrived about fifteen minutes ago, someone dumped the large container of batter over her head, then pushed her head into the chip fryer, and held her down with the large chip scoop. As she was due to start pre-frying chips, the oil was up to temperature, and I'm afraid that's not very good for the complexion.'

'Oh, my good God!' exclaimed Falconer, unable to quite comprehend what he had been told. 'I'll have to take a look, for the sake of procedure, but now I know what happened, I know I'm not going to like it one little bit.'

Slowly, like a child who is afraid that someone might jump out at him, Falconer approached the other side of the counter, and moved towards the huge bulk of what, until nearly midday today, been Mrs Sylvia Beeton.

'Can you give me a hand to turn her over?' he called to Christmas. 'How did you manage it? She's a very big woman.'

'I got Green to help me,' explained the Doc, and followed Falconer behind the counter.

'That would explain why he looked so bilious when I got here,' replied Falconer, more as something to say to keep his mind off what he was about to see.

The two of them manhandled the body, so that they could look at its face, and Falconer came out in a cold sweat. 'Whoever it was, has literally fried her face, and in batter,

199

too,' he managed, in a rather high-pitched voice, letting go his hold on his half of the mighty Mrs Beeton.

Christmas lowered his end too, and said, with a nervous little giggle, 'She's definitely been battered to death, then! And it looks like she was held down in there at the back of the neck, as I just said, with the chip scoop. I haven't touched it, just left it for you to put into an evidence bag, in case it's got fingerprints on it.'

'Don't joke about it, Philip. It only makes it worse. And I'll just get that scoop bagged up now. Thanks for noticing that. God, what a ghastly way to end up!'

'What a dreadful thing even to contemplate doing to another human being,' commented the medical man, and they both fell silent, and stared off into nothingness, horrified by this seemingly random and unspeakable act.

So deep were they in a brown study that they didn't hear the door open, and before either of them could do anything about it, Carmichael sprung up like a jack-in-the-box beside them, full of enthusiasm, as usual, to see what was afoot; and, unfortunately, from this distance, he could do just that.

As he began to heave, Falconer yelled, 'Nooo!' and rushed, over in the vain hope that he could stem the inevitable flow. 'Footprints, man!' he shouted. 'Evidence!'

Hearing the inspector's voice, Carmichael swivelled his noxious spray a hundred and eighty degrees, and the last of his offering landed on the highly polished tops of Falconer's immaculate shoes.

'Now look what you've done, Sergeant! Muddied any forensic evidence on the floor. And just look at my shoes,' he finished, reaching for a roll of kitchen paper that sat on the shelf behind the counter. 'Why on earth didn't you wait?'

'Urgh!' groaned Carmichael, took a step forward to assist Falconer and slipped, landing on his back on his contribution to 'Dirty Floor Day.'

'And now you've fallen in it! Get yourself into the little

cloakroom out the back, and see what you can do about cleaning yourself up!'

'You know I've got a dicky tummy, sir,' Carmichael pleaded, then, thinking again of what he had just seen, and went for it again with enthusiasm. But there was no ammunition left for him to shoot, and he stood there, in a pool of his own breakfast, dry-heaving like a pump fresh out of water.

'Sometimes I wonder why you joined the force!' snapped his boss, wiping lumps of the vile substance from his shoes, making a little moue of distaste, and making sure that he was breathing only through his mouth.

'Because I wanted to catch criminals, sir,' answered the sergeant, gingerly making his way towards the indicated cloakroom, and removing his jacket as he went.

'Well, that's ruined any evidence of footprints, this side of the counter!' said Falconer, a little later, looking daggers at his sergeant, who was perched on one of the old chairs at the back of the shop, his head between his knees. 'Why couldn't you have had a light breakfast for, once? Just look at the mess you've made of the crime scene!'

'Sorry, sir,' replied the ghost of Carmichael's voice. 'I couldn't help it. I'm surprised it didn't have the same effect on you, too.'

'Leave it, Sergeant. I suppose *I'll* have to clear this away as best as I can before the SOCO team arrives, and I'd rather hoped to warn you to stay the other side of the counter before you came round here, but you just appeared out of nowhere, and it was too late by then.'

'What sort of evil person does that to someone?' Carmichael managed, his thought processes slowly re-gathering, his rinsed-off jacket in a chip shop plastic carrier bag at his feet. 'What sort of imagination could even think of doing something like that?'

'Don't ask me, Carmichael. Most people are all right, but a few of them, out there, are mad, bad, and dangerous to know, to coin a cliché. They're either just pure evil, or off their heads.'

'Hear, hear!' sounded, from where Philip Christmas was seated at another table, talking quietly into a recording device to aid his post mortem some time later.

PORTION THREE

Saturday 17th April – afternoon

Neither Falconer nor Carmichael had been able to face any lunch, and when the SOCO team had arrived they left them to it and called into a coffee shop at the other end of the parade for a shot of caffeine.

'Oh, God, sir! I've never seen anything like that in my life before,' Carmichael almost breathed. 'All that bubbling! And her eyes! Bugger!' He suddenly went silent, and seemed to have a silent conversation with his innards, eventually adding, 'I think that's going to give me nightmares! Sorry about the language, sir.'

'Don't give it another thought, Carmichael. I think you've earned a bit of a swear after what you've witnessed this morning. Me, I think it was the batter that made it worse,' Falconer opined, in a low voice, so as not to alert too many people already in the coffee shop that they were police. 'And I agree with you. I think my sleep might be a bit disturbed for a few nights after this morning's little adventure.'

As Carmichael made a characteristic shrugging motion identical to the one he had made only a minute ago, Falconer looked at him in alarm, and hissed, 'And don't you dare be sick again. You can't have anything left after that magnificent demonstration back there!'

The sergeant sat as still as a statue for almost thirty seconds, his eyes closed, making a herculean effort to regain control of his internal muscles, then took a sip of coffee. 'So, where do we start, sir?' he asked. The spirit was willing, and the flesh recovering, at last.

'We ought to start with the owner, see if she made any enemies out of the customers. And I believe there are tenants in the upstairs flat. It might be worth having a word with them. Then we're going to have to have a look at where she lived: the usual stuff, although it was anything but a usual death, even for a murder.'

'While you were in that cloakroom, I got the address of the owner, and of Mrs Beeton, the – er – deceased. I think we should pay a little visit to Mr Carrington and ask if he remembers anything from last night that might have led to what we found this morning. There might also be regulars that she had fallen out with. He said she didn't mince her words, so that looks like our starting point, after the upstairs flat.'

'Mmph, sir.' Carmichael was still working on that internal control.

As the occupiers of the first floor flat above the chip shop were both office workers, they were at home, and not surprised to see the police after all the fuss that had been taking place downstairs since just before midday.

Before either of them could say anything, after the flat door had been opened, the young man who opened it asked, 'It's not about last night, is it? The music and everything?'

Falconer, not understanding what he was talking about merely echoed, 'Music?'

'We sometimes get a bit carried away on a Friday and Saturday night, and you can tell Mrs Beeton that we're really sorry. We'll think about other people in the future. We don't want to lose this flat, as we've only been here six months, and it's perfect for somewhere we can walk to work from.'

'Mrs Beeton asked you to turn your music down last night?' Falconer bluffed.

'Yeah! She was furious, because she had a rush on, and

she couldn't hear the orders with us blaring out with the CD player. We're really sorry, and we'll apologise to her when we see her again. She was a bit of a dragon, though, which you'll know, if you've met her.'

'I'm afraid I haven't had that pleasure, sir. May I take your name, and that of your flatmate?'

'I'm Mark Manners, and my wife's name is Melanie,' he offered, and Falconer was surprised at the use of the term wife. The young man couldn't have been more than twenty-one or two.

'Well, Mr Manners, I'm afraid that Mrs Beeton was murdered a little before midday today, and I'm here to ask you whether you heard or saw anything about that time,' (and to see if her coming up here constantly to get you to turn your music down was enough to enrage you sufficiently to fry her face, he thought, but didn't vocalise).

Manners took a step backwards in surprise, and called over his shoulder, 'Mel, that chip shop woman has been murdered.'

There was a scuffling noise from the interior of the flat, and a young woman joined them, wearing only a dressing gown and slippers, yesterday's make-up a series of smears on her face, and her hair tousled and standing on end. 'What, that old moaning minnie who came up here last night? I don't believe it! Where did it happen? In the actual shop?'

'That's right, Mrs Manners. Just before midday.'

'I was asleep,' she stated baldly. 'Is that what you were trying to wake me up and tell me about, Mark?'

While they were speaking, Falconer had been thinking, and decided that, for now, they were wasting their time here. They could always call again and, if necessary, bring them down to the station for further questioning. If their noise nuisance had been persistent, and they were worried they might lose their tenancy, this might prove sufficient motive for doing away with the complainer.

After all, the owner probably wasn't on duty for the same number of hours that Sylvia Beeton was. What was the use of having a dog, and barking yourself? Maybe this very young couple had decided to take matters into their own hands before things came to a head, and Sylvia told the owner how often she had to go upstairs to tell them to turn the volume down. It was food for thought, at least.

Frank Carrington lived just a few streets away in Crescent Road, a pleasant curved development of detached 1930s houses, his being number nineteen. The garden was positively manicured, a car less than a year old stood on the drive, and pristine white net curtains showed at all the front windows.

'Very tidy!' commented Falconer, as they drew up at the kerb. 'Can't be too much of a hardship, serving fish and chips to the sort of rabble that buy them after chucking-out time, but I wouldn't fancy it on a Friday or Saturday night.'

'Me neither, but I wouldn't mind a couple of portions of his produce after work,' was Carmichael's reply, showing that he had obviously recovered from his unpleasant little outburst of Technicolor conceptual art.

'He did rather give the impression that he had employed Mrs Beeton for her strong personality, shall we say. Anyway, let's see what he can remember about who was in last night, shall we?'

Carrington answered the door almost before Falconer had taken his finger from the bell, and invited them into a house as immaculately kept as the garden. 'I'll just put the kettle on, then we can sit down with a cup of tea or coffee, and I'll tell you everything I know. I want whoever did this caught. Sylvia's been working part-time for me for as long as I can remember, and I want whoever did this locked away for a very long time.

'She started when her husband left her and she still had

206

the kids at home, and when they left, she just carried on. Oh, but she was a good one with handling trouble. I've seen her pick some troublesome lad up by the scruff of the neck and hurl him out of the door without batting an eyelid. I won't be a minute. Go in and make yourselves comfortable,' he concluded, disappearing off into what they could see was the kitchen, another room that sparkled with loving buffing and cleaning.

The two detectives went through a door that evidently led to the sitting room, and found it furnished with plush leather furniture at one end, and an antique dining table and chairs at the other. Settling, each of them, into an armchair, and almost disappearing into its feather-filled cushions, they waited in silence until Carrington returned, a large tray in his hands.

'I didn't ask you what you wanted, but I thought tea would be all right? I can make coffee if you prefer, though,' he declared, setting down the tray on a marble coffee table.

'Tea's fine,' confirmed Carmichael.

'Just the ticket,' agreed Falconer, and Carrington began to dispense the fragrant liquid.

'Milk? Yes? Right. Help yourselves to sugar,' he suggested, as he handed them their cups, then stared on in disbelief as Carmichael added six spoonfuls of sugar to his cup, nearly emptying the little sugar bowl.

'Don't worry about me,' Falconer hastily stated. 'I don't take sugar,' as if this would be consolation enough to their host. He was used by now to Carmichael's preference for sticky tea that could almost, but not quite, be sliced.

'Me neither,' muttered Carrington. 'Now,' at a more normal volume, 'How can I be of assistance? I've made a note of anyone I saw or heard misbehaving yesterday evening, and of any Sylvia mentioned when we were chatting, clearing up. It's the usual suspects, I'm afraid, and she actually had to take the unusual step of barring one of them, 'Dogger' Ferguson, last night. I don't think I've known her ever do that before, but I don't know whether I can back that up, now she's gone.'

So, Sylvia Beeton had been employed to be the chip shop 'heavy', and Mr Carrington was one of those weak men whom he would like to advise to 'grow a backbone'. Hiding behind the stronger personality of a woman was despicable, in his opinion.

Suddenly, Carrington looked woebegone and lost, and Falconer realised how much he would miss the woman, if she had worked for him for as long as he said she had. 'Let's have those names then, sir,' he requested, and Carmichael extracted his notebook, after having made short work of the plate of biscuits that had also sat on the tray, and was now sadly decorated with only a few crumbs.

Noticing this for the first time, Falconer exclaimed, 'Carmichael! You've eaten *all* the biscuits!'

'Oh, sorry Mr Carrington, but I lost my breakfast,' he shuddered as he remembered, 'and I didn't feel like any lunch.'

'Don't worry, Sergeant. A few biscuits isn't going to bankrupt me. I've got a little list here: 'Spike' Ellis, 'Dogger' Ferguson, 'Troll' Norman, 'Darkie' Collins, 'Chalky' White, and 'Curry' Khan. They were the main offenders. I've known them all since their mums used to bring them along in their prams and pushchairs to get a bag of chips for their tea.

'And nice kids they were, too, but you know what happens to them these days, once they get to a certain age. Once the acne gets them, they discover fags, booze, joints, and girls, and suddenly they're all like Jekyll and Hyde, especially on Friday and Saturday nights. They've got really mouthy over the last year or so.'

'But Mrs Beeton kept them in line, did she?' asked Falconer.

'As best she could, but they were getting worse. She

wouldn't stand for any nonsense when she was serving, and she gave as good as she got. Her father was a sailor, and, boy, could he cuss! She learnt well from him.'

'Anyone else you can think of who might bear her a grudge?' was his final question.

'No one. She was a fine specimen of her kind, and she'll be sorely missed in the shop.'

Back in the car, Falconer turned a suddenly optimistic face to Carmichael, and said, 'I recognise most of those names. They've all been in trouble at some time or other over the last eighteen months or so, so we'll have no problem with their addresses, and the ones not known to the police will be easy to find, because we'll make sure we get their addresses from the others.'

'That'll save a lot of time. We can just look them up on the computer, and we'll be able to go there knowing what they've already been up to.'

'Just so! Forewarned is forearmed!'

PORTION FOUR

Saturday 17th April – later

Back at the station, they looked up the records of the names of the four youths that both of them were familiar with, and it was the usual story of the times, for between them they had been brought in for: taking a motor vehicle without the owner's consent, being drunk and disorderly, breach of the peace, brawling, possession of cannabis, and a bit of shoplifting, just to add spice to the mix.

Dogger Ferguson had narrowly missed being prosecuted for assaulting a police officer, but as the officer was PC Merv Green, who was soft-hearted underneath his gruff exterior, he had not pressed charges, and the incident merely remained on file.

The two names currently unknown to the police were Darkie Collins and Curry Khan, but Falconer had every confidence that they would pick up their addresses from their mates. The other four all lived on an estate consisting mostly of blocks of flats; not high-rises – only four floors – but even these were a blot on the Market Darley/Upper Darley landscape, and a source of much of the trouble caused by teenagers and tearaways in the town and in the surrounding area.

Their first call was to the home of Spike Ellis, seventeen years old, and with three convictions for shoplifting to his name. The flat was in Robin House, as this was the Wild Birds Estate, and on the top floor, the lift, of course, being out of order. The entrance hall smelt of vomit and urine, and

Carmichael clapped his handkerchief to his mouth and nose as soon as they entered.

'Don't touch the bannister rail,' warned Falconer, who had been caught like this before. Some clever individuals, in their cups, found it hilarious to smear bannister rails with faeces, and others, of a more pathological bent, liked to embed bits of broken glass in them, or even razor blades.

The top landing had four doors, all desperately in need of a coat of paint and, from the door with the number sixteen on it, (in drunken brass numerals, their original quota of fixing screws now reduced to one each) blared loud music, the sound of a baby yelling, and a female voice shouting abuse at one of the other occupants.

Falconer left it for Carmichael to use his mighty fist to knock, and when that produced no reaction from within, shouted himself, 'Open up. Police!'

There was a sudden silence within, with the exception of the wails of the baby, and a woman with dyed blonde hair, her roots almost half its length, and last night's heavy make-up making an artist's palette of her face, opened the door and grunted, 'Wotcher want? My Spike ain't done nuffink! Whenever it was, 'e was 'ere wiv me. Gottit?'

'Good morning Mrs Ellis,' Falconer opened for his side, and immediately had the legs cut from under him.

'That's *Miss* Ellis. Spike's old man did a runner when 'e found out I was up the duff, and I ain't seen 'im since, if yer must know.'

Falconer tried again. 'Good morning *Miss* Ellis. I wonder if we could have a word with your son – er – Spike, if it's not too much trouble. It won't take a minute, if we could just step inside.'

Miss Ellis turned, and bellowed, 'Spike, you get your arse out 'ere this minute. Wot you been up to now, yer little bastard?'

As they entered the flat, Carmichael wishing he could use

his handkerchief here, too, a spindly, spotty youth with his hair dyed orange came out of one of the doors and stared at the visitors, perplexed.

Falconer took a moment to adjust to the smell and, surreptitiously looking round what he could see of the flat, took in overflowing ashtrays, empty beer and lager cans, and at least three rolled-up and very used disposable nappies just lying on the floor. The curtains were still drawn, there were newspapers and baby toys scattered across the floor and the furniture, and a collection of mugs and plates, unwashed and discarded after use.

''E's only seventeen. You've gotta 'ave me present, cos I'm what they call an appropriate adult,' Miss Ellis informed them, picking up the baby and lighting a cigarette at the same time.

How well their social workers taught them these days, thought Falconer, before turning his full attention to Spike, who looked very wary now, and beat him to it, by announcing, 'I ain't done nuffink! You can't pin anyfink on me, cos I ain't done nuffink.'

'I only want to know where you were first thing this morning, Spike, and to confirm where you were yesterday evening.'

'D'yer wanna sit down?' interrupted Miss Ellis, intent on being as much of a nuisance as she could. She might have been yelling her head off at Spike just a few minutes before, but he was her baby, and she would protect him fiercely to the end.

'No, thank you,' squeaked Carmichael, determined not to draw a deep breath in this flat.

'Spike?' Falconer encouraged the youth.

'I've only just woke up,' Spike mumbled. 'That's what me mum was yellin' about when you come knockin' on the door just now.'

''E's a real lazy little sod sometimes,' added his mother,

213

as an aside, then added, "'e didn't come in till Gawd knows what time last night, then 'e can't get up in the mornin'. Just like 'is dad 'e'll turn out. Never 'old down a job, nor nuffink like that. Waste o' space, 'e is at the moment.'

'I'd rather you didn't interrupt during questioning, if you don't mind, Miss Ellis. It's Spike I would like to give me information,' said Falconer, his temper rising.

'Sorry for breavin',' Spike's mother snapped back at him. She sat down on a filthy, food-stained armchair and stubbed out her cigarette on a ketchup-stained plate.

'Where did you get up to yesterday evening, Spike?' Falconer asked, mentally keeping his fingers crossed that the youth's mother would butt out of the conversation and let him get on with his job in peace.

'Not a lot,' Spike answered. 'We got Dogger to blag some extra-strong cider from the offie, and some real head-bangin' lagers. We drunk a few, then went round the old car ports and smoked a joint or two' – this young man knew about the changes in the law that no longer made smoking a little cannabis a prosecutable offence – 'then o' course, we got the munchies, so we stashed the booze, and went down the chippie on the parade.

'After that, we went back to the car ports, and finished off the booze. I was wasted when I got in, and I've just woke up, like I told yer.'

'And who was with you?'

'Dogger, like I said, Troll, Chalky, Darkie, and old Curry. That's us. The cool dudes!'

'So, let me get this straight. You got one of your friends to buy alcohol from the off-licence, for under-age drinkers, then you smoked some drugs, then went to the chip shop, came back to the estate, and continued to drink until you came home.'

'That's it. Wot else d'yer wanna know?'

'Did you wake up earlier than just now, and go to the

parade to visit the chip shop again, possibly because of something that happened when you were there yesterday evening?'

'Shit! I told yer. I din't wake up till just now. 'Ow could I 'ave gone out, when I never woke up?'

'Thank you very much. We'll be on our way, then. Goodbye.'

'So much for family life in the enlightened twenty-first century,' Falconer commented to Carmichael as they finally reached the blessed fresh air again, and headed for the car.

'How can they live like that?' asked Carmichael. 'No wonder we have so much trouble with the kids today, if they come from places like that. And she's got a baby. Imagine having to get a pram or pushchair up and down all those stairs, when the lifts are out of order!'

'Which is always,' said Falconer, concluding the conversation.

Four more of the names they had been given came from similar blocks on the same estate, and the interviews began with either a youth only just risen, or, in two cases, not even out of bed yet, and the day was getting on. Their trail led them variously to Blackbird House, Starling House, Goldfinch House, and Jackdaw House, and each block was as depressing as the first had been.

The only positive information that they received were the addresses of Darkie Collins and Curry Khan, neither of whom lived on the Wild Birds, and which they decided to visit after they had had a look at Sylvia Beeton's house and spoken to her neighbours.

They had obtained the keys of her house from her handbag at the chip shop, and set off now for Meadow Road which, now that they thought about it, wasn't too far from Crescent Road, so they should, logically, have gone there first, before taking themselves off to the Wild Birds Estate.

Meadow Road was a little less up-market than Crescent Road, but was comprised of tidy pairs of thirties semis. Sylvia's was a left-handed one, as one looked at the pair, and was in stark contrast to the condition of its mirror twin.

In fact, the gardens all along that side of the road were well-kept, with flower beds, displays of roses and shrubs, and lawns green and rich. Sylvia's was the exception. The beds that existed had only shrubs in them, although they were not overgrown and neglected, and the lawn, though neatly trimmed, was more weeds and moss than grass. It was perfectly tidy; just not planted and pandered to with the obsessiveness evident in the neighbouring gardens.

To the right of the boundary with the right-hand semi rose a veritable Everest of Leylandii hedging, beautifully trimmed right up to the edge of the path next door, but sprawling right over the path leading to the door of Sylvia's house, and even infringing on the lawn in the middle of its length.

'Definitely not an avid gardener, then, like her neighbours,' commented Falconer, picking his way to the door. 'More 'just keeping it tidy', like the average mortal.'

'Surprised she could get her bike up the path,' added Carmichael, thinking of the bicycle that still resided in the area at the back of the chip shop.

'You can see the tracks of her tyres on the lawn from where it was wet earlier in the week,' Falconer pointed out, removing her door key from his pocket and opening the door. 'I don't know what we expect to find in here, but we'd better have a look around, in case she had any threatening letters or anything like that.'

'Wouldn't she have confided in Mr Carrington?' asked Carmichael. 'They'd worked together for years.'

'You're probably right, but let's just take a quick look round, then we can pay a call on the neighbours and find out what they have to say about her.'

The inside of the property was in much better order than

the garden, and it appeared that Sylvia Beeton had led a clean and tidy life behind closed doors. Even the cup and bowl that she had presumably used for her breakfast this morning were standing, rinsed, and upside down on the draining board, the dish-cloth hung over the mixer tap to dry.

After less than half an hour of poking and prying, Falconer called it a day. 'Come on, Carmichael,' he said, summoning the sergeant from working his way through the sideboard. 'We'll go next door and find out what sort of a neighbour she was.'

A cold welcome awaited them at the property to the right of Sylvia's house; the one with the regimented garden that looked like it had had its lawn trimmed with a manicure set. Its owner, David Mortimer, was a man who appeared to be in his mid-fifties, his grey hair close-trimmed, rather like his grass. He had a small toothbrush moustache and wore a cardigan and slippers, highlighting, thought Falconer, the fact that this was a Saturday and, for him, at least, a day of leisure.

'I'm calling about your neighbour, Mrs Sylvia Beeton. I don't know whether it's been on local radio yet ...?' Falconer began his questioning, after introductions had been carried out.

'It has, but I really have no opinion on the matter,' replied Mortimer, his eyes cold and disinterested.

'We just wanted to get an idea of what she was like as a neighbour – you know the sort of thing. Had she fallen out with anybody, to your knowledge? Had there been any trouble at the house, recently?'

'I keep myself to myself, Inspector. I do not waste time gossiping with the neighbours, and have no interest whatsoever in the ins and outs of their private lives. I'm afraid I can't help you at all,' he announced, and swiftly closed the door in their faces.

'What a miserable old sod,' said Falconer. 'People aren't usually that unhelpful.'

At the house to the left of Sylvia's, the occupant introduced herself as Mrs Hare (but call me Maude, everybody else does), who patted at her hair in a coquettish way as she spoke to them, even though she proved to be a widow, and was in her early eighties.

'And what can I do for you two young gentlemen?' she asked them, smoothing down the wrinkles in her skirt.

'We're here about your neighbour, Sylvia Beeton,' Falconer informed her.

'What? You'll have to speak up, young man. I don't hear as well as I used to.'

'SYLVIA BEETON,' Falconer repeated.

'Oh, you'll be asking about that hedge at her property,' said Mrs Hare, with a knowing nod of her head. 'Well, I don't get involved with anything of that sort.'

'NO!' roared Falconer, SHE'S DEAD!'

'She's done what, dearie?' asked the elderly woman, cupping a hand to an ear and leaning forward.

'SHE'S BEEN MURDERED!' shouted Falconer.

'Oh, that's nice for her. I hope she enjoys herself. Well, I mustn't stand here on the doorstep gossiping and letting the heat out. Thank you for telling me, young man,' and with that, Mrs Hare closed the door with a smile, and just the hint of a twinkle in her faded old eyes.

'Bloody marvellous!' exclaimed Falconer. 'We come out here to find out about the woman's character, and one neighbour lives like a recluse, and the other's as deaf as a post. Let's get off to those other two addresses, and call it a day for today.'

PORTION FIVE

Saturday 17th April – even later

'Darkie' Collins lived in Jubilee Terrace, a string of houses dating from the turn of the twentieth century, and obviously built to celebrate Queen Victoria's Diamond Jubilee. Forming the other side of the street was Victoria Terrace, dating from the same era. The front gardens were minimal, consisting of only a few feet of land between the boundary and the house, but this area of number thirteen was full of spring flowers in pots and tubs.

The woman who opened the door was very dark-skinned, and had one of the widest smiles Falconer had ever seen. How could anyone get so many teeth into one mouth? he thought, as she beamed a welcome at them. 'Mrs Collins?' he enquired, hopefully, and she immediately corrected him,

'Miss Collins. I haven't yet persuaded a good man to put a ring on my finger,' she informed him, and smiled again, as if this was one of the most amusing things she had ever said.

'Miss Collins. I'm here to speak to your son, if he's at home. Is that possible?'

'Winston? What's he done?' she asked, and turned her head back inside the narrow hall and yelled, 'Winston, get your backside down here. Now!' then turned her hundred watt smile back round to the two detectives and said, as sweetly as they could have wished, 'would you like to come inside for a cup of tea?'

She showed them into a tiny sitting room, where the chairs and sofa were covered with bright throws, and vividly-

219

coloured abstract paintings hung from the walls. As she disappeared off to the kitchen, a clattering down the stairs announced the arrival of Winston, and he came straight in to see what was happening.

Winston proved to be much lighter-skinned than his mother, but his complexion confirmed why his friends called him 'Darkie'. When asked why he tolerated this, his reply was pragmatic. 'Well, it's better than "nigger", which was what they called me before they got to know me. And you've got to be part of the hard crew, or you get beaten up. It's self-protection, innit, mate?'

His mother reappeared carrying a tin tray with four mugs on it. 'I made one for you, too, Winston,' she informed her son, then continued, 'What you been up to, boy? You in trouble?'

'I just want to know where your son was this morning, Miss Collins,' Falconer informed her.

'He's old enough to speak for himself now,' she said, looking at her son as he lounged in a chair. 'And sit up straight when we've got visitors.'

Winston hauled himself into a vaguely upright position, and replied to Falconer's query. 'I've been upstairs all morning doing my homework.' His accent had definitely lost that twang of Jamaican that it had had when he had first spoken.

'Did you know Mrs Beeton, who served in the chip shop, on the parade?'

'Sure I know her. I've known her since I was a little tiny kid. She shouts loud, but she doesn't mean nothin' by it.'

'Did you see her last night?' Falconer was approaching the nub of the matter.

'Sure I saw her last night. Me and my mates went there for some chips, and to hang out and chill,' he replied, without any hint that he knew what had happened.

'Did you and your mates fall out with her?'

220

'Sure, we had words, but dat's de game, innit? It don't mean a ting, man. Jost de banter and stoff.'

'Winston, don't you use that silly accent under my roof. I've told you before, you've been brought up properly, so you speak properly too.'

'Sorry, Ma,' he apologised, then disarmed his mother with a huge grin. 'Gotcha!'

Interrupting this tender parent/child moment, Falconer asked, 'Did you know she was dead, Winston?'

'No way!' he shouted.

'She can't be!' exclaimed his mother. 'Was it an accident, or a heart attack, or something like that? She was a big woman.'

'I'm sorry to have to tell you that she was murdered, late this morning.'

There was a silence that threatened to cause a real hiatus in the interview, until Falconer gave it a little nudge by asking, 'Did you, by any chance, slip down to the parade this morning, Winston?'

Two voices angrily assured both policemen that the boy hadn't left his room, except for two cups of coffee and a bathroom break.

'Did any of your friends have a particular grudge against her, for something she'd said or done?' he continued.

'Nuh! But Dogger Ferguson did say more than once that she needed a good slap, like all women.'

'Winston!'

'Well, he did! He's an animal, always saying things like that, but he doesn't mean anything by it.'

Three heavy sighs followed this casual reference to violence and women, and this time it was Miss Collins who broke it. 'It's that estate!' she said, obviously referring to the Wild Birds. 'We used to live there, too, when I was left on my own with Winston, but I scrimped and saved to do an Open University degree, and then trained as a social worker

221

so that we could have a better life.

'I bought this house for a song, seeing as it was number thirteen, and so many people have silly superstitious natures. We moved here three years ago, but Winston still hangs around with the old crowd from the blocks.

'I can't believe old Sylvia's dead, though. She's been serving me since Winston was in his pushchair.'

'Mum!'

'And you're absolutely certain that Winston never set foot outside this house this morning, Mrs Collins?'

'I would swear it on the Bible, Inspector.'

'And you can't think of anything that happened, that might have triggered off a fit of rage in one of your friends, Winston?'

'No, man! Not even Dogger would waste anyone!'

'Curry' Khan lived in a large modern detached house in the fairly new development, King's Acre. There was a Mercedes parked on one side of the double drive, a BMW on the other, and an elderly man working away in the garden, clearing away dead growth so that the spring flowers could grow uninhibited.

'Very nice,' was Falconer's comment, as they parked.

'Too flash!' was Carmichael's simultaneous opinion.

The door was opened by a tiny woman in a sari, who immediately went to fetch a man they presumed was her husband. 'Mr Khan?' enquired Falconer, holding out his hand in greeting.

His assumption was correct, and soon they were all four seated in the large sitting room at the back of the house, from which a fair-sized conservatory opened out.

'I wonder if I could speak to your son, Mr Khan. I'm afraid I don't know his real Chr ... hrmph! His forename, as we've only ever heard him referred to by his, um, nickname.' Falconer had nearly put his foot right in it, by referring to the man's son's Christian name. Life was so much more complicated these days!

'What? Curry?' asked Mr Khan, beaming at them as he said this. 'They might call him that because of his ethnic origins, but if they knew how much I make from my Indian restaurants – I've got three, you know – they might use it as a term of respect, for he will have a very good inheritance.'

'How lovely!' Falconer congratulated him, not quite knowing how to respond to a reference to circumstances under which his current host would be dead. 'Is it possible for us to have a word with him?'

'Of course, Inspector. He is in his study, doing his schoolwork. Indira will fetch him for you.' The tiny woman left the room on this errand, returning shortly with a slim and elegant young man who introduced himself as Sanjeev, and took a seat looking expectantly at the two visitors.

'Good afternoon,' Falconer greeted him formally. It seemed like that sort of household, to him. 'I wonder if you could tell me where you have been this morning – all of it,' he added, in case the lad had slipped out before attending to his homework.

'I had a shower and ate my breakfast,' Sanjeev began, talking the question literally, 'Then, I went to my study to attend to my homework. When I had finished that, my mother brought me a cup of tea, and I did some research on the internet. I was still engaged in that activity when you rang the doorbell,' he explained, precisely and succinctly.

'You didn't leave the house at all?'

'Not even for one minute, I assure you.'

'What does this questioning concern, Inspector? I would like to know why you are visiting my house today,' asked Sanjeev's father.

'A woman who worked at the chip shop on the parade has, most unfortunately, been found dead this morning, and we are of the opinion that she was murdered, and that your

223

son was in the chip shop last night.'

'No! Sanjeev?' shouted Mr Khan, rising from his seat.

'I'm so sorry, Papa! I'm so sorry!'

The boy's face was crumpled in anguish, and anger suffused his father's expression, his face red and his fists clenched.

Falconer's eyes widened at what was unfolding in front of him, and Carmichael was so startled in the change of atmosphere that he dropped his pencil, and had to grovel around under the wooden dining chair on which he was sitting to find it again.

The inspector began to rise from his seat, steeling himself to administer a caution before arrest, when Mr Khan spoke again. 'So, you have been buying chips again; when I have three restaurants from which you could get free food whenever you wanted it. My *son*! *My* son, *buying* chips! Oh, the shame of it!'

'I am so sorry, Papa. It was only because I was with my friends. I won't go in there again. I promise. I promise you, on my word of honour, Papa!'

Falconer sank back into his chair again, and gave a small cough of embarrassment. 'I think I have all the information I need from your son, and we'll take our leave of you now. Don't worry: we can see ourselves out,' he squeaked, and he and Carmichael fairly scarpered back to the car.

Once back behind the wheel, Carmichael gave Falconer a long stare of bewilderment, and the inspector turned to him and said, 'There are some cultural gaps too wide to cross, Carmichael.'

Back at the station, Falconer asked his sergeant to go through his notes to see if there was anything in there to give them a pointer. The four interviews he had conducted on the Wild Birds Estate had left his head in a whirl, with all the shouting, the bad language, and the squalor and he could remember little of what was actually said.

'Well, nobody actually owned up to anything, and I don't have a lot of notes, because I left out all the swear words.'

'There are decent people living in those blocks, Carmichael. It just happens that the ones we spoke to today are particularly, um, deprived,' Falconer stated, being absolutely fair. 'They only represent a minority of the flats' tenants.

'None of them liked Mrs Beeton that much. They all thought she was loud and mouthy. And bossy, too. And that couple who lived over the shop weren't too keen, either.'

'She had to be, working in a place like that. I expect that was why Mr Carrington has kept her on for so long. He needs, or needed, someone who could not only serve and give change, but could act as a bouncer as well. It would seem that Sylvia Beeton fulfilled all these criteria.'

At that moment, the telephone rang, and Falconer grabbed at the receiver. 'Inspector Falconer: Market Darley CID. How may I help you? Oh, Philip it's you. If I'd known it was you, I'd have blown my whistle down the phone and hung up.'

'Ha ha! Very funny! You're only sulking because of what happened to your shoes at the locus. You can't fool me, Harry, old boy,' replied the doctor.

'What can I do for you?'

'I just felt I had to phone you, to say that I've never had a body before that I didn't know whether to douse in salt and vinegar or examine. I shall dine out on this story for months, thanks to you.'

'Philip?'

'Yes, Harry?'

'Go away, before I commit another murder in the area; one that you won't be able to be around to deal with,' he threatened, and hung up.

'What did the doc want?' asked Carmichael.

225

'Nothing. It wasn't important.' If he'd told Carmichael what Philip Christmas had just said, there was no telling how the sergeant would react, and he'd only just got his shoes clean again. 'Have we got anything at all?'

I don't think so, sir. It must have been some passing nutter, I suppose.'

'I don't buy that, Carmichael. There's more to this than meets the eye, and I'm going to get to the bottom of it, if it's the last thing I do.'

PORTION SIX

Monday 18th April

Over the weekend, Falconer had had a recurring dream: one that forced him to revisit Sylvia Beeton's house and stare at it long and hard. There was something tickling at the back of his mind, and he needed it to jump forward and declare itself. The answer was within his grasp: he just hadn't recognised it yet.

Monday morning found him in the office very early, making a list of telephone numbers, which he worked his way through shortly after arriving at the station, hoping to catch people before they left for work.

He hit paydirt on his fourth call, then made another call, to round off his activities for the morning, being passed from department to department until he found what he was after. After a few minutes' reflection, he dialled again, to ascertain that he would be able to carry out what he wanted to do, then sat twiddling his thumbs until Carmichael arrived, too excited to settle to do anything, yet exasperated at how slowly time was crawling by. The sergeant wasn't due on duty until nine thirty this morning, and Falconer snorted his disgust and chagrin that the man had not been rostered for an earlier shift.

The hands of the clock slowly ground their way round to five, four, three, two minutes to the half hour, then the door of the office burst open, and a bright and sunny figure lolloped into the room, shedding its jacket as it went. 'Morning, sir. Anything happening?' it asked.

The tension suddenly left Falconer's body now that his partner was there, and he slumped in his chair. 'Yes, Carmichael. I've solved the case!'

'You've done what?'

'I know who killed Mrs Beeton from the chip shop!'

'You what?'

'I know who did it, Carmichael. Am I speaking Swahili or something today, or are you just incapable of understanding me anymore?'

'Sorry, sir,' said Carmichael, sitting down.

'Now, you listen up, my lad, and listen good. I'm going to tell you a little story – but not all of it, yet – then we're going out to make an arrest,' Falconer declared, and proceeded so to do.

David Mortimer submitted, without fuss, to being arrested, merely taking one more look at his immaculate garden as he was led away, and pausing to spit over the garden gate at his next door neighbour Sylvia Beeton's house. There had been no resistance at all, and he had readily admitted what he had done in a fit of rage and depression.

'So it was as simple as that, was it?' asked Carmichael, after Mortimer had been taken away in a squad car, and they were driving back to the station.

'We got nothing from those boys, no matter how intimidating their behaviour might have been when they were out in public, and I couldn't see any signs of guilt from any one of them. The only thing that stuck in my mind was what that deaf old lady – what was her name? Maude Hare, I think – said when we arrived.

'She thought we'd come about a hedge. I thought she was just rambling, because of her age and lack of hearing, but I did notice that she had a neat little privet hedge, and Mrs Beeton had a fence, so I just dismissed what she'd said. And then, both nights at the weekend, I dreamt I was being consumed by a giant hedge, and I couldn't find any way out of it. It wasn't like a maze, you understand: just a huge hedge.

'Well, then I remembered that, at Mrs Beeton's house, the hedge between her property and the one on the right was a huge monstrosity of Leylandii, and that her side of it grew right across the pathway, which was at odds with her usual tidiness, but on the other side, it was carefully trimmed and kept in shape.

'Did Mrs Hare think we were from the council, I wondered, and today, after I'd made a few other calls, I phoned up the local authority, and got myself on a real merry-go-round of extensions, until I found out that a complaint had been lodged some time ago.

'I'd already phoned the tree surgeons I was able to find in the Yellow Pages, and, on the fourth call, I found one who had an appointment to go to Mrs Beeton's house this week and cut down a hedge of Leylandii. The council had told me there was nothing they could do for the woman, and advised her to go to the Citizens Advice Bureau. It wasn't her hedge you see.

'They'd told her she could trim the offending branches, and even put the cuttings on to her neighbour's land, to prove that she hadn't stolen his property, but she wanted to find a way to get rid of the hedge altogether, because it blocked so much light from the front of her house, and it looks like she was willing to pay to get the job done without permission.

'A further search of her house produced a file of letters between their solicitors about removing the light-blocking eyesore. They were in that sideboard I called you away from, when I mistakenly thought there was nothing there for us. The situation had come to an impasse, however, and another visit to Mrs Hare, with the word 'hedge' shouted very loudly, produced the information that they – Mrs Beeton and Mr

Mortimer – were frequently going hammer-and-tongs at it about the hedge, out on the street.

'Mortimer said – you heard him yourself – that she told him this morning that she was 'going to have the bloody things cut down and burnt', and she'd like to see him stop her. He spent a couple of hours working himself into a real rage and downing shots of scotch, then went round to the chip shop and confronted her, and that was that. What a waste of both lives! And the fool had left his fingerprints all over the chip scoop, so there was no chance of him bluffing his way out of it.'

They were just passing the end of the pedestrian High Street, when Carmichael suddenly yelled, 'Stop!'

Falconer did a fairly good impression of an emergency stop, and looked at his partner quizzically. Whatever is it, Sergeant? What's the matter?'

'I just fancied a bag of chips, and there's a chip shop on that corner back there. I might even have a battered burger with it.'

'Well, it has been at least two hours since your breakfast,' replied Falconer, then leaned out of the car window and shouted, 'Could you get the same for me as well; and lots of vinegar, please, Carmichael.'

THE END